THE LIGHTHOUSE KEEPER OF ANGLESEY

CAROLINE YOUNG

Storm

PUBLISHING

Ebook ISBN: 978-1-80508-913-1
Paperback ISBN: 978-1-80508-914-8

Cover design: Emma Rogers
Cover images: Shutterstock

Published by Storm Publishing.
For further information, visit:
www.stormpublishing.co

ALSO BY CAROLINE YOUNG

Welcome to Anglesey

The Forgotten Farmhouse by the Sea

Secrets at the Cottage by the Sea

Coming Home to the Windmill by the Sea

To my three daughters, Bethan, Rhiannon and Mari; by far my greatest achievements in life.

"Life always offers you a second chance. It's called tomorrow."
Dylan Thomas

PROLOGUE

Lloyd Evans sat alone on the smooth-pebbled beach and gazed out towards the horizon, far beyond the lighthouse. It would be dark soon, as night came early on Anglesey in February. Lloyd knew these treacherous rocks and the weed-swathed, shadowy depths around them better than anywhere on earth, and loved them more. He had spent years sharing the seas around the island with keen sea-fishermen and boat trips full of excited visitors each summer. His father Aled had been the coastguard at Penmon, the wild easternmost point of Anglesey. His grandfather had been one before him, and his great-grandfather a lighthouse keeper, a proud profession before automation dispensed with it, and with him. The sea around this island was in Lloyd's blood, and he saw it as his closest friend, his only friend, one that whispered its secrets to him, and listened as he whispered his.

Once, he'd had dreams beyond this place, but they had long since faded. When he lay dying, Aled had made his son promise that he would stay at Penmon so that their family's intimate knowledge of the sea that surrounded them passed down through decades, would not be lost. Lloyd had kept this promise, suppressing other opportunities, other lives, but it had cost him dearly. He had hidden here, guarding a tragedy that made him too sad to leave his memories behind.

Today was Lloyd's sixty-fourth birthday. He had been alone for almost thirty years, since his much-loved wife Kate had left him one summer day without a word of warning. Their daughter, Seren, named after the Welsh word for "star", would be a woman now – a beautiful, successful one, he felt sure. Her very existence proved that love had once been a part of his life, and it consoled him for the fact that it had ended so brutally, and without any reason being given.

Whenever he closed his eyes to sleep at night, he could still feel Seren's tiny hand in his, and see her brown eyes looking up at him, full of hope and trust. He had loved his child, however little he had been able to show her, or others, that he did at the end. He had given her up so she would be happy, and never tried to reclaim her in his guilt, but it had ripped him apart. Yes, Kate had broken his heart when she had left, but Seren had taken all the pieces of it with her and she still had them, wherever she was now.

When darkness finally fell, and the scores of whirling seabirds were silent, the only light remaining was the steady blink of the lighthouse. This gave Lloyd a small degree of hope that night, as it did every night, because he knew it would not cease its lonely, life-saving pulse until tomorrow dawned.

PART 1

DREAMS AND DECISIONS

ONE

ST THOMAS' HOSPITAL, LONDON, FEBRUARY 2023

Seren opened one eye and looked quickly down at her chest. There was the same bland hospital gown she had been wearing earlier, the same green blanket was laid over her, but there was a soft mound where her left breast should no longer be. A flicker of panic that they had removed the wrong one was allayed when a quick poke of both reassured her that the right one was still flesh. The other mound must be dressings, padding, as she had not been offered reconstruction, but she touched it gently, just to be sure. There was no feeling at all.

At thirty-two, she was very young to be diagnosed with breast cancer, or so a panoply of consultants had told her. Did it run in her family? they wondered. She'd answered "no", as the only family she had ever really known was Aunt Alice's, and they were all very hale and hearty. Did she have a healthy lifestyle? they'd asked. And she'd said "yes". It was too late to be truthful now, either with the medics, or with herself. She had tried, and tried hard, to ride over the waves of depression without medication, until she'd met Finlay and he had shown her the tempting oblivion of booze. Now, she drank only rarely, but took her tablets faithfully, one white, one blue; she knew that they, and Enya, her little girl, had saved her life.

"Is my daughter allowed to come and see me yet?" she blurted to the nurse. "She's nearly five, and I know she'll be missing me. She's very shy, very quiet, you see. She's with my aunt until I'm discharged, but I feel fine already."

"Ah, yes. It says, 'Next of kin: Mrs Alice Montague' here," the staff nurse said from the end of the bed, glancing at her records. "No, not yet, dear. The anaesthetic will still be in your system, and you might be a little *unpredictable*. We don't want to scare your daughter, do we?"

Seren knew better than to argue. And no, she didn't want Enya to be scared.

It was only three months since she had left Finlay, Enya's father, but doing so had crystallised plans that had been simmering in her mind for years. As an adopted child, there had always been a huge, parent-sized hole in her life, one she had always known she had to fill. She had to get better, fast, so that she could finally take them both away from all her mistakes and misjudgements, somewhere she could heal and think and her little girl could thrive. Cancer had shown her that time was a limited commodity and that the moment to *act* on her feelings was right now, but where she needed to go, she did not know. The right place existed, she felt it in her bones. Her challenge was to find it.

Seren closed her eyes and let her thoughts drift. Hours passed, and the muted daylight in the ward became the glare of strip lights whenever she opened her eyes to check where she was. Images of Enya's sad, pale face mingled with the sounds of traffic on a busy street, the smell of frying onions from a take-away shop, and she flinched involuntarily at the memory of a man's face inches from hers, shouting, accusing her of the crime of not loving him enough. Sitting bolt upright, she felt a sharp twinge in her chest. The anaesthetic was wearing off, which –

though scary – did mean she would see her daughter soon. No pain was worse than Enya feeling abandoned for a second longer than was necessary. She knew more than most how terrible that felt.

Seren had no idea when she surfaced next, but she sensed it was in the very depths of the night as there was silence from the blanketed hummocks in every other bed on the ward. Her sleep had been troubled, crammed with strangely familiar images and imaginings that she could still see with a vividness that unnerved her.

A nurse doing her rounds smiled at her, and whispered, "Here's something to help you sleep, love. Press the buzzer if you need me," before vanishing into the orange gloom of the ward.

Seren put the tablets in the bin. She wanted to revisit her dream; she knew it held the key to unlock a mystery that had threaded through her life. At its heart, was a lighthouse, and a surging sea. It was always the same dream, and she had seen these wisps of memory many times, but that night they had seemed so clear, she had almost expected the squat black and white lighthouse to be at the end of her bed when she awoke. There had been noises this time, too, the regular, low tolling of a bell, a sound that had punctuated a life she could not quite remember, and the shrill rush of the wind. In her dream, she saw the ocean and watched the water frothing against the stone tower in an unending rhythm, almost like the low beat of a drum, summoning her. White birds dived from the sky like arrows to spear a fish for supper, or so a man's voice she did not know had told her, her small hand warm in his. But where was that place, that lighthouse... and who was that man?

· · ·

Seren's enquiries about her early life, before she had come to London, had always been rather brusquely dealt with by her aunt and uncle. At first, this puzzled her, as their kindness in taking her in was obvious. Instead of clear answers to her questions, she was reminded of how she was going to be happy here, and how lucky she was to have been brought up with her older cousins Melissa and Alex, but she did not feel either happy or lucky. She always felt apart, and that her feelings were of less interest and importance in the household; it was an attitude that hardened as the years passed. An awkward, quirky child, she had amassed several piercings and tattoos by the age of sixteen and delighted in playing loud music in her room and ignoring the yells of protest from her always-revising cousins. Her interests centred around art, and she took thousands of photographs on a basic camera she had been given one Christmas. An uncommitted student at the expensive private school she had been sent to, she adored her Rastafarian art teacher who asked pupils to call him "Mistah Marley". Her far more studious cousins had, as expected, both got into Oxford and graduated with Firsts, but Seren's dreams of photographing the natural world were dampened by Uncle Neil who told her, albeit kindly, how difficult it might be to make a living from "taking snaps of birds and trees". After a long tussle, she took his advice and started a biology degree in London. Within weeks, she was skipping lectures and missing deadlines with aplomb, delighted to be able to prove him wrong.

"Life is out there, but I'm missing it all!" she wailed whenever her aunt quizzed her gently about why she didn't seem to be engaging with her studies. "I need to follow my dream, don't you understand?"

Meeting Finlay O'Neill in the West End pub he was working in, abandoning her degree course in the second year and moving in with him within a month, was a predictable rebellion against what she called "domestic tyranny". It ended as many such protests do – in disaster. Finlay was a lonely, insecure man in his thirties who had left his rural home in the west of Ireland at sixteen to seek better fortune in London, but had found only petty crime and disappointment. He'd hoped that Seren would fill the gap in his life where a loving family should have been, he told her, but she could not. She, in turn, had dreamt that this man would make her feel *rooted* as nobody else had ever done, but as an uprooted soul himself, he could not. Enya was the only good to come of the relationship, but she was a quiet, wary child, damaged by her father's unpredictability and fierce temper. Time and time again, Seren had wanted to leave him, but pity had stopped her. For all his flaws, he'd had dreams that life had shattered, just as it had done hers. No, Finlay was not going to be an easy man to leave.

Outside the hospital, she heard the beginnings of the day. A van reversed, beeping insistently, and a few brave starlings chirped. But the sounds in her head were so much louder, a cacophony of seabirds and wind and waves that she did not want to quieten. They felt more real than anything else in her London world and the lighthouse and its sonorous bell were beacons, calling her. It was somewhere she had known once, she was certain – a place she had felt safe and needed to return to. It was home.

TWO

Alice and Neil Montague had lived in their three-storey Victorian townhouse in Wimbledon, South London, for over thirty-five years. Neil never tired of telling people they'd got it for a song back in the day, but that it was worth millions now. To Seren, it had never felt like home, and she had spent many lonely years there fantasising about her *real* home and her *real* parents. Flickers, shadows in the corner of her memory, were her only clues as to where she came from, and they corroded her peace of mind like acid.

The clearest memory of the sea change that had occurred was of being lifted out of bed and into a car that smelt of something floral, and an endless, dark car journey wrapped in a scratchy woollen blanket. She had been very young, only four years old, and her early questions about her past were smothered in bland reassurances while she settled down. She soon learnt that it was pointless to ask what was happening to her, or why, and this lasted for years, until she felt she had no choice but to press for answers.

"This is what your mother and your father wanted," Aunt Alice, her mother's sister, always said. "And it's for the best."

But Seren was never convinced.

Her aunt Alice came to visit the morning after her surgery. A thin, anxious-looking figure, she was waiting at the door before visiting time had even begun. Seren's only thought was that she must have set off incredibly early. To her fuddled, post-operative brain, the older woman resembled a grey heron, hunched and poised to pounce. Alice had not reacted well to her diagnosis, and had been near hysterics when Seren had told her what lay ahead. It was as if she had prodded a still-raw wound, but Alice refused to explain or reveal what it was.

"How are you feeling, dear?" she said, leaning over to kiss her niece's cheek, and letting her eyes flicker over her chest. "I'm so very sorry this is happening to you. Does it hurt an awful lot?"

"Not really. They give me lots of great drugs. How's Enya?" Seren said. "Is she missing me? Does she know I'm OK?"

Alice sat on the plastic chair beside the bed. "Yes, she's absolutely fine. She drew this get-well card for you too. She did ask about you, but I told her you needed to be left in peace and that there were lots of poorly people here. I hope that was appropriate."

Seren flinched. Alice was in complete control of Enya while she was alone at her house, and she felt she could not say it did not feel *appropriate* to keep her daughter from visiting her. In fact, it felt rather unkind.

"OK. I should be discharged in a day or so. Can you tell her I'll be... *home* soon?"

Alice nodded. "Of course, dear. But I want to know about *you*, and what the doctors have said... about, well, what happens *going forward*." She leant forward, her face taut with urgency.

Seren smiled. She was such a mystery, this woman, such a mixture of well-meaning and uptight. Had her mother been the same? she wondered. She had never been told, as Kate was never mentioned in Wimbledon.

"They've said they caught it early, and that I should be fine," she replied. "Thank goodness I took your advice, though, and went to the GP about the lump straight away. How did you know it might be cancer? I'm very young to get it, or so everyone keeps telling me."

"A lump is a lump, however big it is and however old you are, and it needs to be taken seriously," her aunt said, and Seren felt one of her hands gently covering her own. "Yes, thank goodness indeed that you listened to me and got it checked straight away. So many women don't, and, well, yes..."

There was a slightly awkward pause, as if neither woman knew where to take the conversation next. They had rarely *had* a serious discussion in the past, so this was very new to both of them. Embarrassed, Seren moved things on.

"Aunt Alice, I had a... well, I want to call it a *vision* rather than a dream, after my surgery, and I know it will sound a bit kooky to you." She stopped, unsure, until she found a foothold again. "It's made me want to ask you some questions, and I need you to give me honest answers to them."

"You want to talk to me about a dream you had?" Alice said. Her more usual, guarded manner had returned. "Aren't you a bit old for all that now?"

"It's a dream I've often had before, but this time, it was so clear it flowed, almost like a narrative, a story that I was a part of," Seren said. "It ties up with the few things I remember from before I came to live with you."

"Remember that you've had a general anaesthetic, dear," Alice said. "Things are bound to seem a bit... muddled."

"I know, but it all seemed very real to me. I saw a lighthouse, the sea, and a man too; he was tall, and dark-haired, with a big brown beard and he was holding my hand... I could *feel* the rough skin of his fingers on mine."

A hesitation, a clearing of the throat, before Alice said quietly, "I think you may be recalling a distant memory of your father, who took care of you before you came to us, until he became too... *ill* to do so any more."

Seren took a quick breath. "You've told me so little about him, or my mother. I know you thought that the less I knew, the less it would upset me, but I need to fill in some more of the gaps now, I really do. What was his name? You've never even told me that."

A pause. "His name is Lloyd Evans," the older woman said softly.

"He's still *alive?*" Seren exclaimed, and the patients on either side of her tut-tutted. "Where is he, and what does he do?"

Another, longer pause, followed by a sigh. "He told us that he was the son of a coastguard and the great-grandson of a lighthouse keeper I believe – all very romantic. He had a boat back then, I think, and a thing for poetry, both of which attracted your mother like a moth to a flame."

Seren ignored her aunt's obvious discomfiture, and pressed on.

"Lloyd Evans is a Welsh name, isn't it? That's why I'm called Seren, which I know is Welsh for 'star', because I googled it, but was I actually born in Wales? I know I have a connection to it, and my surname is Evans, for crying out loud. Who am I?" She was flushed and gabbling now.

Her aunt looked at her knees and didn't reply. She hated anyone getting agitated. Eventually, she murmured, "You need to calm down, Seren."

"Sorry, I know it will sound weird to you, but I saw things last night that have filled my dreams all my life, rising up to the surface like bubbles in water," Seren said. "You have told me snippets, but I need to know *everything*."

"It seems you've inherited Lloyd's poetic touch," Alice muttered.

"I'm an adult, for God's sake, and I am being treated for cancer, which sharpens anyone's sense of urgency. Whenever I've asked things, such as why my mother left so suddenly, or how she died, you've always dodged my questions, but you don't need to protect me from the truth any more."

Aunt Alice blinked, as if she was a nervous animal about to bolt. "Don't I? I'm not so sure about that. It was all such a long time ago, and you were very young when you came to us. And remember that you have Enya to think of before you dredge up things that might upset you, that might make you... unwell again. Think about it very carefully, dear."

This reference to her long struggle with depression was not lost on Seren.

"I know the risks, but I feel as if a part of me is missing, as if there's a hole at the centre of where 'Seren Evans' should be. I have always felt that, but after... all this," she pointed at her dressings, "I can't ignore it any longer. When the doctors here asked about my parents, my medical heritage, I had no answers and you still refused to give me any, but you are the only person who has them. Please, Aunt, I need to know."

Alice's shoulders slumped. "I'll try, as you are so insistent. Just believe that we always did what we thought was best at the time."

Seren nodded her agreement, but a flicker of impatience undercut it.

"You were *traumatised* when we got the phone call to come and get you about six months after your mother left Anglesey. You could hardly speak to us. You sat trembling in the back of the car all the way home."

"But who called you? Was it my father?"

"No, it wasn't, but it was someone who cared deeply about both of you. When we got there, your father was in a terrible state. He had lost control, and was raging and crashing around the place."

"I don't remember that, as I hope Enya won't remember some of the things Finlay did," Seren murmured.

"Your father had just received my mother's letter telling him of Kate's death, and grief had utterly overwhelmed him. It was not a safe place for a child to be any more, and he knew it."

Seren gasped as something clicked into place in her memory. "Is that why he was so distressed? Is that why he sent me away? Because he'd just found out that my mother had died? I'm not surprised he lost it!"

"Oh goodness, perhaps I'd better start from the beginning," Alice said, flustered. "But I need to ask you again, do you really think now is the right time to rake over the past? You need to focus on feeling better."

"Yes, I do, but knowing the truth will *help* me feel better."

Alice sighed again. "If you're sure, but there are some things even I don't know, and can't tell you, so just hear me out, please." She paused, and laid her folded hands in her lap. "Your father, Lloyd, lived on a small island off the top of North Wales, called Anglesey. Still does, for all I know. Kate, my sister, met him when she went up there for a summer job and she bewitched him, they bewitched each other, from what I could gather. They had a blissful few months, and then she got pregnant. They got married on a clifftop in a howling gale, I remember, as my hat blew into the sea, and lived in a tiny stone cottage by a lighthouse. Then you arrived. That's the gist of it, really. It was a romantic story cut short in the cruellest of ways."

"But why did she leave him, leave *me*?" Seren whispered. "How could any mother do that?"

Alice hesitated and Seren saw her left eyelid twitch, as it always did when she was caught off guard. "To be honest, none of us ever really knew why Kate did anything. She was always the flighty one in the family, and she made decisions I could never understand." There was a painful pause in which Seren knew she was supposed to compare the sisters and find Alice superior, but she said nothing. She did not have enough memories of her mother to pass judgement on her, but the mystery of her departure throbbed at the centre of her, a painful wound that would never heal until she knew the truth.

"But my father, Lloyd Evans, he tried to bring me up on his own, didn't he?"

"He did, yes, for several months, until it all got too much for him that night when he heard she was dead and would never be coming back to him. I'm quite sure that Lloyd loved you, in his own way, and he worshipped Kate, but she broke his heart." She paused. "Yes, she was good at making life incredibly difficult for other people, especially people who loved her. They were always left to pick up the pieces in her wake."

Seren saw a shadow cross her aunt's face. Had Kate hurt her sister's feelings too?

"I kept in touch with Lloyd after she left you both, and some of your mother's friends were incredibly loyal to her, and kept an eye out," Aunt Alice went on. "I let your father know that we would help him in any way we could if he needed it. When he realised I had come to take you that night, he knew you would be better off with us, that you needed a proper *family*."

A pause, in which unspoken words lurked. Alice poured herself a cup of water.

"How did my mother die, Aunt? Tell me, please."

"All I know is that she was on a motorbike and crashed into a motorway bridge. It was instantaneous, and nobody else was involved. Our parents agonised that she'd done it deliberately, because she was troubled about something, but we never discussed it. Our family didn't do feelings, you see. Nothing was ever the same after that, for anyone."

For the first time, Seren thought she saw genuine sadness in her aunt's face.

"My mother wrote to tell Lloyd that Kate had died, as I said, and I think that's what pushed him over the edge. He was a gentle man, and his total collapse was so dreadful. I will never forget that night."

"Did he ever try and get in touch after I came to live with you? Did he know how I was doing?" Seren asked. "Surely he wanted to know?"

A second's hesitation. "He sent postcards at first, a book of poetry on your eighteenth, a photograph on your twenty-first, but a clean break seemed best at that point, for you both. We asked him to stop trying to make contact and let you live your life. It wasn't an easy decision, believe me, but I feel sure it was the right one."

Seren breathed deeply, trying to calm the waves of anger that were now flooding her. "I can see that you believe that, but I'm not so sure, to be honest," she said. "And why did you never show me any of the things he sent? I would have wanted to see them."

"Seren, I showed you a postcard once when you were little, and you were terribly upset for days. You refused to eat, or go to nursery – we were so worried. We decided that it was best that you forgot about him, as I had to forget about my sister."

"I see," Seren replied, but she had to steady herself before continuing, saying each word slowly to help her stay calm. "You and Uncle Neil have been good to me, and I know you always meant well, but I want to meet my father again now. If my cancer returns, I will never have the chance."

Aunt Alice pursed her lips and all the colour drained from her face. When two nurses scurried in and pulled the curtains around another patient's bed, it filled the awkward silence between the two women. Both were grateful for the pause.

"This might be where my life's meant to go next, Aunt. I need to find somewhere I feel I *belong,* and where Enya can grow up safe and happy," Seren said. "Surely you can see that?"

"I do, of course I do, but couldn't that be here, with us? Enya needs a stable environment after all these upsets, and she's such a delicate little thing. Do you really think Nirvana is waiting for you both at this lighthouse by the sea, with an old man you've not seen for almost thirty years? He couldn't be a good father to you then, and perhaps he can't now. Is it really worth taking such a huge risk?" Alice's voice was shaking, and her eyes were moist.

A fly buzzed desultorily around the ward, bouncing off the closed windows. Neither woman spoke for a few minutes.

"Look, I don't know what will happen, but I do know there are pieces missing from the puzzle that is my life, and I need them, to feel whole again," Seren said, looking down at her bandaged body. "Though I know I never truly can be."

Alice got up slowly. "I had wondered if this day would come, and a part of me is glad it has, actually. I'll get your father's letters together, and see if I still have a contact number. I don't remember if he never had a phone, so it was the local shop, I seem to recall. For now, rest and recover, please." She kissed her niece on the cheek once more. "And please, please don't expect miracles, dear. They don't exist."

But as her aunt walked away, a small voice inside Seren's head murmured that, just perhaps, they might.

THREE

Seren was discharged two days later, and returned to the house in Wimbledon armed with bags of painkillers, a soft fabric fake breast and reams of appointment letters for the weeks ahead. She was tired and sore, but her body told her when her pain medication was wearing off, so she let herself trust it. She spent the days resting in the stuffy attic room she had slept in as a child, and nights with Enya on a camp bed on the floor next to her. It felt odd not have her little girl's body curled up against her back like a baby monkey as she had always been between her and Finlay, but Alice had insisted on it.

"She might have a nightmare, and hit out at you without meaning to."

Enya had hardly spoken a word since they had both left her father just before Christmas in the darkness of the small hours. She had been very slow to speak, probably because her early efforts were frequently drowned in shouting, but this long period of near-silence frightened Seren. Was her daughter irrevocably traumatised by her father's rages? Had she somehow internalised her mother's fear of him? Could she even have become *mute*? Finlay had texted Seren a few times, asking first about Enya, and then "how the cancer stuff was going", but never asking her to return as "life was pretty fun" without her "nagging him and looking miserable all the time". Aunt Alice and Uncle Neil were militant in their avowals that they would never, ever let him into the house as they had dried too many of Seren's tears, but she knew it was only a question of time until their loyalty would be tested and he would drum his heels, demanding their return. For now, Finlay was playing nice.

As March began, the first hints of spring stalled in the city, and heavy rain streamed down the Velux windows in the loft and pummelled on the roof. Mother and daughter hid in their warm cocoon, watching Enya's favourite cartoons again and again, and Seren felt her daughter's body relax a little more every time they got to the "happily ever after" part of any story. She had seen and heard too much in her short life to believe in such things, even in stories and movies, so was always on tenterhooks, just in case they didn't.

Images of blissful walks along beaches and fresh, clean air gradually became more and more vivid in Seren's mind. Challenges lay ahead, but this was time to accept the possibility of a happiness she had never dared imagine, with a member of her *real* family, her long-lost father who had been haunting her dreams since girlhood. *He had loved her, in his own way,* Alice had said, and those words filled her heart with hope.

One afternoon, about a week after her discharge, her aunt came into the bedroom carrying a cardboard box sealed with peeling parcel tape.

"Here are all the things your father sent over the years. There's not much, but I kept everything, in case you ever wanted, well... just in case, really."

Seren carefully flattened the duvet to create a space.

"Would you mind just leaving the box with me, please?" she murmured. "I want to look through everything in my own time."

"Sure," her aunt replied. "I'm afraid I don't think you'll learn much about him from a few postcards, though. I visited them once on the island, apart from their pretty chaotic wedding, and your mother seemed as happy as I'd ever seen her. She seemed to have some very good friends as well, but Lloyd was always an intensely private man, as I've told you. He gave nothing away."

I recognise myself in those words, Seren thought. "Well, it's a start," she said.

"Oh, and I remembered that Lloyd always spoke as if he was reciting verse, rhythmic and slow too. I thought you might want to know that."

Seren did. "Are you still in touch with those good friends of my mum's?"

"Oh no. I felt it was best not to keep in touch after, well, after you came to us," Alice said, with a deep sigh. "But they did care about your mother, and about your father, very much. They were good people, trustworthy and loyal."

As soon as her aunt left the room and closed the door, Seren peeled the tape off the box, and her breathing quickened. Her *father* had written these words, sent these things, but she had no idea what to expect from them. An outpouring of love, of grief, of regret? News from the island, pleasantries, or a boring commentary on the weather? When she gently prised the lid off, a wave of mustiness was released, a smell which reminded her of libraries and hymn books in assemblies. Then came a second wave, of spiciness, of old men in high-backed leather chairs in a London club she had once worked in. She pulled out a small package of postcards first. The perished rubber band around them snapped the moment she touched it, and the cards scattered across her lap like dry leaves.

Colour was her first impression: blues, greens, white and

black, each one sharp and defined. Every single postcard had the same image but on one, particularly yellowed card, the pompous-sounding caption read: *"Trwyn Du*/Black Nose, the literal translation of the Welsh name, and the one locals use for Black Point and the lighthouse at Penmon on Anglesey". The angles were different, the photographs sharper, and colours more vivid in some than others, but the place remained the same; it was the one in her dream.

Turning over the postcards one by one, Seren read each of them very slowly. Her aunt had been right in saying that Lloyd was a man of few words, but she could feel that he leant towards poetry in every one he used. She read his enquiries as to her well-being and her progress at school, and titbits about his daily life – taking boat trips out in the summer night fishing for mackerel or sea bass, and working on local farms whenever they needed extra help to gather in the sheep for the winter months, or get a harvest in. She relished his descriptions of the sea, of the richly varied wildlife around him, and above all, she felt how much he missed her. His phrases danced across her imagination, and some lingered longer than others.

I still feel your soft little hand in mine, Seren.
I loved you, even though my heart was broken.
The seagulls miss your generosity with our stale bread.
You are the best of your mother, and of me.

When she had savoured each card, she pulled the book he had sent for her eighteenth birthday out of the box. It was *The Collected Poems of Dylan Thomas*, and he had written on the frontispiece in a messy, boyish hand:

To Seren, because you, too, are Welsh, you will feel these poems in your heart. Dad, Crigyll Cottage, Penmon.

As she had always known, the lighthouse existed, and her father existed.

Leafing through the crisp, yellowed letters sent to her, but kept from her, Seren could almost hear the deep, sonorous voice she dimly remembered. She knew some of this great Welshman's most famous play *Under Milk Wood*, but tears began to stream down her face at the beauty, the rawness of the poetry, quoted by her father in his letters:

Light breaks where no sun shines;
Where no sea runs, the waters of the heart
Push in their tides.

When she came to the bottom of the box, she found a faded photograph of a young man, his face half-hidden by a luxuriant brown beard, standing next to a pretty, blonde woman in a flowing white dress and a big straw hat who was smiling and waving and holding an equally smiling baby on her hip. On the back of the photo, her father had written the words:

Y teulu ni/Our family, Penmon, 1998. *Penblwydd hapus, Seren fach*/Happy birthday, little Seren.

She had had a family, a real family, once.

At that moment, Enya burst into the room. She had returned from the playgroup Alice insisted she attend, but hated, spending most of each session under a table. Seren quickly put everything back in the box and closed the lid. The little girl stared at her, and her mother knew the questions her eyes were asking. What were those secret things? Why couldn't she see them? Why were they here and not with Dad? What was going to happen next? Her mother's answer was a simple, but clear one.

"We're going to live by the sea, and we're going to see someone I've wanted to see for a very long time," she said. "I'll tell you about him another time."

"By the sea?" the little girl cried, her eyes alight.

"Yes. And we are going to live happily ever after."

"But what will Dad say?" she whispered.

Seren paused. Despite their separation, she feared Finlay's reaction, and had decided to tell him her plan only when she needed to. "He'll want us to be happy. And we will be."

Enya tilted her head to one side, like a cautious bird. "You promise?"

"I promise."

FOUR

However much she wanted to, Seren knew that she could not leave London until the oncology consultants decided what her post-surgery treatment would be. If it was radiotherapy, or worse, chemotherapy, she would have to stay in the city for several months and Enya would have to start school in Wimbledon in September. She did not want this, for either of them, but going to Anglesey to meet Lloyd Evans would have to wait until she was well enough to do so. Her aunt was truly delighted at this sensible compromise and told her so, which was rare.

As weeks passed, the endless-seeming barrage of medical appointments dwindled until, at the end of April, she was discharged from the care of the hospital faced with five years of the preventative drug Tamoxifen and the feeling that she had got off lightly. She had lost a breast, but she had been granted a future. The consultant mentioned reconstruction as being an option at a later date, but Seren was not keen. She did not want more drips and tubes so that a piece of her back fat could be sewn onto her rib-flat chest to make her feel normal again. That sounded very far from normal indeed. For her, losing her breast was a badge of honour that made her all the more determined to accept, even embrace, what had happened to her. For now, she had survived, and that was something to be deeply thankful for.

"You're so lucky," another woman, her face grey, whispered to her in a clinic waiting room. "You can get on with your life now."

"I know. I'm going to go and live by the sea, where I was born," Seren replied. "Just get to the end of your treatment, one day at a time, and then life will begin again for you too."

As she walked down the overheated corridors, past the all-too-familiar reception desk and towards the exit, Seren felt hope course through her for what she realised was the first time in years. School had been drudgery apart from her art lessons with Mistah Marley; she'd dropped out of her hated university course and never developed a photography portfolio as she'd intended to because of Finlay, and he had become her universe. The few friends she'd ever made had fallen by the wayside after years of neglect and the humdrum admin jobs she had been forced to take to pay the bills had sapped her of any joy or aspiration. Despite her cousins' best efforts to include her in their lives, she never took up Melissa's offers of lunch in Covent Garden, or Alex's for a drink near his office in the City. But that day, as she went out of the revolving doors and out into the air, she was certain that she, Seren Evans, could forge her own path, and she knew exactly where it would lead her: to home, to her father, and to the lighthouse by the sea.

FIVE

Unfortunately, Lloyd Evans, her father, was not an easy man to contact. Aunt Alice had failed to find any helpful landline telephone numbers for him. She had no idea if he now had a mobile and if so, what his number could be, so Seren was forced to resort to more old-fashioned methods. She would write him a letter, introducing herself and telling him of her intention to return to Anglesey. Her words had to be chosen with enormous care, as there was a risk he would reject her, or not reply at all. Aunt Alice had described him as gentle, but intensely private, and he would not be expecting to hear from his long-lost daughter almost thirty years after she had been taken from him at his very lowest ebb. She needed to proceed with great caution.

She decided to try and embed some of Dylan Thomas' words in her own, so that Lloyd would know that she *did* feel herself to be Welsh, as he had written in the anthology he had sent for her eighteenth birthday. Then he would also know that his gift had been both understood and appreciated – even if she had had to wait *fourteen years* to receive it.

Enya demanded her attention during the afternoons,

anxious, questioning, pleading to be allowed to stop going to playgroup, but in the evenings, once her daughter was asleep, Dylan Thomas' words danced across Seren's mind when she read them, conjuring up places she could only imagine. She ordered a copy of *Under Milk Wood* and absorbed Thomas' startling use of language and his obvious love, and understanding, of his homeland. Since the age of four, she had only known the city, with its dirt, noise and frantic pace, and so to read the poet describe a different kind of childhood filled her with even more determination to let her own daughter experience it:

And as I was green and carefree, famous among the barns
About the happy yard and singing as the farm was home.

Enya had rarely been carefree; the toxic atmosphere with Finlay had ensured she was often as on edge as her mother. She wanted more for her, and better.

Before Seren could begin drafting a letter to her father, she did some research into Anglesey, following its rugged coastline with her finger on a map. She always paused at Penmon and the lighthouse, which she felt subconsciously connected to. She'd stuck all the postcards that Lloyd had sent around her bedroom, and the image of the black and white tower surrounded by the sea now surrounded her, both awake and asleep. She contacted some rental agencies on the island, and left them her details, and her requirements, but the replies were not hopeful. She probably had enough savings for a month or two's rent, and once Enya started school in September, she would find work, but until then, would they be able to live? Uprooting Enya for a home that was worse than the one they had left was not an option, but she could no longer settle for a life of compromise. She had to leave Finlay O'Neill behind her for good. Churning over scenarios in her head day after day was exhausting, so she decided to discuss it with her aunt rather than ruminate about it pointlessly. It did not go well.

"Aunt, I've been looking at properties to rent on Anglesey, and it's slim pickings unless you can afford the holiday let prices," she began, in as chatty a tone as she could manage.

"I see," her aunt replied. "So, you're still set on this plan to try and find your father, and discover your so-called 'roots', are you? I must confess we find it more than a little hurtful, Seren. Neil had hoped you felt he was your father now, after all he's done for you."

Seren was stung. She hadn't meant to hurt anyone's feelings.

"I am grateful, you know I am, for all that you and Uncle Neil have done for me, but I need to at least *meet* Lloyd Evans, if only to know for sure that he can't be any kind of father to me. If I don't do that, I'll never know, and always wonder."

"My dear girl, I hate to be so frank, but you last saw him almost thirty years ago. He may be dead by now, have you even considered that? Or he may not want to see *you* again, as you remind him of Kate. I think you need to consider these things before you start looking at places to rent, I really do."

Suri, the household Siamese cat, sauntered into the kitchen, but the atmosphere was so chilly that he sensed no strokes or treats were likely, and left.

"I know it could go wrong, but why are you so against my even trying? You said my father loved me, and it's clear from his cards and letters that he's missed me all these years," Seren said.

"But his last communication was over ten years ago," Aunt Alice said gently, "and he was *mentally unstable* when I last saw him, and that may not have changed. Do you and Enya really need any more of that in your life?"

Seren felt her heart begin to pound. This kindly air of supe-riority was exactly how her asking to study photography, and moving in with Finlay, had been greeted. She felt a flare of the teenage rebellion that had always been her go-to reaction to it. Yet again, having asked for support, she felt judged.

"Look, I simply cannot stay here any longer, and I certainly can't go back to Finlay. He's loving his freedom and getting pissed with his mate Conor every night, he told me," Seren said. "What other choice do I have? I want to make a fresh start, a new life, a *better* life."

"I understand, but we don't see why you can't stay here until you're strong again. Why does everything with you always have to be so knee-jerk, so *dramatic*?"

"Perhaps I get it from my mother," Seren snapped. "She followed her dreams too, didn't she, and she was very happy?"

Her face flushed, Aunt Alice stood up. "Seren, doesn't everything I've told you about your mother make you see how disastrous it is to make impulsive choices? Kate destroyed our family for a selfish, childish whim. Please don't do the same to yours. Take some time to really think through what you're doing. We *care* about you, Seren, whatever you may think of us." Her fingers were gripping the table edge so hard that the skin on her knuckles had whitened.

Guilt washed over Seren, and she went over to her aunt and put her hands on both her shoulders. "I know you do, Aunt, I really do, and I hear all your caution, but I know what I need to do, and I need to do it now, while I still can," Seren said. "It would be great if you could wish me luck on the biggest adventure of my life. I feel that's what your sister would have wanted you to do."

And in the warm hug that her aunt then gave her, Seren knew she was right.

SIX

Writing to Lloyd Evans, a man she had not seen for so many years, was one of the hardest things Seren had ever done. For a start, it felt alien to be writing a letter on paper, with a pen, and the fact that she could not edit and delete as she could on her laptop, was maddening.

"How the hell did people manage before computers?" she muttered to herself, as sheet after sheet of notepaper hit the wastepaper bin.

Another problem was language. Was her father's English good, or was he primarily a Welsh speaker? This would affect the words she used. Deep in her memory, a song was lodged, and a few words of Welsh that she must have heard as a small child, but nothing more. Was Aunt Alice right in thinking he might not want to see her, because she'd dredge up unhappy memories? Had he married and had other children and was now happily nearing retirement? Or was he, as her aunt had said, perhaps no longer even alive, having spent years pining alone for her mother, and for her. That possibility broke her heart, but in effect she was writing to an almost-stranger.

She wrestled to find the right words to write for days, and

her longing to meet her father grew ever stronger, so that they could talk face to face. She told him about Enya, and how she wanted her to grow up somewhere safe, with family, but every sentence seemed inadequate, or hackneyed. In the end, she chose to explain how she felt with some of Lloyd's favourite poet's words:

All things are known: the stars' advice
Calls some content to travel with the winds.

'I am content to be called to come home, Dad, and to travel with the winds alongside you', she wrote after the quotation. It seemed fitting, in every way.

Finally, she ventured back into the practicalities of finding a home to rent near Penmon that they could afford. She emphasised that she was in no way asking for money, and asking for his help did not come easily, but he knew that part of the island as nobody else did.

When she eventually sealed the envelope, she was not entirely happy with her letter, but she knew that it was fuelled by the desire to know the truth about her past, and love for her own daughter. She hoped with all her heart it would reignite her father's love for his.

The days that followed were tense in the house in Wimbledon as Seren waited nervously for a reply. Aunt Alice was still a little hurt and Uncle Neil slunk around the house trying to stay well out of both women's way. Enya, sensing another imminent change, pestered her mother with endless questions. When were they going to live by the sea? Could she have a dog there? What if Dad did want to come with them? In searching for a response to this last enquiry, Seren marvelled at her daughter's capacity for forgiveness.

"No, love, Dad definitely wants to stay here in London," she said as calmly as she could. Having now texted Finlay to say she was thinking of leaving the city for a while, but without telling him where she was going, his response had unnerved her:

> You need some space, but I need to see Enya, so don't go too far.

Over a week later, a letter arrived postmarked Llangoed, which she recognised as a village near Penmon. The white envelope was soft and slightly stained at the corners, as if it had been kept somewhere moist. The handwriting was old-fashioned, each letter precise and measured. It reminded Seren of the frontispiece of a first edition of a Charles Dickens novel she had once seen in a museum. Her hands trembled as she slit open the envelope and began to read. It was not a long letter, but its tone was open and almost whimsical. Lloyd Evans was obviously an unusual man, as her aunt had said, but as she read, she warmed to him more and more. As her eyes skimmed over his words, a few leapt out at her:

We need to meet, and begin to know each other again. Then, as Dylan Thomas puts it:

My one and noble heart has witnesses
In all love's countries, that will grope awake.

He also responded to her subtle cry for help in finding affordable accommodation on the island with a generosity she could never have anticipated:

You ask where you could live. My cottage is not an ideal place for us to begin again, but a friend here has a small cottage on his farm that he intends to convert in the autumn. Until he does, it is yours, if you want it.

And his final words reassured her that she was doing the right thing:

I long to see you again, and meeting Enya, my granddaughter, is a joy I had never dared dream of.

"Me neither, Dad," she whispered.

When she had read his letter several times, Seren closed her eyes and felt peace flood through her body, slowly releasing the tension it had held inside, like a clenched fist, for so long. She was going home.

SEVEN

The rain was torrential on the day Seren and Enya left London. Her cousin Melissa agreed to let her borrow her bright yellow Fiat 500 for a few months, as she had been promoted and was going to work in the New York office. Aunt Alice tearfully said that she hoped that her niece would always feel able to come home if things didn't work out, but when Seren drove away from Wimbledon, with the tiny car packed to the gunnels, she knew that whatever lay ahead, coming back to that house and that life was not an option.

It took them almost an hour and a half to reach the outskirts of the city, as the stop-start morning traffic was predictably terrible, and Seren, who had barely driven for several years, was very nervous. Once they hit the motorway, the little car seemed to sense it was being given a challenge, purring along at a steady 70mph. Enya was asleep by the time they reached Watford, and Seren was able to loosen her rictus grip on the steering wheel.

As she began to relax, she realised that casting off into the unknown had not been as difficult as she'd anticipated – perhaps because she felt as if she had already done so when she left Finlay and their flat. She'd not dared to go back to ask him for any possessions, and Enya had just grabbed her few toys when they'd left, but it saddened her to think how easy it was to shuck off years of her life. She had loved that man, but he was too damaged to love her in the way she deserved, and Enya was better off fatherless than with him as her father, sad as that sounded.

When Seren looked ahead, she had only the few grainy photographs of the cottage on the farm they were going to live in that Lloyd had sent her and some recent ones of the light-house, always the lighthouse. Whatever else, that little tower symbolised permanence and safety – a still point in a turning world. Everything else was blank, a *tabula rasa* waiting for the future to be written on it. Only the conviction that it had to be better than the past kept Seren's fears and doubts from bubbling up and overcoming her newfound courage. Even if her reunion with her father did not go well – as Aunt Alice had warned her it might not – Anglesey would be a beautiful place to raise a child.

She had arranged to settle her and Enya into their new home before meeting Lloyd, worried that it would be too over-whelming for all three of them if he was waiting on the doorstep when they arrived. They had exchanged a few brief, largely practical, messages, passed on via the landline of a woman called Gwen Hughes, who owned a local café that Seren had eventually found on Facebook, but both father and daughter knew how huge seeing each other for the first time would be. She wanted to put Enya's well-being before her increasingly urgent need to reconnect with her father. Her little girl deserved that, and much more.

The rain that had started at Telford petered out when they passed Shrewsbury and crossed the border into Wales. By the time Seren drove over the Britannia Bridge that spans the strip of sea between the mainland of Wales and the island of Anglesey, the sky was clear of clouds and everything was bathed in soft, spring sunshine. Looking to the right, she glimpsed the elegant span of Thomas Telford's suspension bridge, the other crossing onto the island. Between the two, a white-sailed yacht was gliding silently on its way, leaving a silvery snail-trail in the deep blue water. Enya's face was bright with excitement as she realised that her mother had kept her word; they really *were* going to live by the sea! When they drove down the hill towards the town of Menai Bridge, Seren glimpsed a tiny church on a small, wooded islet, resplendent amidst all this and with the mountains of *Eryri*/Snowdonia as its backdrop, like a small gem in a setting of breathtaking beauty.

The road that led to Penmon was one of the most stunning Seren had ever driven. It took them along a windy, wooded road until they reached Beaumaris, a town in which a row of brightly painted Georgian houses proclaimed its grandiose history as a seaside retreat as you approached. Then the road went on, past the squat castle Edward I had built over 700 years ago, out alongside the lapping waters of the Menai Straits, and on towards *Trwyn Du*/Black Nose. Seren saw the lighthouse long before they reached it.

"Oh, there it is!" she exclaimed. "Just like in my dreams. Oh God! Oh my God!"

"Is it nice to see it again?" Enya said, a furrow of concern on her face.

"Yes, yes, it is, love, sorry. I was just surprised to see it there, the same as I remember. I didn't mean to scare you," Seren said quickly.

The little girl nodded cautiously and her mother smiled at her. She knew that surprises were not usually good things in her daughter's experience.

They followed the single-track road towards Penlôn Farm, where Lloyd Evans had told them that Mrs Ruthie Edwards would be waiting to let them into their short-term home, endearingly called *Bwthyn y Dryw*/Wren Cottage. She and her husband Dafydd were old friends, he said, and had known him since childhood, so they were more than happy to help. When they pulled into the farmyard, Seren saw a plumpish, middle-aged woman wearing a grubby apron and wellies standing by the farm door holding a basket of washing on one hip and waving enthusiastically with her free hand. What was most astounding about her were her vivid rosy cheeks and her thick mane of chestnut curls. She was the epitome of the jolly farmer's wife in so many children's books Seren remembered.

"That must be Mrs Edwards," Seren said to a wary-looking Enya. She hated meeting new people, or having to talk to them. "Shall we say hello together?"

But Enya scrunched herself into a ball in her seat. Seren reached back and stroked her arm gently – so much change in so little time. No wonder the little girl was unsure what to do. This was overwhelming for both of them.

"You stay here if you want to, love. That's fine."

Mrs Edwards walked over towards the car, a broad smile on her face, and Seren shook her hand, a warm hand, roughened with hard work.

"*Croeso 'nôl*/Welcome back, Seren. After all this time, you've come home at last!" Mrs Edwards said, and Seren saw the glitter of tears in her eyes. "Lloyd has told Dafydd and I all about you, and we know... well, what happened when you were a girl, so don't feel the need to fill us in. It's all been a bit much for Lloyd, I think. It probably is for you, too, *dweud y gwir*/to tell the truth." She paused and looked into the car. "And who's this little treasure? Enya, is it? What a beauty you are with those green eyes and your shiny hair. Ooh, I can see your *Taid*/Grandfather is going to spoil you rotten!"

Enya wriggled, but a small smile spread across her face. Her father had always praised her Irish eyes and glossy, dark hair.

She'd decided, as only children can, that this was a woman to trust. Seren had never seen her respond to any other adult like this, not even Aunt Alice or Uncle Neil, and she marvelled at it.

"I have something to show you that I think you'll like, *Enya fach*/little Enya," she said with a conspiratorial wink. "But you'll need to come out to see it."

Seren watched as Enya opened the car door and stepped gingerly onto the cobbled yard. When Mrs Edwards put two fingers into her mouth and whistled, the little girl looked startled, but when the farmhouse door opened and a bundle of young collie pups tumbled out and charged towards her, fluffy tails wagging, their whole bodies aquiver, she knelt down to take them in her arms. For the next few minutes, both women watched, laughing, as Enya was licked and snuggled from all directions and both she and the pups yelped in delight.

"Mum, puppies! Look! Can I look after them now that we live here?" she said, when her mouth was finally free enough to speak. "They love me already!"

"Course you can. I need all the help I can get," Mrs Edwards replied, smiling at Seren, who mouthed "Thank you". "Now, let's get you both settled in."

Bwthyn y Dryw/Wren Cottage was a few minutes' walk from the main farmhouse, but it was built of the same large blocks of dark grey stone and roofed with the same locally quarried slates that kept almost every home in the area dry. The moment Mrs Edwards opened the front door and Seren walked into the living room, she felt as if she was enveloped in *solidity,* with its walls inches thick and floors made of knobbly stone flagstones that spoke of a different age. Like the lighthouse, it felt permanent, and *safe.* The small windows meant it was a little gloomy, but Mrs Edwards assured her that, when the sun hit the front of the cottage each morning, these rooms blazed with sunshine.

The kitchen was well laid out, with a table and chairs at one end and the living room boasted a huge, stone inglenook fireplace which was "big enough to stand in", or so Seren was proudly told. There was one, small double bedroom, and a single one up above the main living area. Mrs Edwards led them into that one first.

"This room gets lovely and snug when the fire's lit downstairs," Mrs Edwards said, "so I think this is the one for you, Enya."

The little girl dropped onto the bed happily and spread her arms and legs as if laying claim to the space.

"Mrs Edwards, thank you so much for letting us stay here," Seren said. "I'll find a job soon, I hope, and be able to rent somewhere else, but right now…"

"Call me Ruthie, please. And you are more than welcome. My mam Enid was a good friend of your mother's, and our family owes Lloyd more than a few favours, so we're glad to repay one of them."

"Your mother knew mine?" Seren asked. "Gosh, that's amazing."

Ruthie paused and looked a little unsure. "A very long time ago, yes, she did. But today, what's more important is how do you feel about meeting your *dad*?"

"I'm not sure how I feel, to be honest. I do have some memories of him, but it's been a lifetime since we saw each other. Does he still have a big brown beard?"

"Well, it's a grey and white one now, but it's still there, and bigger than ever!"

"Then I'll know it's him. Part of me can't quite believe that he really exists, as he's just been this mysterious figure in my dreams for so long."

"Oh, he most certainly does, and he asked me to tell you that he'll come here tomorrow at 11 a.m. I think Enya will be just fine on puppy duty with me and my youngest, Sali, while you two chat, if you're happy about that?"

"I am. And thank you again, Ruthie," Seren replied. She sighed, and looked around her contentedly. "So our new life begins right now, and I finally meet my father again tomorrow..."

"Yes indeed. I don't know what's brought you here now, and I don't need to know, but it sounds like it's going to be a bit of a rollercoaster ride, for both of you," Ruthie said gently, adding, in an even quieter tone, "He's suffered, you know, and he's been waiting for you for such a long time. We're all, well, over the moon that you're finally here."

As she watched this kind woman walk back to the farm-house, pups bundling around her ankles, Seren felt the same.

PART 2
NEW BEGINNINGS

EIGHT

Spring in London seemed ludicrously muted when compared to the blaze of colour that greeted Seren as she pulled back the curtains on her first morning on Anglesey.

"Jeez, Ruthie was right about the sunshine coming in," she murmured, squinting at the light streaming into the room. When she could focus properly, she slowly took in the scene in front of her. The sky was the clearest blue she had ever seen, a distilled colour as if on an artist's palette, vivid and pure. Just beyond the walled garden around the cottage was a beautiful horse chestnut tree. Its branches were resplendent with pink-tinged sticky buds that would unfurl to reveal soft, new leaves in the day's growing warmth almost as you watched them. Seagulls cruised the thermals, their full-throated cries celebrating the freedom to fly where they wanted to, when they wanted to. Breathing deeply, Seren felt her heart lift, this place really was a little corner of bliss, and it was *hers,* for a while, at least, and it was so remote that Finlay could never find them here.

Enya was already dressed when she raced into her mother's bedroom, her face shining with the prospect of a morning playing with puppies. Seren didn't have the heart to tell her that her T-shirt was on back to front and her hair looked like a scarecrow; it didn't matter, as there were more important things on the agenda for both of them today. At just after 9 a.m., there was a knock at the cottage door. Seren opened it but was surprised to see nobody there – until she looked downwards and saw a little girl beaming up at her with more gaps than front teeth and a scree of freckles across her nose.

"Hiya," the girl said. "I've come to collect Enya. Mam told me to, so I hope it's OK. Is she ready?"

Her accent was one Seren had never heard before, but assumed was North Welsh. It sounded rather nasal, with drawn-out vowels punctuated with sharp consonants, but she decided she liked it. Of course, if they stayed, she had no doubt Enya would soon adopt it too.

"That's fine, yes. Are you Sali?" she replied.

"*Ie, Sali dw'i*/Yes, I'm Sally – oops, sorry, you don't speak Welsh, do you?"

"Not yet, but we'd both like to learn it," Seren said with a smile. "It will help Enya when she starts school if you can teach her a bit."

But as she watched the two little girls scamper across the farmyard towards the delight of a day with pups, Seren felt her first wriggle of nerves. Her decision to come here had been made so quickly in the end that she had put the fact that Enya would be taught only in Welsh when she started school at the back of her mind. Research she'd read had shown that it was a good thing, that most children thrived, but it would be a huge ask for her daughter, who found speaking her own language difficult at times and had not responded well to Finlay trying to teach her a few words of Gaelic, his native tongue. At least they had several months to prepare for it, as she wouldn't start school until September. That should give her ample time to lay the foundations of a happier, more secure childhood for Enya before she faced the challenge of using a brand new language every day.

She looked at the clock on the kitchen wall: 9.25 a.m. In about ninety minutes, her father would be knocking on the door. She would open it, and see him for the first time in so many years. The very thought made her shiver with excitement, and a bit of dread. What if he wasn't actually very nice? What if they didn't get on? What if she disappointed him? She focused on making toast and coffee to dismiss her doubts, there was little point in them now. What would be, would be.

The day was such a lovely one that Seren decided to meet her father outside rather than in the cottage, which was darkening again after its morning bath of sunshine. There was a small wrought-iron table and two chairs set up in the little garden which seemed a light, warm spot for such an important event. At 10.50 a.m., she carried a cafetière of coffee, two mugs and a jug of milk outside and sat down, hands placed in her lap to stop them fidgeting, and waited for Lloyd Evans to arrive. Her heart was thumping so hard against her ribs she was not sure if she would be able to speak to him when he did. The weight of emotion pressed on her chest and squeezed her throat, leaving her almost gasping for air. She took some deep breaths in an effort to calm herself. This was huge.

When she first glimpsed a man, an older man, wearing a very well-worn beige macintosh and a tweed cap walking towards her, her brain did not connect him with the image she had formed of her father at all. This man looked tired, almost dishevelled, very far from the strong figure she remembered looking up at as a child. His gait was uneven and his back slightly rounded, which made him appear stooped. His beard was almost snow-white with an edging of grey, and it hung from his face in matted hanks. All in all, he exuded defeat and sadness rather than the energy and hopefulness Seren remembered, and had been expecting, until now. And he looked so *old*.

She stood up, trembling, took a step towards him and smiled, as she could not help but do. His face lifted instantly, and she watched as many of the shadows and lines seemed to melt away as silently as the wind shunts clouds across the sky. His eyes were alight now, and a deep, soulful brown, just like hers.

"*Seren fach*/Little Seren," he murmured, coming towards her with his arms stretched wide. "How beautiful you are, *fy nghariad*/my darling."

"Dad," she whispered, feeling his voice hum as they reached each other. That deep, sonorous voice was the voice in her dreams. "It's really you."

Whenever she looked back on this moment, Seren could not remember whether she'd walked into Lloyd's arms, or he'd enveloped her as she stood, stock-still, waiting for him to reach her. The memory was a blur of warmth and closeness, and a release of pent-up feelings so enormous that tears were their only possible expression. Father and daughter clung to each other for what seemed like a second, and an eternity, and when they slowly drew apart, both were crying, and it was a moment of bliss for both of them.

He looked different, and yet the same, Seren decided. In the deep crow's feet around his eyes, she saw many years of watching, waiting, looking out to the horizon, perhaps searching for her, hoping she would return. Now, finally, she had come back to him. Never had anything in her life felt so right – and he soon told her that he agreed.

"This is our destiny, to meet again here, on this glorious morning," he murmured. "Oh, I hoped this day would come for years, but I never dared believe it would," Lloyd said, now holding her at arm's length as if to drink her in. "*Duw*/God, I can see so much of my Kate in you. I can see her spirit, her determination."

"Oh, I need you to tell me more about her – no, everything about her. Where you met, where you got married, what she liked to do... *everything*! Start with when you first met, please."

Lloyd sighed. "Can I sit down first, and brace myself?" he said with a wry smile.

And so, they sat at the table and chairs outside the cottage and began to talk.

"We met at the lighthouse, of course. It draws people to it, I've always thought," he said, and Seren nodded her understanding. "Well, she was about to go for a bloody swim right next to it, wasn't she? I had to haul her out as the currents are so dangerous there. Then we went for a *panad*/cuppa at mine..."

"You saved her life on your first date?" Seren said, laughing.

"I always say that she saved mine. We were so happy, it was as if fate had sent her to me. I think we knew from that first day that we would be together forever," he paused, and sighed. "But we weren't, of course. When she left, every ounce of my joy in life went with her, and when I found out from your grandmother that she was... never coming back to us, I thought I couldn't go on. I think the only reason I did, year after year, working on the boat, reading my books, farming the land, was because I was waiting, hoping, for the day you might come back, my Seren – the star of my life. Your mam would be so happy today, I know she would."

"But what was she like, Dad? Was she beautiful? I've only seen one photo, and she looks lovely to me."

"She was *very* beautiful, with wild curls and a laugh that filled a room, and you look so much like her," Lloyd replied, beaming. "I could never believe that I made her happy, but I did. I know I did – I felt it."

"Aunt Alice said you were happy, yes, but she said Mum

was, well, rather selfish overall. I don't know whether she liked her sister very much actually."

Sipping his coffee, Lloyd's expression changed. "They were so different. It wasn't easy for Alice growing up, because I think Kate, well, *took all the air in the family*, if you understand me. She needed so much love, so much reassurance, so much *excitement* that there was probably very little left for her quiet, well-behaved older sister. She's a good soul, your aunt, but a sad one."

Seren felt some things that had always jarred fall into place. Aunt Alice may have been jealous of Kate, and perhaps even disliked her to some degree, but she had loved her enough to drive up here, scoop up her daughter and bring her up. What a huge act of kindness that had been, and Seren had repaid her with sullenness and sulkiness. She blushed with shame.

"Yes, she is a good soul," she said. "I must tell her that, next time I see her."

Father and daughter talked for over an hour, but when they looked back on this, their first reunion, neither could recall much of what they'd said to each other. Seren remembered that Lloyd liked two sugars in his coffee, and he was amazed that she drank hers black, as he had never met a woman who did. She did not tell him about her cancer, or that her partner had made both her and Enya deeply unhappy; those dark things would wait. They had scratched the surface of the past, but this was a day of joy. There were so many questions to ask and answer that their conversation faltered after a while. There were very few common links, after so many years of separation.

"Would you like to see where we lived, you, your mam and me, all those years ago?" Lloyd suggested. "It might help us both remember how things were, and decide how they are going to be now."

"Yes, please. I think it would really help. I've only seen the lighthouse from a distance too, and I remember that more than anything."

"I wish I'd cleared up a bit at home, but you'll have to take it as you find it," Lloyd said with a smile that reached all the way up to his, very vigorous, eyebrows. "We were very happy there... until, well, until we weren't."

Seren nodded her understanding. "I'll just pop over to the farm and tell Ruthie we're going. I'm sure Enya is having the time of her life, with all those puppies!"

Her father met her gaze directly. "I look forward to meeting Enya," he said.

Seren felt a tiny ripple of unease. Her little girl had been through so much upheaval, and was being asked to accept so much more. Meeting a grandfather she never knew existed today might be a step too far.

"And you will, when the time's right," she said. "She's so little, you see, and... very sensitive."

"*Wrth gwrs*/Of course," he replied, before clapping a hand over his mouth. "Oh goodness. You don't speak Welsh any more, do you? I'm sorry."

"Any more?" Seren replied. "So I *did*, when I was little?"

"Your very first word was a Welsh one – *Mam*, which we say instead of 'Mum'."

There was a pause. Every mention of Kate, her mother, sent a shiver down Seren's spine. She really had existed – the pretty woman in the straw hat and the white dress in the photo had been here, had lived here, with them. It was an incredible moment, and one in which she fully realised for the first time that she, too, had once been loved as much as she loved Enya.

"I want to learn to speak Welsh again, and I know Enya will at school, if we stay here," she said, already hoping they could. "Back in a sec, and then we'll go... home, shall we?"

"*Da iawn*/Very good," her father replied. "We've waited long enough, haven't we, my Seren?"

NINE

The walk down to the cottage, and the lighthouse on the point beyond it, was stunningly beautiful. Lloyd took them down a grassy track lined on both sides with high hawthorn hedges frothing with creamy blossom, and Seren breathed in their sweetness as they walked down towards the sea. The nearer they got to the water's edge, the more the air was filled with an energy that can only be found on the coast, an imperceptible feeling of open space both as startling and refreshing as the scent of petrichor on hot city pavements after rain.

Out at sea, snow-white terns dived like quicksilver to catch the unwary fish who gathered in huge numbers in the surging currents around the point. Their high-pitched "*kraaks*" as they scanned the water filled the air with an uncanny sound.

"I remember you telling me about those birds diving for their supper," Seren said, softly, before adding. "And all these years, you have been watching them here while I was growing up somewhere else. I'm glad to be back with you now."

Lloyd glanced at her almost coyly. He was clearly not used to people expressing their feelings so openly, let alone positive ones, and he lived a very repetitive, isolated life, Ruthie had said. This was unfamiliar ground for him. He cleared his throat before saying, "We've had dolphins here the last few summers. Not as many jet-skis here, see, as the currents can be treacherous, so they feel safer, I suppose."

"It does feel like the very edge of the land," Seren replied.

"Dylan Thomas would call it '*Where gulls come to be lonely*'," he replied. "But I love its wildness, even its loneliness. It's always suited me. It's all I know."

"But not my mother?" Seren said. She still wanted to know more about her, the woman who had given her life, and vanished from it. This need was becoming almost insatiable.

Lloyd hesitated. "She did at first. Said it was paradise, but something changed in her just before she went away. I never knew what it was, and she wouldn't tell me. It was the only secret she said not even I could know."

"And then she just left?" Seren said.

Lloyd's face darkened. "One morning, she was gone, yes."

A pause, while both of them took in this bald, sad fact.

"But I don't understand. We all look so happy in that photo you sent me," Seren said, shaking her head. "It doesn't make sense."

"No, it never has. Why on earth Kate was riding a motorbike the day she died is another mystery to me. She couldn't even drive a car, and never wanted me to go fast in mine."

Seren looked at him. "I didn't know that. That's a bit, well, *weird*, isn't it? I thought she must have been some kind of speed freak."

"Far from it. She was impulsive, but when she made up her mind to do something, like living here with me, her pace was slow and mindful once she'd settled – like a butterfly, really. Then she spread her wings wide and soaked up the sunshine. Yes, she did everything with her whole heart, your mam." He stopped, and then said words that Seren realised she had waited years to hear. "And she loved you so very much, *Seren fach*/little Seren. I don't know why she went away, or did what she did, but I know that for certain."

"Thank you, Dad," she replied. "That means more than you can ever know."

The cottage where Seren had lived with her father, and which Alice and Neil had driven her away from on that terrible night, was set back from the shore. A cliff loomed behind it, which meant one half of its roof was covered with thick moss and it was in shade for much of the day. It looked out over the sea with a view interrupted only by a few, straggly bushes, blown into otherworldly shapes by the onshore winds that often blasted this side of the island. Built of the same local stone as the farmhouse and *Bwthyn y Dryw*/Wren Cottage, its wide, slate-covered eaves gave it a glowering look, as if thick, dark eyebrows overhung its face. Seren was disconcerted to find that, despite the magnificent view from the front of the cottage, it did not look as welcoming as she had imagined. In fact, it looked rather bleak, and very uncared-for. Given that Lloyd had lived there, sad and alone, for so long, she decided that was probably inevitable.

When Lloyd led her inside, and she began to look around at his sparse furniture and the bare stone walls and flagstones on the floor, the oppressive feeling she had sensed on first seeing the cottage grew stronger. This was a place that had set itself against the elements, and was strong enough to endure many harsh winters, but it was not a place of comfort. Seren found herself wondering if her mother had felt the same, and whether its gloominess had contributed to her leaving, and her father's subsequent depression and isolation. It felt insensitive to ask him this, but as she moved from room to room, she found herself longing to be outside, in the air and sunshine, and not in this dark cottage.

When they went up the narrow stairs to the little bedroom where she had slept as a child, her feelings intensified as dim memories began to stir, tectonic plates buried deep beneath the subsequent years of her life. Her low, wooden bed was still where it had been when Aunt Alice had lifted her out of it that night, and a well-hugged teddy bear was propped up on the pillow, as if the child she had been when she'd loved it was expected back at any moment. She tried desperately to remember this simple emblem of a past life, and to imagine herself holding it close, but she could not. To the right of the bed, she glimpsed a sheet of paper stuck on the wall, a child's drawing of three stick figures, their spider-like hands interlinked.

"Did I draw that, Dad?" she whispered. "Is that us – you, Mum and me?"

Lloyd nodded. "You did, and it is."

Going nearer, Seren saw that the paper was criss-crossed with yellowed sticky tape. Someone had slashed the drawing between the man and the woman and child, and then taped the pieces back together. She did not need to ask her father who had done it, but a sudden image of someone hovering over her, his face flushed in anger and flecks of spittle hitting her eyes, made her shiver. Bad things had happened here, in this little room, in this house. Its very stones emanated a sadness that the years had neither eradicated nor softened.

Blurred images of things she had heard, and seen, in the cottage flickered across her mind like a cloud of tiny, dancing gnats on a summer's evening. Her imagination and her senses were on overdrive. She could almost *feel* the confusion she had felt here as a child when there had been nobody to ask what was happening, or why. Things had not been good here in the end, and Lloyd had been very ill indeed. For the first time, Seren understood that and accepted that she had been taken from him because there had been no other choice. But who had called Aunt Alice and Neil to come and get her? She felt she could not risk opening old wounds by asking her father and in the long run, it hardly mattered.

Whatever had happened, it had not been either sensible or safe for her to stay here, just as Enya had not been safe growing up with Finlay O'Neill. Only now did she fully understand how such terrible, instinctive choices sometimes needed making in life and that the ripples they caused lasted for years.

Her father led the way down the stairs, through the living room, past the faded armchairs and a dust-covered piano and out into the bright sunshine of a late spring day. Seren closed her eyes as she felt the sun on her face, and she began to feel calmer as her memories ebbed and faded. These strong feelings were not what she had expected at all, and her father knew it.

"It must be very hard for you, coming back after all this time. This has not been a happy home for a long time, and you feel that, don't you?" he said. "The night you went away, and the weeks before it, were... *dark* times, for me, for both of us. I am more sorry than I can say about that, and that your life in London has not been the contented one I wanted for you, but life is rarely fair, I find."

The lump that appeared in Seren's throat was unexpected, but it released the slight tension that had sprung up between them and put raw emotion in its place.

"Yes, I do feel that here, and I don't think I want to dwell on... how ill you were – at the end, I mean. But I was scared. I do remember that."

"I know, and I understand, but I hope you feel we have brighter days ahead of us now," Lloyd said with the slightest note of pleading in his tone. "Shall we walk down to the lighthouse together, like old times – old, *happy* times?"

Seren smiled to reassure him. It had been a lighthouse she

had seen in her dreams, after all, not this dark cottage redolent of stress and sadness. Throughout history, it had been a symbol of safe passage, of perils avoided, of a guiding hand throughout centuries of storms and history. Yes, it was time for her to see *her* lighthouse once again.

TEN

Trwyn Du/Black Nose, the rocky point where the island meets the sea at its most easterly edge, is far from black. The beaches that surround it are pebbled with bright, white stones, and the headland is covered with freshly unfurled green bracken and soft tufts of pink thrift as April becomes May. Scores of seabirds live and breed around the lighthouse each year, and on the tiny rocky outcrop beyond it, Puffin Island. The chug of an approaching boat sees them rise up like a cloud and fill the sky with their celebratory cries, an expression of pure joy that had heartened Lloyd even in his darkest days. Fat seals lounge on the rocks on the far side of the island, and in the summer, puffins dart above the waves before returning to their cliffside nests with food for their gaping-mouthed chicks. The sea, the lighthouse and the cacophony of the birds were what Seren vividly remembered as they walked towards them that day, and she sensed her spirits lifting as they watched the waves crash around the rocks, and felt it spray their faces. They stood in wonder, and in silence, for several minutes.

"But it's *quiet,* the lighthouse," she commented. "I

remember a sound – a bell clanging, always there in the background to our lives."

"They got rid of the bell a few years back, much to the dislike of those of us who live here," Lloyd said. "I miss it, sad as it was to listen to sometimes. *Mournful*, was the word most used about it."

"Oh, wait, I remember we came here once in the dark, and the sea was, well, *blue*," Seren said, amazed at the return of this vivid memory. "Can that possibly have happened?"

"Ah, yes, we did. 'Sea sparkle', they call it. *Bioluminescent plankton* is the scientific term, but I like the more magical one," her father replied with a soft smile. "I often fish here at night, and if I'm lucky, I see it from time to time. The sea is full of surprises, and it can never be tamed, as my father always told me. He passed his respect for the ocean onto me, and it has sustained me through everything. His father lived here, and his grandfather lived over there, in one of the coastguards' houses. Magnificent, aren't they? Airbnbs now, but they should be busy family homes, as they were meant to be, and they were for my forefathers. I hope they will be again someday, though I doubt I'll be here to see it."

Seren looked to her right, and saw two huge, white stone houses, facing out to sea in defiance as they had done for centuries past. They looked well-maintained, and their lawns were mown, but there were no flowers, no signs of a vibrant life.

"It's a shame. They deserve to be loved and lived in, don't they?" she said.

"They do indeed."

Looking out towards the horizon; on the very edge of the rocks, she saw a man hunched over a fishing rod. He was so close to the water that the waves sometimes broke over his head, but he did not flinch. She could see that his shoulder-length wet hair was plastered against his head, and his flimsy clothes were sodden and clinging to a strong-looking body.

"That man is dangerously near the edge, isn't he?" she said. "Do you know him?"

Lloyd nodded slowly. "I do. And he likes to court danger. Says it makes him feel better, ironically. He came here just under a year ago, from Scotland. He said he couldn't bear to stay there any longer."

"That's a bit intense. What's his name?" Seren asked.

"His name's Jamie, and he has his own story, as we all do."

"Ooh, how intriguing! Any more intel to share on the mysterious man from 'somewhere in Scotland', Dad?", Seren said with a playful grin. "He's very handsome, I can see that. He doesn't seem to fit in here, though."

Lloyd frowned at her flippancy. "Jamie keeps himself to himself, so you won't see him around much. And he knows he doesn't really fit in, but he likes it here, nonetheless."

Seren blushed. "I didn't mean to be rude, but..."

"But you were, as people often are," Lloyd said, irritation writ large on his face. "He and I sometimes fish at night together, when the fish bite best, and we talk a little. He doesn't say much, but what he does say, is worth hearing. I hate gossip, and people who indulge in it."

"And I didn't mean to, honestly," Seren said, mortified. "Everybody has the right to their privacy, but the fact that he needs to feel in danger 'to feel better' is a bit, well, concerning."

"I agree with you there."

They watched as the lone fisherman slowly packed up his things and began heading up, towards the beach.

"Can I ask where Jamie lives?"

"There's a row of tiny fishermen's cottages just around the point, and he lives on his own in one of them. They're all pretty run-down except the one that an elderly couple from Manchester visit once in a blue moon. Been in their family for decades, they told Jamie. He keeps an eye on it, does bits of maintenance for them; he's a kind man, despite everything life's thrown at him."

"Despite what?" Seren asked, unable to suppress her curiosity.

Lloyd positively scowled at her now. "That's not my business, and it's not yours. I don't know details, but I know he's been through tough times."

Feeling tears prick at her eyes, Seren felt awful. Her father was angry with her, a horrible feeling she now remembered all too keenly. Harsh words, fierce faces, slamming doors. She tried to move the conversation on, to make peace. "Has he been kind to *you*, Dad? That's the only thing about him that matters to me really."

After a second or two, she saw calm return to Lloyd's face. She was forgiven.

"Oh yes, he has. He has *listened* to me, Seren, and few enough people do that. I worry about him up there, as they're pretty basic little places, but he says he likes the isolation, and doesn't even mind the cold. Says it's warmer than where he comes from, in fact!" Lloyd said. "He carries a lot of guilt, I think, and he's a lonely soul. We have that in common, I suppose."

As the man neared them, he raised one arm in silent greeting when he saw Lloyd, but did not break his stride to speak to them. Lloyd waved back, and Seren smiled, but the man did not acknowledge her at all. She noticed that he was incredibly lean, with well-defined muscles on his calves, as she watched him pass them and clamber up onto the headland path. His reddish-brown hair was long, tied in a loose ponytail and his face was thin, with sharp cheekbones above a thick beard. But what struck her most were his large blue eyes, which, even at some distance, seemed to tell of a deep sorrow. It was not for nothing that Shakespeare had called the eyes "the window to the soul", she mused. When she began to wonder what had brought him here, to lead such a lonely life, her thoughts quickly returned to her own, now-single, situation, and to her child and she felt a prick of guilt. Her father was right, everyone had their own story, but she was here to rewrite her own.

"I must get back to pick up Enya now," she said. "She only met Sali this morning and may be finding it all a bit much. She's a quiet girl – *reserved,* I suppose you'd call it. You have to win her affection rather than assume she will give it."

"That sounds fair enough to me, and I'm sure it's worth waiting for. Can I ask, though – where's her father? Will he come and visit, do you think?"

Seren hesitated and looked away. Now, it was her turn to feel her right to privacy being challenged, and it did not feel good. Of course she was going to be asked these questions, probably many times, but she had not prepared an answer that went anywhere near explaining what their life as Finlay O'Neill's partner and daughter had been like, or how much she dreaded him finding them. She should have been braver long ago, for all their sakes.

"He's still in London, and I dearly hope he stays there," she replied slowly. "Unlike Jamie, he's *not* a kind man, Dad. I don't want to see him, or for him to see Enya, ever again, if I can help it."

"I thought as much. You came so quickly, and without him. What's his name? What kind of man is he? Now, it's my turn to be nosey."

"His name is Finlay O'Neill, and he's from the West of Ireland, but the famous Irish charm I fell for was superficial, and very short-lived." She paused, to prepare herself for what she needed to say next. "I had cancer, Dad. Breast cancer. And that's how I eventually found the courage to leave him." Registering the shock on his face, she went on. "It's OK. I've finished the treatment and I'm on medication to help me stay clear of it, but it made me realise that life is too short not to do what feels right, and stop doing what feels wrong. He loves Enya, and I think he loved me once, in his own selfish way, but we had to leave him because he, he *hurt* me, Dad. He bullied me."

Lloyd pulled at his beard, clearly upset by what he'd heard. "Bullies are always cowards. I will take care of both of you now, *cariad*/darling, as I should have done when you were a girl. Finlay O'Neill will not harm either of you whilst I have life in my tired old body, and you will get better here. As Dylan Thomas said:

"Love drips and gathers, but the fallen blood

"Shall calm her sores.

"We have all suffered, but we will all heal together," he concluded.

When Seren took his hand, as she had done as a child, and father and daughter walked back towards her cottage, she so wanted to believe him.

ELEVEN

Within two weeks of their arrival on Anglesey, Enya told her mother that she was in Heaven. She'd become firm friends with Sali, and adapted to a way of life, a way of *childhood*, at polar opposites from the one she had known in London with a speed that astounded her mother. Having had no freedom in the city to do or say or feel whatever she wanted to, she relished every moment of it here.

The girls were allowed to roam the fields around the farmhouse as long as they could be seen from it, Ruthie told them firmly. This gave them access both to a swing Dafydd had hung from an old oak in the top corner of one field, and a chance to search for tadpoles in the stream that trickled through another one. Seren found it far from easy to allow her daughter such freedom, but gradually, under Ruthie's relaxed and kindly tutelage, she learnt to do so. The results were so convincing, how could she deny her delicate but now-happy girl the chance to bloom in splendour?

"We can see them, and we can certainly hear them if they yell," the farmer's wife told her repeatedly. "This is how childhood used to be – remember? You went out to play and only came back when our bellies were rumbling."

"No, I don't, actually, as it sure wasn't like that for me in Wimbledon," Seren replied. "But I do want it for Enya, and I wish I'd had it for myself."

"I'm sure it's what your mam would have wanted, God rest her soul," Ruthie said, pausing for a moment before turning the mound of bread dough she was kneading. "Kate loved it here, my mam always told me. Loved the fact that you were born up here and would always belong here, as she felt she did."

"A shame it didn't work out like that," Seren said, adding cautiously, "Do you remember her, my... mam?" The Welsh name felt new, but right. Kate had been a mam, not a mum.

"Well, I'm a few years older than you, but I was still a nipper when she left. I remember her being very smiley, and wearing amazing clothes. Colourful dungarees and loads of strings of beads that clattered when she walked," Ruthie said. "She smelt nice too – sort of fresh."

Seren gasped, as a wisp of memory stirred. She remembered a pure, salty scent, one that she had never again identified despite the many snatched hours she had spent squirting perfume testers in the department stores in London trying to do so.

"But *why* did she go, do you know? It broke Dad's heart, and his mind too – which meant I had to leave too." She paused, her brow furrowed. "A butterfly, Dad called her. She took a while to settle, but when she did, she was *glorious*. Why would someone like that just vanish?"

The farmhouse kitchen was unnaturally quiet for a minute or so, and the only sound was of the slap and pull of floury hands on dough.

"That's a question I can't answer for you," Ruthie said. "I was very young at the time, but I do remember Mam and I meeting her a few days before she left. She was alone, without you, up on the headland. I remember Kate seemed strange, not her usual self at all. She didn't want to stop and chat for long, and she looked so tired. When I asked if she was all right, Mam said that Kate had a few *private worries* and to mind my own business, but I do remember them both being upset. I never dared ask about Kate again."

There was a longer silence. The mystery surrounding both Kate's departure and the dreadful way she had died had undercut Lloyd's life and threaded through Seren's, but nobody was answering her questions, whoever and however she asked them.

"I guess it's positive my mother had such good friends, ones she could confide in if she couldn't confide in her husband," she said. "But I don't think that was very kind."

Ruthie was shocked, and took a few moments to compose herself, and respond.

"*Ydy wir*/That's true, but my mam's a loyal woman and yours was an enigma. If you ever met my mother, she'd probably see a lot of Kate in you, Seren," Ruthie said. "You only tell who you need to tell, and you never tell everything."

Seren blushed. Ruthie had hit a nerve, but when she added, in a kinder voice, "But I want you to remember above all that your mother would be very proud of you, for being brave enough to do this, and come back," the tension lifted.

"I'd love to meet your mam – Enid, isn't it, her name?" Seren said, but her friend did not answer, preoccupied with slashing the top of her loaf, ready for baking.

"Anyway, I'm determined to try and find out why Kate left. As mothers, we know how impossibly difficult it would be to leave a child, but she did it. I wonder if those 'private worries' had anything to do with it?"

"Look, I'll help you in any way I can, Seren, but I do think you need to focus on getting to know Lloyd, and helping Enya settle in, poor little mite, before you start digging around in the past," Ruthie said with a firmness of tone she had not used before. "The past is sometimes best left there, I think. Enjoy the *present* instead – you've waited long enough for it. Right, I must get on now."

Seren got up to leave. The conversation had obviously finished.

June brought some bright, sunny days interspersed with a few warm, showery ones. The fields around the island changed with incredible rapidity, as winter-planted crops thrived in this mixture of sunshine and rain. Hedgerows exploded with colour, and shoulder-high cow parsley formed a lacy coverlet over the brambles spooling alongside the small roads around Penmon. Each day followed a similarly open-ended routine: Enya woke early in her "crog" loft, delighting in the novelty of having a bed on a raised platform, like a balcony, from which she could survey everything going on in the cottage below. She then lay in bed singing or chattering to herself for half an hour or so as she watched the outside world wake up through her tiny roof window before going down the rickety wooden stairs to see her mother. Seren was usually awake, listening to her, but it brought her such joy to hear her daughter happy that she did not get up for the cup of tea she craved and risk missing it. In only a matter of a few weeks, Enya had grown so much more confident, and less fearful of men in particular. She did not flinch when Dafydd came into the farmhouse kitchen any more, and laughed when the pups' mother barked a warning if they nipped too hard when suckling. Before they had come here, she would have burst into tears and found a place to hide at any loud noises. It was as if she had grown into her own skin at last, and was increasingly happy in it. Seren decided that it was finally a good time for her to meet Lloyd, or *Taid*/Grandfather and was thankful for the fact that their paths had not yet crossed, as Penmon was remote and such coincidences, unlikely.

She tried to prepare the ground by explaining why she had not grown up with her father, the question she knew Enya would ask first. The simpler she tried to make it sound, the more complex it became.

"So you left your dad like I left mine," the little girl said with the miraculous clarity of a child. "Did he get cross all the time too?"

Seren was unsure how to reply. "No, or not *all* the time, but he wasn't well enough for me to stay with him, so I went to Aunty Alice's instead, which was... *better* for me."

"Like I've come here, where it's better for me?"

"Yes, I suppose so," Seren replied. It was as simple as that.

"Is he nice, your dad?"

Seren felt a catch in her throat, and unheard the unsaid words 'unlike mine'. "Yes, he's very nice, love."

Seren had warned her father that Enya could be shy, and slow to trust men in particular, so he suggested an activity for them to do together to make her feel more at ease when they met for the first time. Questions could come later – they needed to make friends first. The idea he came up with intrigued Seren, but when he explained in more detail, she was deeply touched.

"Jamie once told me that his wife used to make miniature gardens on one of their tea trays with their daughter, using pebbles and flowers and things they found in their garden," Lloyd told her. "She loved it, he said."

"That sounds perfect. Jamie must miss his family, and his home," Seren replied, fully alert to the past tense he had used, "loved", but reluctant to probe.

"I think he does. He sometimes tells me things about their life in the darkness, when we're fishing. He's lost them both, but I think he can't bear to let me see him crying in the light, and I understand that."

"Will he ever go back, do you think?" Seren asked. The memory of that defiant, lonely man sitting on the rocks as the sea crashed over him was still vivid.

"He says he came from a really rough part of a city, where it's hard to make good, and that there's nothing for him to go back to. No, I don't think he will."

"Makes me think of *Shuggie Bain*, that wonderful novel about a little boy growing up surrounded by misery and deprivation," Seren said. "Did Jamie come from Glasgow, by any chance?"

Lloyd hesitated. "Not sure he's ever specified which city, to be honest. I don't need to know, and he doesn't need to tell me for me to understand how he feels."

A raft of questions popped up in Seren's mind, but she suppressed her growing desire to quiz her father about Jamie. The young man's air of resolute endurance in the face of obvious loss made her want to know more about him, and help him, if she could, but she sensed her father would not welcome it. Such things often backfired, and made things worse; she had learnt that in London, when kindly neighbours had heard her crying and tried, in vain, to help her.

If she was meant to know more about Jamie, it would happen in good time and if not, it would not, she tried to tell herself. And yet, despite all her efforts at being patient and philosophical, she could not stop thinking about him, or his sad, blue eyes. She already sensed that they shared something invisible, but powerful: the need to be loved.

Seren need not have worried that Enya would be wary of her father. She stared at his beard (washed and trimmed for the occasion) and noticed the hole in one of his shoes that exposed his big toenail, but she quickly accepted that he was Mummy's dad, and was perfectly happy to sit down at the table with him as her mother hovered behind them with tea, juice and biscuits. When he produced first a tea tray and then a small bag of earth from his holdall, she watched in silence, but when he then emptied lots of little stones, shells, fragments of sea glass, flowers and twigs onto the kitchen table, she laughed in delight at the mess he'd made. Seren had decided to let Lloyd lead things this afternoon and to sit outside the cottage so that he could relax, and to let Enya decide for herself what she thought of her newly discovered *Taid*/Grandfather. As she left the room, she heard him begin to explain what they were going to do, his voice low and gentle. When she returned half an hour later, her daughter's head was bent low over the tray, which was now a clearly demarcated little garden with a pebble path, a pond of misted sea glass, twiggy trees and a crop of daisy-heads nestling in soft earth.

"Look what *Taid*/Grandfather and me did," Enya cried. "It's a garden!"

"That's fantastic," Seren replied, beaming at her daughter's easy use of his Welsh name, *Taid*/Grandfather. "I'm glad you both had a lovely time together."

"And he says he's going to take me fishing soon," the little girl said. "You can come too if you like. He says we're going to go *at night*, to catch the best fish!"

When Lloyd Evans looked up at his daughter sheepishly, and mouthed "Well, at *evening,* actually", his face was happier than she had ever seen it.

TWELVE

The tantalising fine, summery days they had enjoyed so far did not last, as they were followed with a series of overcast, humid ones that promised blue skies but produced only warm showers. The night-fishing trip was put on hold until Lloyd could guarantee a dry night. Enya was up for a wet one, but Seren most determinedly was not, and she was adamant that she would accompany them.

"I can't imagine anything worse than fishing in the dark in the rain," she told her father. These flippant words she came to regret a few days later, however, when something much worse happened.

Mobile signal was very patchy at Penmon, so Seren had not heard from anyone, including Finlay. When her phone pinged late one afternoon as she was shopping for supplies for her and Enya in the lovely art shop in Beaumaris, she feared the worst. Only a handful of people had her number.

"I should have got a new phone," she mumbled, as, sure enough, there was his name on her screen. "Why can't you just leave us alone? It's *over*, Finlay."

For these few, treasured weeks, they had been free of him,

and she had watched Enya open like a delicate flower that feels the sun on its petals for the first time. She had even done a few sessions at the little village *cylch meithrin*/playgroup, and, despite a lot of Welsh being spoken there, she enjoyed going, as Sali was there to support and translate. Now, all that could be under threat, and the horribly familiar ache of dread replaced the carefree joy she had allowed herself to taste on the island. She did not want to open his message, or think about him at all, but knew if she did not, more would follow.

For years, she had avoided baring her soul to well-meaning people about Finlay. How could she begin to describe the psychological torture she had endured, let alone cite bruises long-since vanished and fractures long-since mended? All this, and the very real prospect of not being believed, as his charm was so convincing, had horrified her enough to postpone leaving him again and again, but now things were different. She had done it, spurred on by the sudden awareness of life's transience that only a cancer diagnosis can provide. Yes, she had escaped a relationship that brought her nothing but misery, and brought her child here, where she now felt strong and hopeful, but once she read his words, her whole body shook.

> I went to Wimbledon and spoke to your snooty relatives. What a pair of losers. They wouldn't tell me where you were, but I've got a hunch. See you soon. F.

Seren closed her eyes and leant back against the shop window behind her. The busy street, a scene of such pleasant daily comings and goings only a minute earlier, now evoked a scene of banal normality that she was no longer allowed to be a part of, but instead stood alone on the outside, looking in. It was a familiar feeling.

"Are you all right, love?" an elderly woman asked her. "You look like you need a sit-down. There's a bench over there."

Seren blinked at her, and felt sweat dribble down between her breasts.

"Yes, I'm fine, thanks. Just very hot, that's all," she managed to say.

"I think we'll have some thunder soon," the woman said. "That'll clear it."

Seren almost staggered down the street to sit on the bench between two amply bottomed pensioners on a coach trip from Stockport, or so they told her pale, blank face. All her nascent feelings of safety and belonging had vanished, destroyed as quickly and easily as a pin pops a balloon. She ran through her main worries in her head, an endless cycle, on repeat.

Could he find her? Her phone was a basic one, and she had no idea if he could track her from it. Would Alice and Neil be OK if he got nasty, as he could do if they irritated him? She seemed to have become an unwitting expert in doing so herself, but Seren knew just how vulnerable her aunt and uncle would be to a malice they would neither understand nor feel able to counter. Would he remember all the times she had told him about her dreams of the sea, of a black and white lighthouse and of holding a man's hand as a small child, back in the early days, when Finlay O'Neill had seemed her saviour and she had trusted him? As the pensioners around her chatted and licked their ice creams, a few of Dylan Thomas' words sprang to mind:

Now my saying shall be my undoing...

Life had taught her so many things, both good and bad, and having cancer had brought them all into sharp focus. That day, looking out over the choppy waves and bobbing yachts as she waited to feel calm enough to drive home, Seren realised that one of the most important life lessons she had learnt of late was to be very, very careful whom she trusted.

· · ·

For half an hour, Seren sat quite still, her hands in her lap, noticing nothing and nobody, until she felt her breath slow to a low, regular pulse, like the tolling lighthouse bell from her childhood. Only then did she feel any semblance of peace return, but she was still very agitated when she got back to the farm. She asked Ruthie to keep Enya for a little while longer as she had something she needed to sort.

"That's fine. She's with our Sali, up in the field, watching Dafydd start training the first of the pups with the sheep, and having the time of her life. Oh, and she said *cylch meithrin*/playgroup was *bendigedig*/fantastic today," Ruthie said, but her eyes were fixed on Seren's face. "Is something wrong? You look, well, *hollol annifyr*/completely awful is the Welsh phrase for it."

Seren could not risk saying anything, lest she reveal the depth of her distress. Ruthie would not know what to do with it. Surely relationships took time to be strong enough to withstand such shocking revelations as gaslighting or domestic abuse? Yet again, she wished that navigating friendships was not so very new to her, but Ruthie deserved some kind of answer. She took a deep, calming breath before saying:

"I can't tell you about my past, or what brought me here, yet. But I will, in time, I promise."

"That's fine with me, *cariad*/love. You take all the time you need."

Seren set off down the leafy track Lloyd had shown her on the day they'd first met, leading down to the lighthouse. That was the only place she wanted to be, right on the edge of land where it blends with the sea, feeling the elemental force of the wind and waves battering against the rocks and filling the sky with their sound and fury. Always a place of solace, and of safety, she prayed that it would give her the courage to face whatever lay ahead with Finlay, which would surely seem tiny when compared to this permanence and strength.

By the time she reached the rocky outcrop that led out to the lighthouse, a keen wind had sprung up and grey clouds were racing across the sky, as if they all had an urgent appointment to get to. A few spots of rain began to fall, peppering the rocks around her and Seren noticed that the sky had suddenly darkened to a thick, pewter-grey. Today, the lighthouse was *Trwyn Du*/Black Nose indeed, as if covered with a thick caul of brooding cloud. Sealed and locked years ago, it seemed to be surveying the restless sea like a watchful parent.

Having gone shopping in shorts, a T-shirt and flip-flops, Seren shivered in the sudden change in temperature, but she did not turn back. She needed to get right to the very edge of the land, to the place where her parents had first glimpsed each other all those years ago, and where their love affair had begun. Looking back to the beach, she suddenly saw a tall figure turn and walk away. Jamie. He did not return her wave.

She stood quite still for about ten minutes, feeling the panic ebb, before venturing out towards the base of the lighthouse. Then, with one hand on its flank to steady herself, she pulled her phone out of her pocket, carefully took out the SIM card and flung it as far as she could into the roaring water. It barely made a splash. When she turned to return to the beach, however, a wave crashed against her feet with such force that she fell backwards into the water, flailing with her arms, mouth wide. The sea surged and sucked around her, and she felt the force of it pulling her away from the beach, and towards the churning open water. Her only thought was that she had to get to solid ground again, she could not die – she had a child. Spluttering, she hauled herself into a sitting position on the rocks and clung on with numb fingers, and all her might. Blood was running down both her legs from deep gashes, but the cold water meant she could feel no pain yet, only a strange, salty stinging. When the next wave came, it was even more powerful, but just as she felt her body being peeled off the rock before being flung out to sea, a hand took hers and held on to it tightly.

"I lost you once. I will not lose you again, my girl," her father shouted into the wind, his face contorted with effort and his beard whipping around his face as the wind buffeted them both. "I met Jamie, running along the clifftop, and he told me you were here, and I knew that there was a storm coming. Follow me, and don't look back."

The old man quickly led his daughter onto the beach, where they both collapsed on the pebbles, coughing, gasping and then breathing deeply still holding each other's hands as tightly as ever. Behind them, Seren saw once again the outline of Jamie heading out towards the rocks and the darkness, with one arm raised in parting.

THIRTEEN

Lloyd led a shivering Seren back to his cottage and spent the next hour or so making sure she was warm, dry, and that the cuts on her legs were clean and covered. He bustled around making her tea, stoking the fire and gently drying her hair with a towel as she was shaking too much to do so herself. Stripping off her wet clothes in his bedroom and borrowing an old flannel shirt and a pair of very baggy trousers felt odd to her, but also comforting, once she had got over their unusual smell – not unpleasant, but one she did not recognise.

"What's that smell, Dad? It's kind of smoky but spicy too," she asked, as the second cup of hot, sweet tea began to do its work and warm her core.

"Snuff," he replied. "I gave up smoking a pipe before you were born, but I still like a pinch of snuff from time to time. Tranter's of Bath know me by name now, and know exactly which kind I like – *Country Doctor*, it's called. Beautiful stuff it is too."

"The smell's growing on me. Actually, as weird as it sounds, I think I remember it." A faint image of a black car dashboard covered in a thin layer of brown dust, and that rich smell in the air stirred deep in her memory. Yes, she could remember it now – that spiciness, mingled with a fresh, salty tang. Kate's perfume.

There was so much to learn about her parents. They had missed out on a lifetime together, and putting the myriad missing pieces of the puzzle together to form a whole would take time; she only hoped she was granted enough of it.

When her father eventually sat down in front of the fire, his hair still damp and his beard in wild disarray, he looked older, and more tired, than Seren had ever seen him. He, too, had had a terrible shock and she wondered if he had just relived rescuing a young Kate from the waves, in exactly the same place? However romantically fateful the coincidence now seemed, she was sure it would have triggered all kinds of memories for her father, both good and bad.

"Thank goodness Jamie alerted you," she said, putting one of her soft hands on top of one of his gnarled, veiny ones. "Why didn't he help me himself, instead of calling you, Dad? He's young and strong and he could have pulled me out much sooner..." She stopped, as her father's expression had changed. Again, he looked angry with her.

"It took courage for Jamie to run and tell me he'd seen you, and was worried about you. He stays away from people and all their demands and complexities as much as he can, I told you. He's like a wild animal, licking his wounds and needs to be left in peace."

Seren nodded. "I understand, and I'll remember that," she said, sipping her tea. She did understand, and she would remember it, but a guilty part of her yearned to get closer to Jamie even more strongly, because she knew with absolute certainty that he had sensed her vulnerability because he shared it. He needed healing and the comfort of companionship, just as much as she did, and she longed to offer them to him.

Lloyd sighed. "I don't mean to be angry with you,

cariad/dear. I have gained his trust to some degree, but I know he's been through a lot. As I told you, he had a family once, and he still mourns them, so we need to accept what he can offer us and not expect any more."

A pause, in which logs on the fire crackled and spat.

"But he seems so lonely, and I know how that feels, Dad, just like you and Jamie do," Seren said softly. "I think we recognise kindred spirits in life, even if all we share is sadness and loss."

Lloyd looked at her, his eyes full of compassion. "I think so too, and I am so sorry to hear you have felt those things as well. Tell me more about Finlay O'Neill, Enya's father, the man you're so scared will find you both one day."

"It's not a happy story, I need to warn you," she replied. "In fact, I might need another cup of tea before I tell it. And perhaps even a biscuit, if you've got one."

She watched as her father filled the kettle and opened and closed cupboards in his hunt for biscuits. Outside, the wind had dropped and the first rumble of thunder rippled across the sky. Within seconds, the rain began, heavy from the off and soon streaming down the windows of the cottage in a seemingly endless torrent as the room got darker and darker, as if someone had dimmed the lights. It was like being inside a cave, walled-in with water.

"Here it comes, that storm I felt was on the way," Lloyd called from the kitchen. "I hope Enya's inside, and not still up in the field with Dafydd and the dogs."

Seren felt a shot of fear course through her. Surely Dafydd would get the girls inside as soon as the storm began to rip the sky apart? He rarely carried a mobile as the signal was so unreliable, and she had stupidly just thrown hers in the sea, but he would know the sky, and how the weather changed in an instant on the island, wouldn't he? Enya would be very frightened if there was more thunder and lightning; both had always terrified her, both were loud and unpredictable. In an instant, she knew that telling her father more about Finlay would have to wait.

"I have to get back, Dad," she said. "Can I borrow a mac, please?"

"What? You can't go out in this! You'll get soaked again, and ill. Enya will be fine, believe me."

"But she will be *scared*, Dad. I need to be there. I won't let her be scared ever again," Seren replied firmly. He was right, and going outside was not a prospect she relished, but she had to go. "A mac? Do you have one I could borrow?"

Her father, shaking his head, took a long waterproof coat off a peg near the door and handed it to Seren before pulling on the shorter, yellow one that he used for night-fishing.

"Then I'm coming with you," he said. "We'll go together."

"Thanks, Dad. Surely the worst we can get is wet, after all, and I've already been soaked to my skin once today."

Lloyd raised one eyebrow in thinly veiled disbelief at her naiveté.

The rain was so heavy that it was impossible to see the lighthouse down on the point, or the rocks where Jamie usually sat to fish. Without needing to say so, both Lloyd and his daughter hoped that he was not back there, enduring this downpour in an attempt to purge away his sadness. She had been drawn to the lighthouse for relief, for release, but he would be at risk, as Seren had been, if he was too near the huge swell that often accompanied storms like this.

They walked, arm in arm, dodging the streams of rainwater that had suddenly appeared on either side of the path, carving their way around rocks and through mud and gravel as easily as a knife through butter. The grass was slippery underfoot, and Lloyd clung to his daughter's arm for fear of falling; a hip takes seconds to break, but many months to heal at his age, he had learnt from an elderly neighbour's experience. Lightning crackled overhead, illuminating the oil-sheened sea for a few seconds before plunging it back into inky darkness again. When they eventually reached the farmhouse, the yard was awash with puddles of slurry, muddy water; floating clumps of straw formed little islands in it, blown out of the barn by the gale. The cows and horses were making an incredible noise in the barn as they, too, were terrified. Seren knocked on the front door, and waited, feeling rivulets of cold water trickle down the back of her neck. No waterproof mac could be waterproof enough for rain like this. For a very long minute, nothing happened. Seren knocked again, harder, beginning to panic.

"The lights are on in there, so someone's in," she shouted. "Ruthie! Enya, it's me! Hello in there!"

The door burst open to reveal Ruthie, with four, small arms wound tightly around her legs like ivy around a tree trunk; it took Seren a few seconds to realise that the arms belonged to Sali and Enya.

"Sorry. Bit tricky to get to the door with these two hangers-on," she said, looking up at the sky. "Hmm, it's a nasty one. Come in, both of you."

"We'll get your floor very wet," Lloyd said, reluctant to come inside.

"Who cares? It needs a good mopping anyway," Ruthie shouted, adding, when he still hesitated, "Lloyd, *tyrd i mewn, rwan*/come inside, now, or we'll all get washed away!"

Inside the kitchen were more people, dogs and cats than Seren had ever seen in one room at one time. When her eyes had adjusted to the gloom, she saw Ruthie's husband Dafydd, with their toddler son Harri on his knee and their eldest, Jac, playing Playstation with a blonde, young-looking boy she did not know on the floor in front of the range. A wheelchair seemed to be parked in the corner too and there was a cat asleep on it. At least four, rather damp, sheepdog pups were lying next to the radiator, and several more cats lounged, oblivious to the chaos, on the warm windowsill above it. Ruthie, Enya and Sali still formed a homogenous six-legged whole as they shut the door again, but Enya ran into her mother's arms as soon as Seren took her hood down and was recognisable.

"There's a giant stomping around in the sky, Mum!" she cried. "Ruthie told me. And he's got a wand that sends out forks of fire, but it's OK, because his fire forks can't reach us in here."

Ruthie smiled at a puzzled Seren, and mouthed "Sorry, it seemed to calm her down". An exhausted-looking Lloyd sat down on the chair next to Dafydd and tried to ignore the pools of water that appeared beneath him as his coat dripped onto the floor. Seren felt a flicker of guilt that she had put him through such an ordeal, and was alarmed at how old he suddenly looked.

"*Arglwydd, mae'n fudr allan heddiw*/God, it's nasty out there today," Dafydd said with a wink at his old friend. Lloyd laughed so loudly that all the pups' ears flattened against their damp little heads and then everyone else in the room laughed fondly at *them*.

As Ruthie made yet more tea and toasted some thick white bread, Seren hugged her daughter close and looked around the room at the people who had welcomed them both so openly into their lives. She had never, ever felt like this before – accepted for who she was, as she was. Her upbringing in Wimbledon had never been loving enough, and she had been bitter and resentful. She had always been on the periphery of friendship groups in school, awkward and insecure as she had always been. Adulthood had not given any long-term friends either, because Finlay had sequestered her away so that she could never keep them, insisting that he was all she and Enya needed. It had taken cancer to force her to realise that all he offered her and their daughter was a cage, for which he had the only key. That was no life – but this warmth, today, in this kitchen, *was*.

The adults chatted and all the children played quietly

(except when the blonde boy almost fell out of his wheelchair when he tried to get the pups to pull it along like a team of huskies and then filled the room with his hysterical laughter).

"And this is the famous Gwyn," Ruthie said, gently helping the boy get up off the floor . "No wonder his mam asked me to keep an eye on him this afternoon so she could get her hair done. She never gets a moment's peace!"

Seren smiled at Gwyn, and he winked back at her. As a wave of happiness flooded her body, she dared to believe that not even Finlay could spoil this bliss as it felt so natural, and so immutable. He would never find them here, and if he did, surely she would be strong enough to send him packing with people like this on her side?

But a small voice still said that she would never, ever be strong or brave enough to do that. In fact, it whispered that she would never be strong or brave at all.

FOURTEEN

High summer was so different on the island to those she had spent in London that Seren could hardly believe they were called the same season. Whereas in the city, blazing hot sunshine had been a source of torture, something to keep out with blinds and curtains, here on Anglesey it was something to celebrate and embrace, as it made all the colours of the landscape come alive. It did not shine brightly every day, and fine days were still punctuated with cooler ones, and sometimes, even downright wet ones, but when it *did,* it did not bring the stifling humidity of the city. Seren recalled going to manicured London parks in search of some contact with nature and then lying, slicked with sweat, for as long as she could stand it before coming home to hide from the sun. Enya had so rarely been outside in the hottest months of the year in London that her mother had to learn from Ruthie the importance of sunscreen, sun hats and bright, UV-protective swimsuits that meant that kids could now play on the beach all day without fear of burning. It was a revelation.

"My mam slathered camomile lotion on us every evening, because we always got burnt, but now, kids don't actually need to burn at all, which means we can relax and enjoy the heat when it comes... on about two days a year, that is," she told Seren.

"I have a very vague memory of a sunny day as a baby, and a really big hat on my head, but Enya never really wanted to be outside in the city, so avoiding the sun hasn't been an issue."

"Well, we can't keep Enya inside any more. She's desperate to get out!"

"I know. I can't believe the transformation. She's a carefree, even mischievous child now, not one that cowers in corners and won't speak to anyone," Seren said. "Oh, Ruthie, I should have done this years ago – come back, I mean."

Ruthie put a hand on Seren's arm. "Look, we all put off things we're frightened of. It's natural. And Enya knows that – or she will do, one day."

Indeed, the changes in Enya in the time they had been on Anglesey were nothing short of miraculous. Encouraged by a fearless Sali and her older brother Jac, she learnt to love swimming in the sea and Seren had never seen her so happy as when she ran, shrieking, into the shallows with her friends and let the water crash against her legs. They helped Gwyn into the water to paddle too, having been given strict directions by his mother Angharad as to how to support him so that he could share the fun. Jamie, intrigued by the noises that echoed off the cliffs around the beach, started joining them on the beach, and Enya quickly admitted him into her circle of trusted people. Whenever the children were in the water, an adult was always stationed on the shore, ensuring nobody ventured out of their depth, but to hear her daughter's piping voice, surrounded by other children, ringing out loudly for the first time in her life, was like nectar for Seren.

"I thought you said she was shy, especially of men," Lloyd

said one morning, as he came to relieve her at the water's edge. "She's best of friends with Jac and Gwyn, and Jamie and me, of course. It's great to see."

Lloyd spent a great deal of time with them now. Most summer days, he took tourist boats out around Puffin Island, but whenever he was free, he was with his daughter and grand-daughter. There was nowhere else he wanted to be, he said.

"She's become a completely different child," Seren replied. "I always think she's like a flower, that's finally dared to bloom. I reckon she'll be fine when she starts school, even with the Welsh. I've heard her using a few words with Sali already."

"Of course she will. She belongs here," Lloyd murmured. "She's lit up my life, just as you did all those years ago, and I can't imagine life without her now. Or rather, I *won't* imagine it."

Seren turned to him and smiled. "I don't think we're going anywhere, anytime soon, but I do need to find a job, Dad. I feel bad, not giving Ruthie any money for rent. I've signed on for benefits, but they take ages to come through and my savings are almost all gone. I think I'll have to get a new mobile phone too, as nobody can reach me if they need to. I do want to start taking photos too, of things I see and places we go, as it's all so gorgeous and iPhones have great cameras these days."

"Many of us manage perfectly well without phones up here, you know. I just hope it doesn't bring trouble for you, getting another one," her father replied.

"I know what you're saying, but it's not fair to worry Aunt Alice and Uncle Neil. They're probably frantic, trying to reach me on my old phone. I'll give them a call from the café to let them know what's happening. I feel I ought to, really."

But Seren wished with all her heart that she did not have to re-establish contact with her old world, the one beyond this perfect sanctuary. She had barely been in touch with her aunt and uncle since their arrival. Getting a new phone, and thus being reachable, was a risk, but she knew she had to take it.

A few days later, she bought a new phone – a more sophisticated one than she had intended to buy because the salesperson extolled the virtues of its camera. Jamie, who had called in to the cottage with a storybook for Enya, spent an hour helping her slot in her SIM card and explaining how to use it. Seren was incredibly thankful. The sunset had been astounding earlier, and she had been thrilled at her first attempts to capture some of the beauty that surrounded her, but as soon as she had finished taking photos, she turned it off. Sending her first text to her aunt and uncle was nerve-wracking, and she half expected reams of angry messages from Finlay to spew out of it once she turned the phone on again, but nothing happened, of course, as he did not have her new number. Simply seeing his name on her list of contacts still sent a shiver through her, however. Slowly, she typed a message to her aunt:

> Hi there. Sorry not been in touch for a while. Phone trouble, but I have a new one and this is my new number. Please don't give it to anyone else. All still great here and our cottage is wonderful. Enya is in paradise, as am I. Hope all's well with you. Love from S and E xx

Within minutes, her phone rang, a jangly, unfamiliar sound she didn't recognise and which felt horribly intrusive in her little home. It was her aunt, of course.

"Seren, thank God! We've been so worried when we couldn't reach you! He came here – Finlay I mean, last evening. He marched up to our door and harangued Neil on the doorstep, prodding his shoulder and demanding to know where you were," she gabbled, hardly pausing for breath. "It was so menacing, and he said he'll be back next week! What on *earth* are we going to do?"

Seren's mind whirred, but as she had no obvious answer, she said nothing.

"We don't want to be involved in all this, we really don't. Neil said he'd never met anyone so rude, and his shoulder was actually quite bruised afterwards. We know Finlay can get nasty if he's not happy. He didn't seem too... affected by drink, mercifully. Please get in touch with him and tell him to leave us alone. Will you do that for us?"

Seren felt as if time had stopped, and her aunt's voice, still talking, faded into nothingness. She sat back in her armchair, closed her eyes and listened to the seagulls cruising above *Bwthyn y Dryw*/Wren Cottage as blue-black darkness fell around her. For a few, blissful, seconds, she dared to imagine that nothing had changed and the days ahead would be as wonderful as the ones behind them. That all ended when she heard her aunt say:

"Seren, are you still there? Please, tell me what are you going to do about this... situation? It's really none of our business."

"I know, and I'm really, really sorry he's bothered you, Aunt, but I don't want to contact him. I don't want him to know where we are," she replied quietly.

"I know, and I completely understand, but he told Neil he'd guessed you'd gone to find where you were born, but luckily he couldn't remember where that was, so you have time..."

"Time to do what? Run away somewhere else?" Seren muttered.

There was no point in telling her aunt to contact the police and ask for their protection. She had done so herself, several times, and no help had come, but she'd heard real fear in Aunt Alice's voice and recognised it.

"I'll do something, I promise, and I'm sorry again. You don't deserve this."

She hung up before her aunt could exacerbate her guilt by agreeing with her.

There was no way she was going to admit Finlay back into their lives, but she had to make sure her aunt and uncle were safe from him. The only possible solution filled her with absolute horror; she would have to go back to London and beg him, finally, to leave them all in peace.

PART 3

GATHERING CLOUDS

FIFTEEN

Seren had never left Enya with anyone until her hospital admission for cancer surgery had forced her to. She had never trusted Finlay enough, though he loved his daughter when he was free of his crippling anxieties. He'd always dulled the pain at the centre of his life, the hole where he wanted love to be, with alcohol. She had never known when his rage would break through his thin veneer of control or when drink would fuel his fury. Now, the thought of leaving her little girl with someone she had not known for very long at all was enough to make her nauseous, but she had precious little choice, she would have to ask Ruthie to look after Enya while she went back to London, which was a big ask for all concerned.

She reckoned that if she caught the 7.15 a.m. train from Bangor, she would be in Euston by 10.30 a.m., but she would need to leave very early in the morning and would be back very late. This meant it probably would be best for Enya to stay with Ruthie for two nights and follow her kids' routine, but this felt almost unbearable. She could meet Finlay somewhere neutral and public, say what she needed to say, then go and see her uncle and aunt in Wimbledon to reassure them before leaving on the 4 p.m. train for North Wales. It would cost a ridiculous amount of money, but it had to be done, and the sooner the better.

She could not ring Finlay from her new phone, as that would give him her number, so she emailed him from an internet café in Bangor and put her plan to him. She suggested Covent Garden piazza as a venue, as it was public and full of other people. When she pressed send, she knew that he would not be working in the pub until later that evening, but suspected he would be on his laptop accessing sites she'd never dared ask him about right now. She was proved right when his reply came within minutes.

> I assume you don't have a mobile any more. Your uncle said not, but I never believe people like him. Full of shit.

Trembling, Seren lied:

> No, I don't have a phone. See you at about 11 a.m. tomorrow in Covent Garden Piazza.

She bought the train ticket immediately so that there was no going back. The first fly in the ointment was the fact that Ruthie said she was taking her kids to see her parents in Ruthin the following day, so could not have Enya. This left only Lloyd, but would her elderly father be able to take care of an energetic five-year-old for that length of time if, in fact, he wasn't scheduled to be working on the boat? His answer was emphatic:

"I would be *wrth 'y modd*/absolutely delighted to look after my granddaughter, but I have two provisos. First, Jamie must be here too, just in case. He doesn't have to know where you're going, or why, but I'm too old to be on my own with Enya. Secondly, that I'm allowed to spoil her rotten."

"Ruthie told her you might do that, so she'll probably hold you to it," Seren replied with a nonchalance she did not really feel. To keep her daughter safe, she had to be able to trust her father and she did not have time to quibble about Jamie staying with them too. If his company made Lloyd more confident, it was probably sensible.

"It will mean her sleeping at yours, or you sleeping at ours, for two nights, Dad. I need to leave very early in the morning, and I won't be back until well past her bedtime."

"I think she should come here, and I know exactly which bed to put her in," Lloyd replied. "I knew I was right to keep your old teddy on high alert for just such an occasion. Jamie can go on the sofa. I know he'll agree. He's very fond of Enya, you know."

Leaving Penmon that evening was difficult, but when Seren saw how hard her father had tried to tidy up his cottage, and when he showed her the treats – some healthy, some far from it – he'd bought for them all to have a "midnight feast" together, she was glad that her little girl was going to have a lovely time. Jamie had agreed at once, and she felt as sure as she could be that these two kind and caring men would keep Enya safe until she got home. She resisted the temptation to tell her to "be good", as a large part of her hoped they got up to as much mischief as possible simply because it was something her daughter had too little experience of.

Covent Garden was heaving with people when she arrived the following morning, but a quick scan revealed that Finlay was not amongst them. He was late. "Same old, same old," she muttered to herself as she bought a hugely expensive coffee and sat on some stone steps to wait for him. When she finally saw him ambling across the piazza, her heart leapt involuntarily. He was so handsome, in the way Irish men often are, with thick, dark curls and piercing blue eyes; she had fallen for him instantly when those eyes had met hers across the bar all those years ago. What worried her was that she knew she would do exactly the same, if she met him now. He was as mesmeric as ever.

When he saw her, he gave her one of his finest, most dazzling smiles, which had always been enough to light up any room he entered. He looked so at ease with himself as he approached her in his trendily frayed jeans, checked shirt, vintage waistcoat and strategically tied neckerchief. He had always favoured the "cheeky tinker" look, and Seren had always loved it. She stood up to greet him, heart pounding, but when he opened his arms expecting to enfold her in them, she hesitated. It was best not to go there, now, or ever again.

"Hi, Finlay. Thanks for coming," she said, holding out a hand to shake his.

"Jeez, aren't we being formal today?" he said, grinning as their hands met. "You're looking well, so. Wherever you're living now, obviously suits you."

Seren felt a twinge of alarm. If he was going to press her to tell him where that was, she wasn't sure how long she would be able to hold out. He could not punch her in public, but he could reduce her to jelly with a few well-chosen words.

"Thanks. Let's find somewhere quieter to talk, shall we?"

"We could go home, Seren – to our flat, I mean," he replied, pushing his floppy curls back of his face and looking at her directly. "It's private there at least."

She shook her head. "No, not there. There's a pizza place round the corner where we can have something to eat and I can say what I came here to say."

She saw his bespoke good-humoured expression fade. She had become so expert in reading his face, his moods, and watching them change like quicksilver.

"Right. Sounds like fun," he said with a weak smile. "Lead the way, boss."

. . .

They talked for almost an hour, or rather, Seren did, and Finlay listened, which was rare. She did not tell him where they were living, but she watched his face fall when she told him how happy Enya was there, how she had gained so much confidence and even made friends, something neither of them had ever seen her do in London. As she described the changes in her, how truly happy she now was, Seren was sure she saw a glint of longing in his eyes, and even jealousy; he wanted that for himself, but never had it. She felt herself begin to pity him.

"She even loves swimming in the sea," Seren said. "Like a little fish, she is."

"Oh, so you live near the sea, do you? I guessed as much," Finlay replied, a sudden, sharp-eyed look on his face. "That's nice. I'd really like to visit you both."

Seren hesitated, her heart pounding. She had slipped up. She had to stick to the script she had practised on the train down, the one that persuaded Finlay that it was best, for all of them, if he left them alone to live their new lives without him. Luckily, their pizzas then arrived, which gave her some time to calm down.

"I don't think that's a good idea," she said. "We haven't been happy for such a long time, and you know it. When I faced the possibility of my life *ending*, when I got my diagnosis, I knew for certain that you can't be a part of my future, Finlay, or a significant part of Enya's. That's the way it has to be, for all our sakes. Surely you get that?"

Finlay's face twisted into a tortuous mixture of sadness and fury and his eyes brimmed with sudden tears.

"I see," he said. "Yes, of course I do. Yes."

Then, holding up a proprietary finger to the waitress, he mouthed "a bottle of red" and Seren felt her legs begin to shake under the table. Once he started drinking, she knew that his restraint, and efforts at mature understanding would evaporate in minutes.

"She is my daughter too, remember. I do have rights, you know," he hissed, pouring himself a large glass of wine and swallowing most of it in one gulp. "What you are proposing is both cruel and illegal."

Seren slowed her breath, took her time. Panicking now could cost her everything.

"Actually, I don't think you *do* have rights. I've checked. Your name isn't on Enya's birth certificate, as you were off in Galway on a bender the whole month before she was born, and I'm never going to agree to you having regular access to her, so don't even ask me to."

Finlay refilled his glass, and a small rosette of pink appeared in the centre of both his cheeks after he'd emptied it in one. He said nothing.

"You have never given me a penny either for myself or for her, and you *scare* her, Finlay – you always have. She knows what you're capable of when you're angry and I can't have that threat in her life any more. Those days are over."

He was blinking blearily now, as the wine hit his bloodstream.

"That's complete crap and you know it! We quarrelled, sure, but you always exaggerate things, you stupid little attention-seeker," he slurred, a spiteful look in his eyes. "Perhaps she isn't even mine, as she's such a wimp. You probably slept around quite a bit back in the day. God knows, you had little else to offer a man."

As he sneered, instead of cowering, surrendering as she had always done in the past, Seren felt a white-hot rage burgeoning inside her. She'd had enough of this – of him.

"Crude insults – always your first weapon of choice, your second being your fist or your boot," she replied quietly. "You pursued *me*, begged me to come and live with *you,* remember? You believed I could give you the love you needed – and I tried, as hard as anyone could bloody try, but it was never, ever enough. Nobody can fill that hole at the heart of you, or rather, only *you* can. Then, perhaps, you can love and be loved, but you've got things you need to sort out first."

Seething, Finlay drained his glass again and then emptied the rest of the bottle into it. The atmosphere between them had changed completely. Any warmth had vanished, replaced by blatant mutual contempt. Now that he was very drunk, Seren decided she needed to be more cautious, and row back a little in case he hit out, as he so often did. She had not come to insult or goad him, but to try and make this man *understand* what had gone wrong and how they needed to part for good. Getting him to agree that was essential.

"Look, it's time to go our separate ways, for your sake as much as mine," she urged. "We tried, but it's never going to work. We've wasted too many years trying, haven't we?"

But just as Finlay began shaking his head mournfully, Seren's phone rang in her bag. He stared at her, mouth open, his face full of hatred.

"So you *do* have a mobile? Another lie to add to your collection," he spat. "Aren't you going to answer it? Might be your new man. I expect you have another one on the go by now, knowing you. Once a tart, always a tart."

Mortified, Seren slowly pulled out her phone. It was not a number she recognised, but before she could end the call, Finlay snatched the phone and immediately pressed a series of buttons. She was so stunned that she could not react, but when his phone then rang, Seren knew what he had done – he now had her number. She had to stop him setting up a tracking option, as he had done in the past, but she sat completely paralysed as she watched his skinny fingers spider over her phone, his face rigid with determination. Standing up, her legs quaking, she finally found the strength to grab it back from him.

"Stop playing stupid games, Finlay. We are *adults,* remember? I came here to ask you to promise to leave Alice and Neil alone and that you won't harass me and Enya, or try to find us. We are happy, and we don't need you to ruin that," she said, utterly oblivious to the stares of other diners. An unfamiliar strength was flowing through her body, sporadic, sometimes guttering, but it was enough to render Finlay speechless. This was no longer the cowed, timid woman he had dominated for years, and he was weaponless against her, emasculated in the face of her courage. "Think of Enya, if not of me. Give her a *chance*, if you love her at all, and get on with your own life, find your own path. Please, don't call or message me. Let us go."

Finlay was deeply shocked and began to cry. Seren felt another stab of pity, but she could not risk offering him comfort. She had been there too many times before, and it had never, ever worked out, for either of them. This man could neither sustain compassion nor receive it without exploiting it for his own ends. Sadly, very sadly, he did not know how.

"Goodbye, Finlay," she said, leaving a ten-pound note on the table to pay for the pizza she had hardly tasted. "And good luck." His continued tearful silence was strangely reassuring. Could it be that he had listened to her and would do as she'd asked? she wondered. God, she hoped so.

Walking out of the café and into the crowded street, she did not look back. When her phone rang again half an hour later and she saw Aunt Alice's name on the screen, she breathed a sigh of relief. Perhaps a tiny shred of moral rectitude lurked inside him, a shred of the man she had loved and she had found it.

Anxious faces followed the hugs when she arrived at the house in Wimbledon, but she quickly reassured her aunt and uncle that they would not be threatened by her ex-partner again. Over the simple familiarity of a cup of tea and a toasted teacake, she described their cottage on Anglesey, her reunion with Lloyd, Enya's newfound confidence and how they were both doing better than ever before.

"You certainly look well, dear," Aunt Alice said. "Got some colour in your cheeks again."

"Better days lie ahead for me and Enya, honestly," she said.

"Delighted to hear it," her uncle said, pecking her on the cheek.

But as she walked away, there was something in her aunt's wave and warm, kind smile that reminded Seren of another woman, also waving and smiling, holding a baby in her arms and wearing a white dress and a huge straw hat: her mother. It saddened her deeply that she would never know what else the sisters had shared, because Kate was gone forever.

SIXTEEN

When Seren arrived home at almost midnight, she could not even consider trying to go to sleep until she knew Enya was safely asleep in Lloyd's cottage, and that all had gone well in her absence.

"It would be really helpful right now if you had a bloody mobile, Dad," she muttered as she set out to walk down to *Crigyll Cottage.*

In summer on Anglesey, the sky is never completely dark. That night, a haze of moonlight lit her path enough to see her way and it seemed churlish to pollute it with torchlight. Rabbits skittered for cover as she walked past their night-time scurryings, and she heard mysterious rustlings that she decided not to let alarm her. How far she had come since the days when she was too afraid to go to the corner shop for milk and bread in Kilburn!

The sea ahead of her reflected the soft, grey blanket of clouds in the sky. A scudding breeze whipped the water into small flashes of white that dotted its surface like pinpricks of light that seemed to be guiding her towards her father's cottage. When she knocked on the door, only silence and dark windows greeted her. A fillip of anxiety in her belly was acknowledged but quickly dismissed. It was early for her father to be in bed, but very late for Enya to be out; perhaps they were simply in the back garden watching the fireflies dance as a treat. But neither the fireflies, nor her father and daughter, were there when she checked, and Seren could feel her breath quickening as panic began to take hold. Then, suddenly, she knew exactly where they were. Lloyd and Jamie had taken Enya night-fishing, as they had promised; she had probably nagged them to on a perfectly clear night like this when her mother could not pour cold water on the plan. There was little point in being angry with her father for capitulating. He had asked to spoil her, after all.

As she neared *Trwyn Du*/Black Nose and Seren saw the pulsing light of the lighthouse flashing over the lead-grey sea, she spotted three figures down on the rocks, and three fishing rods with three tiny lights on their ends bobbing above the water. A gust of laughter reached her – two deep, men's voices and the unmistakably higher, gigglier sound of a child. She crept nearer still, until she could make out the grizzled white hair of one man, her father, and the dark hair of another, Jamie, who had his arm around Enya's back as he helped her cast her line out over the waves. Seren watched as the rod arced in the air, the little light flickered and then settled and Enya sat, as the men did, and all three waited like statues for the fish to bite. It was a magical moment, a snapshot of an experience she knew her daughter would never forget and one which her own father would never, ever have given her. It was not for her to spoil it. In fact, they need never even know that she had witnessed it. The lighthouse beam would keep sweeping softly over them, Lloyd would put her to bed in the little bed she had once slept in, and she would sleep all the better for this adventure.

Tomorrow, she would hear all about it, but tonight, it was their secret. Seren could see that Enya had become one of

Dylan Thomas' "sea girls", and was comfortable both with the ocean's power, and its potential for generosity. It was a wonderful gift to possess.

When she went to collect her daughter the following morning, she found her outside the cottage eating her breakfast (pancakes, thickly encrusted with sugar) with Jamie and her grandfather. There were dark shadows under her eyes after her late night, but Seren said nothing. Too many flares of joy had been extinguished in this little girl's life. She needed to know that good things happened and that punishment did not always follow them.

"*Taid*/Grandfather says I can come for sleepovers whenever I like!" Enya cried when she saw her. "He said I was as good as you were, when you lived here."

"Almost, but not quite," Lloyd added, winking at his daughter. "We've had a wonderful time, haven't we, Enya? *Bendigedig*/Brilliant."

"Yes, and eaten *so many treats!*" the little girl carolled, finishing her last mouthful of sugary pancake with enormous relish.

"You pop inside and get yourself some juice," Lloyd said. "I need to talk to your mam for a minute." When Enya had gone, he added, "So, how did it go with Finlay? You can trust Jamie – he knows the basics, as I had to tell him why we were looking after Enya, but he's very good at keeping secrets."

Jamie looked up, his face still and kind, but he said nothing. Yes, Seren had no doubt at all that she could trust him.

"It was horrible, but I think it was worth my going, and meeting him face to face. He seemed to grasp that we're better off without each other, but it was sad. He does love Enya, and I know he was glad, in his way, that she's settled so well up here, but he's such a complex person. He finds it hard to see others happier than he is. I really hope he can learn, gradually, to let the past go and find his own version of happiness, whatever that is."

Lloyd's expression was one of doubt. "Few leopards change their spots, *cariad*/love, but let's hope this one does."

Jamie looked up again, his face troubled this time.

"I want to believe that people can change for the better, Lloyd. I have to believe that, in fact," he said earnestly.

"I understand, my friend," Lloyd said. "We want to believe it too, don't we, Seren?"

"I *do* believe it," Seren replied, feeling warmth course through her at the smile that then lit up Jamie's face.

As mother and daughter walked back to their cottage on the farm a little later, Enya chatted happily about all she'd done and how Jamie had made up a brilliant story about a seal who couldn't catch any fish. Seren wondered when she would tell her about their fishing trip, but she did not have to wait long, her excitement was too great to be shrouded in secrecy for long.

"And guess what? We went fishing in the dark, just like *Taid*/Grandfather promised me, and Jamie taught me how to put my bait on a hook to catch a fish and I caught one, Mum – it was *this* big!" The little girl spread her hands as wide as she could, and Seren looked suitably awed.

"It was kind of Jamie to help *Taid*/Grandfather look after you, wasn't it?" she said in as easy-going a tone as she could muster. There was something fascinating about that man, a stranger washed up on an unfamiliar shore, a bit like herself. She needed to know all she could about him, even if it meant gently quizzing her child. "What did you both talk about?"

Enya sighed. "I really like him, Mum. It was sad when he told me he had a little girl once, but she died. Her name was Agnes, and she was very pretty."

"That's very sad," Seren said, her thoughts racing. "How did she die, did he tell you? And what about his wife, Agnes' mum?"

Enya paused, her little face clouded with tragedies she could not comprehend. "He didn't tell me those things, but he said he has no family left at all any more. He told me that *Taid*/Grandfather is his only friend in the whole world – oh, and me, of course, so now he has two friends. That's enough, isn't it, Mum?"

"Yes, it is, and I think he is lucky to have friends like you two," Seren replied briskly. This was all getting too intense, so she decided to move the conversation onto less maudlin ground, such as what to have for lunch. She also tried not to feel hurt that Jamie still seemed wary of trusting her as she did him, and did not yet see her as a friend. Perhaps he was reluctant to trust a single mother with a clouded past. Or perhaps his trust was hard to earn, as he had been betrayed in the past, but she hoped it would come, in time. She had no idea what other baggage Jamie carried with him, and Lloyd would not share his limited knowledge, but if the enigmatic Scotsman ever decided to tell her his story, she decided that she would listen and then she would tell him hers.

Enya was quiet for the rest of the walk home, but her mother sensed that she had more to say. Eventually, she said it.

"Can Jamie come to our house one day? He told me his house is horrible, and he's very thin, so perhaps he doesn't even have a cooker. He could come for tea. *Taid*/Grandfather could come as well as he's his friend. Can they, Mum? Can I ask them?"

Seren busied herself unlocking the front door to give herself some time to think. Would it be so terrible to hold out the hand of shared humanity to this lonely man and cook him a hot meal? How could she ever really hope to gain his trust if she did not do so? Would he actually come, as he avoided other people as much as he could? It was a huge leap from the tentative relationship he had formed with her thus far, but if the past weeks on the island had shown her anything, it was that risks were sometimes worth taking.

"I think that's a great idea, but let's not rush things. Why don't we talk to *Taid*/Grandfather about it first and see what he thinks? If he agrees, and asks Jamie when the time feels right, and he says 'yes', we'll cook something together for him. Does that sound like a good plan?"

Her daughter's shining eyes told her that it did.

SEVENTEEN

As easy summer days drifted by, Seren became more and more certain that she wanted to stay on Anglesey for the foreseeable future. Returning to the city was not an option, and Finlay had not been in touch since they had parted in Covent Garden, which was a huge relief. Enya would be starting school in a few weeks, and so Seren focussed on establishing real roots by finding them both a permanent home, and herself a job. Ruthie and Dafydd had not said as much, but she knew that, in the autumn, they would want to begin the work of converting the cottage for the following season, and she would have to leave it. She had no career, as she had always lived hand-to-mouth with zero-hour contracts as a temp, in shops or in basic admin roles since quitting university. She had never pursued her girlhood passion for photography, as Finlay had insisted she stayed home with him and their girl instead of going out scouring the skies for comets, celebrating the glory of an oak tree in full leaf or catching a pair of hares boxing in fields in spring. He, less kindly than Uncle Neil, saw all that as no good for paying the bills. Instead, she was confined to poring over beautifully glossy books in bookshops and marvelling at the pictures taken by photography competition winners.

On the island, however, nobody could censure or constrain her. She took hundreds of photos with her new phone, and was pleased with most of the results, but she knew that making a living from them was probably unrealistic. In these influencer, Insta-ready-days, *everyone's* a photographer, she told herself, and yet when she saw how she had managed to catch the moment an arc of sea spray hit the cliff, or the wing-blurred arrival of a bee on a flower, she felt a surge of pride. She was good at this, as she had always known she could be, but she and Enya needed money first and foremost, so finding a job took priority. Her spirits sank as she scoured the local papers and quickly resigned herself to care work or shelf-stacking when school began for Enya. This was not ideal, but it was a start, and she needed one of those.

Whenever worry, even fear, threatened to overwhelm her, Seren found the sea to be a great healer. She joined Enya in sea-swimming whenever a blasting wind or driving rain did not greet them when they got out. She marvelled at the hardiness and now-voracious appetite of a child who had been on the verge of being referred to a paediatric nutritional clinic in London as she was so puny and ate so little. Now, she hardly stopped talking, and it broke Seren's heart to realise that her silence had been a reaction to trauma, and to fear. The realisation that stress, and distress, had made her child very unwell made her more determined than ever to ensure the rest of Enya's childhood was joyful. She was happy on the island, her daughter was thriving and Lloyd looked years younger than he had when they'd first arrived. In fact, he described her coming back as instigating his resurrection from the dead:

"I was not living, in fact I had no life at all until you came. I was merely existing. I worked because I had to eat; I ate, and then I worked again – sailing the boat, driving a tractor up and down a field without ever looking up at the sky. *Diolch*/Thank you, for saving me from that drudgery," he said to her.

But this closeness came at a price, when Seren began to sense a slight dependency in their relationship when he needed to see her often, even twice a day, or he would become anxious. She became convinced that this cloying adoration could have played a part in his breakdown when he had heard of Kate's death, as if she had been a lifebuoy, keeping him afloat. At times, she felt as if even the faintest possibility of her not staying here permanently would see him collapse as he had on that fateful night when he knew his wife would never return. Had her mother felt that pressure too? If she had, was leaving without warning how she'd responded to it? Lloyd unfailingly described their courtship, their marriage and their relationship as perfection, but Seren sometimes doubted his version of events. All the books, plays and poetry she had ever read had shown her that human beings were flawed, and in those very flaws often lay their richness, their *humanity*. She decided to see if Aunt Alice could be persuaded to say more about her parents' relationship, as she had still told her so little. If her parents had been so blissfully happy here, why had Kate abandoned both her husband and her child and driven a motorbike into a motorway bridge a few months later? It did not add up and if her father would not tell her the truth, perhaps Alice might.

One evening, as dusk bathed the landscape with a soft pearlescent-pink light, Seren dialled her aunt's familiar number. She might be irritated to be called now, to be taken out of the comfort of her present and into the pain of the past, but this was something Seren needed to do.

"Why are you dredging all this up again now, when you're doing so well?" Aunt Alice sighed, as Seren asked yet again for more detail about Kate, the mother she could barely remember. "Why can't you just accept that your mother was, well, rather a fickle woman who put herself before anyone else."

"You've said that before, but I find it hard to believe," Seren replied. "She was loved and happy here. Everyone I meet that knew her tells me that."

"Well obviously she *wasn't*, because she left," the older woman snapped. She was clearly in defensive mode already.

Flinching, Seren pressed on. "But so suddenly, and without any warning. Something awful must have happened for her to take such a drastic step, surely."

Silence.

"Did you hate your sister, Aunt?" she said softly. "It almost sounds as if you did."

A short pause, and some stifled sniffing on the other end of the phone told Seren that she had struck a nerve.

"No, of course I didn't. Far from it, in fact, but we... *did things differently,*" came the eventual, guarded response. "She made her choice, given the circumstances, and that's all I'm willing to say about it."

"But what *were* the circumstances?" Seren said. "There's more, isn't there? Don't I deserve to know it?"

"Stop this, please, right now. Your father has grieved enough... as have I."

"But he doesn't know *why* she left, Aunt, and it's still hurting him."

Seren could hear her aunt breathing, quick and shallow. "Look, I will not say any more about this. I can't. I keep my promises, Seren, however hard it was for me to do so, both in the past, and now. Please don't ask me any more questions about it."

Her voice was low and firm with purpose. The conversation was drawing to a close, with the truth tantalisingly near, but Seren knew she could not reach it without risking a huge argument. Why was her aunt making this so impossibly difficult for both of them?

Neither woman spoke for a second or two, as the enormity of their conversation sank in. Despite their differences, they had shared decades of their lives and a finely knit net of memories. They had lost a sister and a mother, but they had each other, and always had; there was a lot to lose, if Seren pushed too far.

Aunt Alice spoke first. "Don't let ancient history cloud your life, one you've waited so long to be able to enjoy," she said, sounding exhausted rather than angry. "You are well, your father has you home again now, and his granddaughter, which is more than he ever dared hope for. You have a second chance, a chance to do things differently, as your mother never did. *Carpe diem*, Seren – seize the day. It's what Kate always did, and I know she would want you to."

"But, Aunt..."

"But nothing. Good night, and give my love to Enya," Aunt Alice said, and hung up.

For a few moments, Seren sat unmoving as tiny bats flew above her, the click-click-click of their waxy wings punctuating the stillness. She knew without doubt that there was a secret buried deep in her mother's story, but for now, it stayed hidden. Sipping her wine and listening to the landscape settling for the night, she accepted that, for now, that was perhaps as it should be. It was her time to *live,* not focus on loss. And she had so much to live for.

"*Awake, my sleeper, to the sun,*" she murmured, as she went inside and closed her cottage door. "Dylan Thomas always has the words for it, doesn't he, Dad?"

When she slept that night, she slept peacefully.

EIGHTEEN

There are moments in life which, in retrospect, mark a line in the sand, an event after which everything takes a different direction. Jamie being invited for tea was to be one such event for Seren. Lloyd had liked the idea, but agreed that it was more than possible Jamie would not feel willing, or able, to come. In the event, it was Enya who made the decision for him.

As it was still light until almost 10 p.m., Seren allowed her daughter to go night-fishing with her grandfather and Jamie again. Her terms of agreement were simple, even though it had all gone well last time, she insisted that she could be sitting nearby, ostensibly taking photos of the silken summer sky behind them (but in reality, keeping a very close eye). Everyone agreed, and they set off at around 9 p.m., just as the sky was beginning to prepare itself for night. They met Jamie at a corner where the lane that led to his cottage converged with the path to the lighthouse, and for the first time, he greeted Seren as warmly as he greeted the others. Usually, he was far more reserved with her. He seemed buoyant and said he had brought some home-made shortbread for them to share, which he told Enya that everyone ate in Scotland, "especially when they're fishing", which made her smile. When she asked where he'd found authentic shortbread, and he said that he did all his shopping online, Seren was surprised. So he *did* maintain some contact with the outside world, despite his isolated life on the island? Was he still in touch with anyone in Scotland, his homeland? Had he told Enya the truth, in saying that he had no family? She knew better than to ask him, but she was more intrigued than ever as their little group set off into the dusk full of happy anticipation.

"Thank you for letting Enya join us," Jamie said to her as Lloyd led his granddaughter on ahead. "She's a natural... *fishergirl*."

When she laughed at this new word, he blushed, and Seren saw insecurity flash across his face once more.

"Sorry. I often used to make up silly words like that for my... for..."

Seren rescued him. "I think Enya would be *delighted* to be known as a 'fishergirl' judging by the smile on her face this evening," she said. She sensed that he had been close to telling her about his own daughter, who had died. That would come, she felt sure now, but not yet. "I love words too – the sillier the better!"

Jamie's smiling response had a warmth she had not seen in it before.

"Is that a special child-size rod, Dad?" she called out to Lloyd, who was carrying most of their fishing equipment. "For Enya, I assume? That's kind of you."

"Actually, I bought it for you, but you left before you were old enough to use it," her father replied. Seren turned away, as sudden tears pricked.

As they all walked down towards the lighthouse together, clouds of seabirds circled above them, their cries a celebration of the long summer's day that had just been, and the prospect of another one to come tomorrow. The sun had set, but ribbons of pink and ochre still streaked the sky and were reflected in the sea, which was unusually calm that night.

"Thank you for letting me come night-fishing again," Enya said.

"*Croeso, cariad*/You're welcome, love," Seren replied, and Enya beamed at her mother's shy use of Welsh, the language that was so much a part of their new life. Sali had taught them both so much already.

"*Fydd popeth yn iawn, Mam*/Everything will be fine, Mum," she whispered, and squeezed her mother's hand.

The two men, and Enya, settled themselves on a rock too near the water for Seren's liking, but she said nothing. She was near enough to dash in and save anyone who fell in, and there were no threatening waves tonight. Once again, she watched the three of them slowly and carefully bait their hooks and then cast their lines in an almost-balletic movement. Again, she asked herself how this confident little girl could possibly be the same child who had not spoken for days at a time, hidden under tables at playgroup and refused to talk to anyone new? Miraculously, it was.

Happy that all was well, Seren started taking some photos of the sky, and of the birds, the underside of whose wings were now ablaze with the tints of dying sunlight. The lighthouse was bathed in a soft orange glow, and she was almost sure the small black mound she glimpsed in the water to the right of it was the sleek head of a seal, checking on them. When it dived and disappeared, she knew it had been; it comforted her that this beautiful creature felt they were welcome here.

Once the strange, semi-darkness of a midsummer night enveloped the Point, the beam from the lighthouse and the tiny lights on the end of the three fishing rods were the only sources of brightness. The moon was almost full, but its edges were blurred, and the narrow silvery path it cast across the sea was less than the wider arc the lighthouse illuminated every few minutes. It was quiet, but sound seemed to travel clearly through the velvet air, and Seren heard every *"plip"* of hook in water, and even the odd word of the fishers' conversation. From time to time, there was a billow of excitement as one of them caught something, but most things they threw back in the sea. The cool box was opened only once, for a shining, thrashing sea bass. Catching was not the point, it was the quiet waiting that mattered.

"We're only allowed to catch two sea bass a day, so I think we'll treat ourselves to this chap for our dinner tomorrow, and hope we catch one more, shall we, Enya?" Lloyd said with a smile, adding, "Jamie, if we do, you must come and eat them with us at Seren's cottage, she'll cook them better than I ever could."

"Yes! You must come for tea!" Enya cried, but her face dropped, hurt, when Jamie carried on lightly flicking his rod without answering.

Seren crept a little nearer to take some shots of their three hunched backs and bobbing rods, with the lighthouse in the background; she knew these silhouettes would make a stunning photograph, and a fittingly poignant memory of what they were sharing. All of them had endured sadness, and loss, but that night, the quiet bond between them was almost palpable in the chill night air.

She heard Enya's voice again, quieter this time, and gentler in tone.

"Jamie, did Agnes like fishing?"

A pause, while everyone held their breath. "She did, yes. She usually caught more than me, in fact. We used to go to my dad's cabin on the island of Jura every summer, and just swim and fish. It was paradise."

A sudden splash as a fish leapt above the water made them all gasp before disappearing into the darkness. Only a child could ask the next question, and so Enya did: "But why did you leave them both behind and come here?"

Lloyd cleared his throat. "Sssh, Enya. Leave Jamie in peace."

"It's OK to ask, but I can't answer you, Enya," Jamie replied, his voice shaky. "I had no choice. That's all I can say. I should have looked after my family better. I put my job before them and paid a very high price for it."

"No doubt you did what you thought was best," Lloyd said, and Seren saw him put an arm around his friend's shoulders. "That's all anyone can do."

Silently, the moon slid behind a cloud, and there was no light at all except their flickering rods and the swathe of sea the lighthouse beam revealed.

"What was your job, before you came here?" Enya asked.

"I was a journalist. I wrote stories for newspapers," Jamie replied, adding quietly, so that Enya was unlikely to hear his words, "I was interested in things back then, but some of the stories I had to write were about bad things, and bad people."

"They sell newspapers in the village shop," Enya cried excitely. "You could write stories about us!"

"I don't know if I could ever do that kind of work again," Jamie said. "Too much time has passed, and I'm a different man these days. I'm not curious or brave enough any more."

Seren, who had been listening to their conversation, decided it was time to step in. There was a dark undercurrent to Jamie's words that alarmed her.

"So, caught anything yet?" she said, trying very hard indeed to sound light-hearted. "It's getting pretty late, Enya. We should really think about..."

Suddenly, her daughter's voice rang out across the night.

"I've got a fish! Look, it's pulling me! It's *massive*. Help!"

Chaos ensued for the next few minutes, as both men helped

keep her steady on her feet as she landed the sizeable fish, a magnificent silvery-blue sea bass.

"That's my first ever fish! Now, you *have* to come to tea tomorrow, Jamie! Me and Mum are going to cook and *Taid*/Grandfather is coming too," Enya said. There was a silence, in which Seren and Lloyd held their breath, wondering if she had gone too far and offended him. Did he trust them enough to say "yes"?

Jamie said nothing for an agonising couple of minutes, busying himself with his rod, his head bent low. Eventually, he looked up and said, "I'd love to come. Thank you, Enya."

The little girl whooped with joy and high-fived him, and when Seren glimpsed Jamie's face, she could see how much it meant to him both to be invited, and to feel able to accept.

NINETEEN

The following day, the day of their planned dinner, was a hot, sunny one, but it came with a welcome breeze. Seren decided to pick some fresh samphire to cook with the fish that evening, and walked to a small cove that Lloyd had told her was a rich source of the deliciously salty succulent plant at this time of year. Enya wanted to stay with her *Taid*/Grandfather, as she often did these days, so Seren went alone, feeling the warm wind gently lift her hair and caress her face and relishing the freedom. This was how it felt to be truly *alive*; such simple gifts from nature far surpassed the striving for success, possessions and status she had seen in London – and these were all free.

When she reached the sandy inlet, she was disappointed to see a middle-aged woman bending over, obviously cutting and filling a small bag with samphire. Lloyd had told her that it had to be harvested with respect. Would there be enough for her too? She walked nearer and the woman lifted her head and gasped, before clapping a hand over her open mouth.

"Oh, my good God!"

Seren stared at her. "Er, sorry. Do I know you?"

The woman shook her head from side to side, as if unable to

speak. She was clearly very shocked indeed. Seren waited, embarrassed, until she felt ready to let her know what on earth was going on.

"I'm so sorry, it's just that you look so like a dear old friend of mine – incredibly like her, in fact," the woman said. "You must think I'm crazy, and I do apologise. It almost took my breath away, when I saw your face."

Seren looked at the woman as she tried to knot her bag of samphire and then called to a young cocker spaniel who was sniffing further down the sand. She was preparing to leave, but her face was very pale and she still seemed shaken. When a possibility began to settle in Seren's mind, she knew she had to see if it could be true. The woman was now trembling so much she could not fasten the dog's lead.

"Let me help you," Seren said, taking the lead gently. "Before you go, can I ask who you thought I look like? Might it have been a woman called Kate, who lived with Lloyd Evans in the cottage near the lighthouse about thirty years ago?"

The woman looked up sharply, her eyes bright. "Yes, yes! Oh, my goodness! Tell me, are you... could you be...?" She stopped, unable to speak, when Seren smiled. "And you have her smile too. You're Seren, aren't you?" she whispered.

Seren nodded. "Yes, I am. Did you know my mum?" she said. "Were you her friend? I know she had some good ones."

"Yes, I did, and I was. We used to swim here, she and I, and another friend, and all you babies were all sat together on a blanket over there. Oh, I can see it now, such happy, happy times," the woman said sadly. "I'm Catrin, by the way – Catrin Jones. It's strange to see you again, after all this time. Almost a lifetime, in fact; you were so small... and now, you're a woman."

"It happens! But yes. I'm back, and living near my father," Seren replied, emotion washing over her in hot, rapid waves. This woman had actually *known* her mother. Would she be able to tell her why she'd left? "It's great to meet you, but I wonder if I could ask you some questions?"

Catrin's face clouded instantly, her eyes guarded. "I'm afraid I need to get home now. I'm picking up my grandson Max," she said, starting to walk away, pulling her disappointed-seeming spaniel after her. "But I'm sure Lloyd is very happy to have you back."

"But... wait a second, I just need to know..." Seren called, her voice a strange yelping sound.

"I know what you want to know, Seren, but I can't tell you."

"Did she even love me, and my dad?" she shouted to Catrin's retreating back.

The older woman wheeled around. "She loved you both more than anything in the whole world. That was why she did what she did. Believe me."

Frozen with shock, Seren stood on the beach and watched Catrin scuttle up the stone steps and stride off along the coastal path.

When she was calm enough, she began to cut the delicate samphire stems as Lloyd had shown her. Now, more than ever, she was determined to find out what had happened to Kate and why she had died alone, in such a terrible way. These people knew the truth, and she needed to know it too.

When Jamie was very keen to bring a traditional Scottish dessert to the meal that evening, Seren realised that her initial impression of him might not have been accurate. Her image of soulful recluse choosing to live in a run-down cottage, interact with nobody and forage for food was gradually metamorphosing into someone who was trying to learn how to *live* again after a past filled with regret and disappointment. This was something else they shared, a bond forged in suffering; it felt good to know they were travelling along a similar path, towards a better future. It made her feel less alone in travelling it.

The evening was a warm one, so they decided to cook and eat outside. Lloyd was put in charge of preparing the barbecue whilst Seren and Enya gutted the sea bass and made a creamy salad of Anglesey new potatoes and another one of tomatoes, spring onions and leaves from Ruthie's vegetable patch behind the farmhouse. The samphire they would fry lightly, before sprinkling it over the fish.

When Seren saw Jamie coming into the farmyard, she barely recognised him. He was wearing a pristine white open-necked shirt, chinos and he had shaved his straggly beard off. For the first time, she could see his sharp jawline and full lips – both of which had been hidden previously. He was very hand-some indeed. He was carrying a large white china bowl which he presented to her, saying:

"I present cranachan, the best dessert ever," he said with a small bow. "I picked raspberries every summer as a *bairn*/lad, so it seemed appropriate to bring them tonight. And I went easy on the whisky, given the company present."

"Thanks! It looks amazing," Seren said, hoping that Enya had forgotten her dislike of the tiny seeds inside each plump, juicy blob of raspberry. She was so much less fussy now, that Seren felt confident she would.

They ate as the sun began to set over the sea, out beyond the lighthouse and Puffin Island. Swallows looped and danced above them, before returning to their roosts under the eaves of the farmhouse and the air was full of their joyous squeaks. The meal was superb, and everyone congratulated Enya on her first catch, which saw her almost explode with pride.

As Seren watched her daughter chat and laugh with both men at the table, she could not help but wonder if all three of them were somehow compensating for relationships they had had, and lost – Enya, her father; Lloyd, his little daughter and

Jamie, Agnes and, presumably, her mother. Only one moment of tension clouded this easy to-and-fro, and it began unexpectedly, with a simple statement from a child.

"I wish my dad was more like you, Jamie," Enya said, nibbling a samphire stalk.

Jamie hesitated, before asking, "In what way?"

"Well, he *can* be nice like you, but sometimes he hit us," Enya said. "We had to go to hospital a few times and I got a sticker for being brave."

The atmosphere around the table chilled in an instant. Lloyd looked at his knees, mortified to hear this terrible truth from a child's lips. Jamie's jaw tightened, and his eyes flashed with anger, so when Seren caught his gaze, her expression begged him, wordlessly, to say nothing more in front of Enya. He seemed to understand as he did not speak for several moments, before saying, very quietly:

"Thank goodness you and your mother are here now."

"And he *won't* be coming to visit," Lloyd added. "Or so we dearly hope."

Enya looked from one adult face to another, struggling to interpret the new, spikier mood that had replaced ease and friendship.

"No, it's best he doesn't, we think, don't we, love?" Seren said.

Enya nodded, but her face was still a little guarded, unsure. Had she done something wrong? If so, would she be punished for it?

Seren, seeing this, hugged her tightly. "Time for bed, fishergirl. Say goodnight to *Taid*/Grandfather and Jamie and I'll take you up."

When her daughter kissed both men good night, her confidence restored, it was as if she had known them for years. She *trusted* these two men, and that the days of punishment for wrongdoings she neither understood nor deserved were over.

. . .

Returning to the table about ten minutes later, she found Jamie and Lloyd deep in conversation, both with empty wine glasses and brows furrowed.

"Seren, I'm so sorry to hear that from Enya," Jamie said. "It must have been awful, for both of you."

"Don't worry. It's best you know, but I really think he'll leave us alone now," Seren replied, desperately hoping she was right.

"But can you be sure?" her father added. "I don't trust him to play fair."

"He won't hurt you if your father and I are here to protect you," Jamie said with an air of finality. "You have our sworn promise that we will be, Seren."

Lloyd nodded his head slowly, and said, "In Dylan's immortal words:

"Never and never, my girl riding far and near

"In the land of the hearthstone tales, and spelled asleep,

"Fear or believe that the wolf in a sheepwhite hood

"Loping and bleating roughly and blithely shall leap."

"Thank you, both of you," she said, refilling their glasses. "No leaping wolves here, please."

But as they drank, Seren wondered if she could ever be completely sure Finlay would not hurt them again. Enya was worth fighting for, and he was not a man to surrender easily.

TWENTY

After that ground-breaking evening, Jamie visited Seren and Enya at their cottage fairly regularly. He always said he was just passing, but she sensed he now craved company, *their* company to be precise. Mother and daughter soon became accustomed to his quiet presence, and they missed it when he did not come. Sometimes, he sat in the corner of the kitchen watching Seren prepare tea and Enya colouring or painting at the table, but on other days, he was chattier. On those days, Enya sat on his knee, flicked his ears to make him laugh and let him give her piggy-backs up and down the lane, which was lovely, but Seren did sometimes found these vagaries of mood frustrating. Who was the real Jamie? she wondered. As weeks passed, however, she slowly learnt to take what he offered and be grateful for it, as Lloyd had told her to. Whatever lay in his past would be revealed if and when he felt the time was right and the same applied for her, and her past. Right now, they were both learning to live again in the safest way possible – slowly.

Whenever Enya spent time either playing with Sali ("her first ever best friend", as she poignantly dubbed her) or with Lloyd (whom she adored, in every way), Seren and Jamie were now left alone together, whether they wanted to be or not. Neither felt entirely at ease, and both were conscious of tracts of silence and an occasional brittleness to their conversations. Whenever Seren suggested they go for a walk to break the tension, she fretted that this might come across as too forward. Whenever Jamie's response was hesitant, and she looked hurt, he then apologised. Thus, they navigated each other – one step forward, two steps sideways, but neither said how they truly felt or dared to take a risk and seem vulnerable; the past had left them both with robust defences that were difficult to penetrate.

One sunny afternoon, when Enya was playing with Sali on the farm, Lloyd insisted on cooking tea for them all at his cottage. As both the dishes and the muttering in the little kitchen increased, Seren and Jamie agreed to leave him to create chaos in peace. Starlings were filling the sky with their mercurial to-ing and fro-ing as they prepared to roost for the night and they both settled into an easy, companionable rhythm. Walking alongside each other made it feel easier to say things that had felt awkward before. Seren told him of her long-held yearning to become a professional nature photographer, and the impossibility of her ever affording the camera she knew would help her. In turn, Jamie told her a little about the criminality that was rife beneath the surface of Glasgow, and the risks journalists took to expose it, and the police to control it, but he gave no details. They sat down on a rocky outcrop overlooking the bay, as they had glimpsed a school of silver-backed porpoises leaping over the waves. For a few minutes, neither spoke, but appreciated being in the right place at the right time.

"I think it's time I told you a bit about myself," Jamie said softly. Seren nodded encouragingly, but said nothing, lest his courage vanish if she made a sound. He went on, "I came from a pretty tough neighbourhood, a place where most people had said goodbye to their dreams long before they reached adulthood. My mother died when I was six and my father hit the drink, went to pieces, and was jailed a year later for violent assault on a police officer. I've never seen him since. I got dragged into things I'm not proud of. It was all I knew, all I'd ever seen, but my English teacher believed in me. She helped me haul myself out of it and I got in to do journalism in college. After that, I didn't look back – until I did, and I ended up here a year ago." He paused, and the air between them hummed with tension. Much as Seren wanted to, she did not dare ask for more detail, any detail, beyond this broad sweep. He had skirted over that deliberately, but it was strange that she knew about his daughter Agnes only from Enya, but not from him. Eventually, he said, "Until I met your father, I had lost all faith in human kindness, to be honest. He held out a hand to me when I was drowning in my own sorrow."

"I'm glad he's supported you. He will have understood how you felt, I think, as there are things he finds difficult to talk about too," Seren said. This had to be her chance to ask Jamie a question that she had wanted to ask for a long time, especially as he seemed unwilling to talk about himself any further. "Has he told you much about my mother leaving, for instance, and his breakdown before Aunt Alice took me to London? I was so small, I can't remember any of it, but I wish I could."

"Not much, no," Jamie replied eventually. "He told me that he still has no idea why your mother left, but I think her death, and then you being taken away, were nearly the end of him, and I know how that feels too."

Without thinking, Seren laid a hand on top of his. He did not pull away.

"I know. He was left with nothing and nobody, but there's so much secrecy surrounding my mother, it's driving me bonkers. I met a friend of hers the other day who almost ran away when I asked her a question about her. It's a mystery I'm determined to solve, if only for Dad's sake. He needs to know, finally, if he did anything to make her go. He won't have peace until then."

Jamie nodded. "I'll help you in any way I can," he said. "I am so glad you and Enya have come back. Life feels better, for both Lloyd and I, now you're here."

A pause, as these simple words sank in.

"I just hope we can stay. We have to move out of our cottage, and I'm not having much luck finding somewhere to move in to so far."

"Then let me help you. I have money I don't need in my bank account from when I was still earning, still leading some kind of life," Jamie said, quickly holding up a hand to silence her when she protested. "What's the purpose of this bloody life of ours if it's not to help those we care about? I know that now; I just wish I'd known it earlier."

Seren sighed. "I remember a quote from a writer I loved in school, George Eliot:

"What do we live for, if it is not to make life less difficult for each other?

"I am grateful, truly, but I can't take your money, Jamie."

"I want to help you, and that's the end of it. For Enya's sake. She needs a long-term home, and we can all see how she's thrived since you both got here. Don't risk that."

"I know, and I don't want to, but I can never be dependent on a man for money again. I hope you can understand that." ,

Jamie nodded, but she sensed his disappointment.

As she lay in bed that night, Seren was still certain that she could never accept financial help from this kind, wounded man, but she had seen something in his eyes that she had not seen before, an appeal to be close to him and let him be close to her.

. . .

The long, warm days of July and August passed too quickly. Seren and Enya became adept at finding a beach that was not crowded and, when it was fine, basked in the sun and swam like eels. When it was not, they read stories or went for a rainy walk and made crumble from the first, early blackberries they'd picked in the luxuriant hedgerows. All four friends went night-fishing several more times, watching shooting stars streak across the night sky and marvelling at a much deeper darkness than the orange glow of London. On one amazing night, the sea was aglow with the blue bioluminescence Seren remembered seeing in her childhood and tears streaked her cheeks as she watched Enya, rapt with wonder, take in the rare gift of seeing it.

"People here call it 'sea sparkle', don't they, Dad?" she murmured.

"They do indeed."

"It's the most beautiful thing I've ever seen," Enya replied.

On some days, Lloyd took his granddaughter on the pleasure boat he skippered taking tourists around the island, where she proved an immediate hit, pointing out things only her young eyes could spot, such as mottled seals camouflaged on grey rocks or an elegant speckle-breasted curlew tiptoeing along the shoreline looking for food. Seren was always aware that Enya would start school soon and life would change again, but for now, every day was like a sip of precious nectar, and she treasured each one.

Her search for a new home was hampered by the fact that she was determined to stay as near to Penmon and her father as possible. Many of the two-bedroomed houses anywhere near the sea on Anglesey were either expensive bijou holiday lets or second homes, and affordable rental properties were few and far between.

"Where are local people supposed to live?" she asked Lloyd after another fruitless day of house-hunting. "I don't want Enya to grow up miles from you in a grotty flat where she can't see the sea."

Lloyd said little, but she could hear the words he didn't say, "You can always move in with me, and we'll manage somehow", but his cottage was small, and she could not risk their relationship fracturing under the stress that round-the-clock proximity to her father could cause. She was not that desperate – yet. But as September neared, and the school term was imminent, things became slightly awkward with Dafydd and Ruthie, who wanted builders to start on *Bwthyn y Dryw*/Wren Cottage before the end of the dry weather so that they could let it out to visitors in the spring. As the days whizzed by, Seren realised the conundrum she faced – Lloyd had offered to put them up and Jamie had offered money, but she had refused both and could not regret that. She wanted, and needed, to carve out a future for herself and Enya in her own way; this was why she had come here, after all – but time was running out.

There were flickers of hope, but they were few, and dim. Seren got a trial shift at a trendy small plates restaurant in Beaumaris, but her wages would be minimal and the summer season was almost over. Enya was looking forward to starting school with Sali, and was speaking more and more Welsh both with her, and with her *Taid*/Grandfather. Seren was now seriously trying to learn the language, building on the few words she remembered from her girlhood. Ruthie had told her it would help Enya if her mother could read school reading books in Welsh with her daughter and it also would be a huge advantage when applying for jobs. Sometimes, the two women and their daughters sat at the farm kitchen table and attempted a short *sgwrs yn Gymraeg*/chat in Welsh. It was a start, and yes, a few good things were happening, Seren reminded herself, but underlying everything was the aching worry of not knowing where they would live. When Jamie arrived at Lloyd's cottage one afternoon in the last week of August, the fact that he knocked on the cottage door told them that he meant business. Nobody knocked, ever. He came in, greeted them briefly, then sat down, spreading both his palms on the kitchen table. Seren and Lloyd exchanged glances; this was a serious, determined Jamie they had not seen before.

"I have a plan. You need help, and I want to give it to you, as I told you. If you won't take money from me, as I know you won't, so I won't bother offering again, take that at least." He paused. "Can I go on?"

Seren and Lloyd nodded wordlessly. His Scottish accent was much stronger the more assertively he spoke, as if he was using a more strident, confident voice from his past. It was both unnerving and endearing.

"Good. One of the cottages near me is owned by good people, older people, who live in Manchester. I've kept an eye on it for them since I've been here."

Lloyd and Seren nodded their understanding again.

"But these people can't use the wee cottage much any more as the husband is too ill to travel. I asked them if you and Enya can live there until they decide what to do with it, and they've agreed. It's better for them that it is cared for and lived in, and they only want money for the bills. You and Enya will be close to your father but have a place of your own, and I will be nearby too, just in case. Can you accept this as a solution, Seren? Please tell me you'll be sensible, and agree."

Seren could not answer for several seconds, but her smile and brimming eyes made it clear that she agreed.

"*Diolch yn fawr*/Thank you for being a friend to us," Lloyd murmured, slapping Jamie on the back with vigour.

"Thank you for being one to me," Jamie replied.

TWENTY-ONE

On one of the last days before school began for Enya, the weather was so spectacular that Seren drove them all over to Aberffraw, a village on the west of the island that boasted a huge beach, as Enya was very keen to try out her new *"Little Mermaid"* bodyboard in its famous waves. Seren promised to swim alongside her to allay her father's fears of so small a child braving the waves, but part of her wanted her daughter to experience the sensation of being carried into shore by the power of the ocean, and to feel able to *give* herself to it unconditionally. They drove along high-hedged lanes bursting with yellow ragwort and spools of honeysuckle until they reached the grass-covered sand dunes that led to the beach.

"It looks like a desert!" Enya said from the back seat. "Miles and miles of it."

"I haven't been over here for years. Your mother and I came often, to walk and swim," Lloyd murmured. *"Mae'n dal i fod yn brydferth iawn/*It's still very beautiful."

Stopping at the village shop to buy cold drinks and an ice cream for Enya, Seren was pleasantly surprised to see it sold far more than the usual snacks, newspapers and tired-looking fruit and vegetables. It was a treasure trove of local produce, tips, recipes, useful information for exploring the island and posters advertising local events and activities. A flyer advertising photography classes particularly caught her eye. Laid around the central text were stunning close-up photos of seals' whiskery noses, seabirds' feet, flower petals and leaves laced with raindrops, resplendent in all their miniature perfection.

"Dad, I just want to ask about these classes," she said. "I won't be a minute."

An attractive woman with thick, blonde curls was behind the till, a baby on her hip and a pretty curly-haired child colouring on a little table next to her. She smiled, a smile that conveyed a welcome without words.

"Hi there, can I help?" the woman began. "Gorgeous day. Here on holiday?"

Seren suddenly felt very nervous, as the woman's gaze was so sure and steady.

"Er no, actually. We moved up from London in the spring as I was born here, but I was taken away, and now we live in Penmon, but my daughter's heard about the waves over here, so we..." she stopped, aware that she was babbling.

"Welcome home, then. I came back as an adult too, and have never regretted it," the woman said calmly. "I'm Beth Williams, by the way."

"Seren, Seren Evans. Glad to meet you," Seren said, feeling her initial nerves melt away in the face of this woman's natural openness. "I wanted to ask about the photography classes on the poster."

"Ah, that's my husband Ioan's territory. He's a painter, and he runs all the art classes here, but he's recruited a brilliant local woman to start a nature photography course. Mai, she's called. She's had her work submitted for competitions, and lives in LlanfairPG, about ten miles from here."

"LlanfairPG? Is that the place with the really long name?"

"Llanfairpwllgwyngyllgogerychwyrndrobwllllantysilio-gogogoch," Beth said in one breath, then collapsing in giggles. "Yes, it is. Took me ages to learn it!"

Seren laughed with her. This woman's aura of positivity was incredible.

"Well done. It's a real mouthful," she said, spotting Lloyd shifting from foot to foot outside the shop. "Sorry, my dad's waiting outside or I'd love to stay and chat."

"Of course. So, it's the photography classes you want to know about, yes?"

"Yes. You see the photos on the poster imply that this tutor's especially interested in close-up nature photography, which is one of the things that fascinates me," Seren said. "I think it's sometimes called macro photography."

"Well, she takes a lot of different kinds of nature pictures, and they're all amazing in my opinion," Beth said. "The classes will be at 10 o'clock every Wednesday in that building over the square if you're interested, starting at the end of September. Her phone number's on the poster. Go for it, I say!"

Seren looked towards where she was pointing to and saw a large old building that had been stunningly converted into both a light, modern restaurant and an open space for other activities. Once Enya was at school, these classes would be perfect. "Thanks a million for that, Beth. Sounds ideal. I'll contact Mai asap."

"You're very welcome. Hope you like being home as much as I do, but it can take a while to settle in." She winked knowingly.

"Oh, I know, but I'm loving it so far," Seren replied.

"Great. Hope to see you soon, then."

"Yes, I hope we meet again, Beth. I really do," Seren said. And she really did.

. . .

When they reached the beach, however, the mood plummeted. Enya was very disappointed to see that the waves were rippling to the shore, rather than crashing in the big white breakers she'd hoped for. Her reaction was the nearest Seren had ever seen to a tantrum, so they agreed to drive on a few miles to *Porth Trecastell*/Cable Bay, a more enclosed, smaller cove where the wind funnelled the water between the cliffs and made large waves more likely. Lloyd was a little anxious, but Seren effectively silenced him with the words:

"We'll all be watching, Dad. Let her *live* a little. She's never been able to. I've mollycoddled her too much in the past, I think, and she loves the water so much."

A breeze was beginning to pick up on the headland, and the waves were building nicely in *Porth Trecastell* when they arrived. Enya ran straight down onto the beach clutching her bodyboard and waited impatiently at the water's edge for her mother to join her, slather her in sun cream and insist she stay very close to her *at all times*, as she always did. Jamie was in a buoyant mood, declaring this weather "as warm as the Caribbean after a Scottish summer" and paddling in the shallows with his trousers rolled up and a knotted hankie perched on top of his head "like my old *seanair*/grandfather used to wear". Lloyd sat on the picnic blanket, his face furrowed with concern as he watched Enya and Seren ride wave after frothing wave all the way to the shore. He had spotted what they had not – the darkening of the sky on the horizon and the line of wind-battered trees above the beach beginning to buckle and sway.

After about twenty minutes, Seren's teeth were chattering, and she staggered out of the water. That was enough for her, but Enya's face fell; did this mean she'd have to get out too? This was her "last day of fun before school," she whinged.

When Jamie assured Seren that he was more than happy to watch her while she went to warm up, Lloyd stood up, now very concerned indeed.

"She shouldn't be in there on her own," he said in a voice taut with anger.

Seren, who had so often had her enjoyment curtailed by an over-controlling man, suddenly felt angry too. "Dad, please stop worrying. Enya is a pretty strong swimmer now, we're watching her and she won't go out too deep."

"Can Jamie swim, if she does? Did you even ask him that?"

Furious at this challenge to her parenting, Seren buried herself in her thick towelling robe rather than offend her father with another dismissal. Who knew her child best? She did, of course. When, a few minutes later, she saw him going down to the shore to keep watch, she sighed, but settled back on the warm sand to feel it relax her every muscle. This was bliss and everything would be just fine, she told herself as she drifted off to sleep.

The next sound she heard was a terrified yell. She did not even recognise the voice, as it was far too high-pitched to be either Jamie or Lloyd. When she sat up, blinking, and saw Jamie charging into the water, his arms flailing, and a small bobbing head on a distant wave that had to be Enya's.

Screaming, she leapt up and raced past an anguished Lloyd waving his arms in panic at the water's edge and on, into the water. She saw Jamie trying desperately to reach Enya whose head was now disappearing beneath the water for seconds at a time as her strength failed. He could get to her first if the waves let him, but could he swim himself? She had no idea, as she hadn't asked. Shitshitshit. Had she put both of them at terrible risk? Sobs rose in her chest, and she began to wail in distress. The next sound she heard made goosebumps rise on her arm.

"Enya! Enya darlin'!" Jamie shouted, frantically doggy-paddling towards her. "I'm coming!"

A few seconds later, he had grabbed one of her arms and lifted her up out of the water. When Seren reached them, coughing and spluttering, the swell was much stronger and the waves higher than ever. Her daughter was clinging to Jamie with both arms and legs, her face buried in his wet shirt. Seren watched as he staggered against the force of the water towards the shallows.

"Oh, thank you," Seren blurted. "I'm so sorry, I should never..."

But he was neither listening to nor looking at her. His eyes were focused only on Enya, on her breathing, and checking she was still alive. He was shaking uncontrollably, and as white as chalk when she took a huge, gasping breath.

"Thank God. I couldn't bear to see you lose her like I lost Agnes," he murmured.

Seren wrapped her arms around them both, and, holding hands, all three waded back to the beach, pushed and pulled by the waves on the now-outgoing tide but staying inextricably together. Lloyd was waiting with towels and a face ribboned with tears, but he said not a single word to add to his daughter's guilt. He did not need to, as he knew exactly how she would be feeling; he had failed as a parent, and had blamed himself for that for years. They had all learnt a lesson today and adding a layer of guilt or blame served no purpose at all.

A few hours later, when Enya was dozing on the sofa and everyone was contentedly full of fish and chips they'd bought on the way home, Seren knew that she had to ask Jamie the question she should have asked on the beach.

"Jamie, can you swim?"

He looked at her steadily. "I would say no – well, not until today, anyway."

"Thank God I didn't know that earlier," Seren said, shaking her head at her own stupidity.

PART 4

UPS... AND DOWNS

TWENTY-TWO

Leaving *Bwthyn y Dryw*/Wren Cottage, their little cottage on the farm, was hard for everyone. Seren cried as she thanked Ruthie and Dafydd once again for letting them stay there; Enya and Sali clutched each other, weeping, as if they were not in fact starting school together in a week's time, Jac kicked a ball repeatedly at a wall to vent his feelings and toddler Harri screeched on cue.

"This little place has been our sanctuary," Seren said, as she squeezed the last carrier bag into the back of the Fiat 500. "We came here to heal, and we have done."

"Don't you dare be strangers. Come back and see us anytime, won't you?" Ruthie called. "See you at the school gate, Enya!"

Everyone waved furiously as they drove away, and suddenly, they and that wonderful phase of their new lives, were gone. Seren stopped at Lloyd's cottage to pick him up, as he had insisted on helping them unload the car, which she found strange as he was almost certainly not as strong as she was. He had not told her that he and Jamie had already spent a long time making sure their new home was clean and fresh after being empty for months, and so he was excited to see her reaction to that, and to a surprise they had organised for her.

"You're going to love it in your new home," he said to Enya, who was looking unconvinced. "And you won't be far away at all."

When they pulled up outside the row of terraced cottages, Jamie was standing outside the third one, waving enthusiastically.

"Welcome!" he said. "Come on in!"

"I love the yellow front door, Mum! It's like going into a sunflower and you love them!" Enya said, running inside the cottage. Seren followed more slowly, still slightly unsure of her feelings. She remained ill at ease with being reliant on another's kindness, though she knew she had little choice but to accept Jamie's help. Once she was working, she would be more independent and able to manage her life without charity, she told herself. But as soon as she, too, was inside the cottage, her doubts about the decision to accept that help evaporated. It was absolutely perfect.

Light streamed through the windows at the front, filling the large kitchen with warmth and inviting the sunshine inside. The pine table glowed, and she smiled to see a vase of sunflowers placed in the middle of it. Had Enya told them that they were her favourite flowers? She must have, and they had remembered, which touched her deeply. The living room was large, cosy and had a huge open fireplace with a wood burner already primed with logs as September would soon bring cooler evenings. While Jamie and Lloyd waited nervously downstairs, Seren and Enya climbed the wooden staircase to check out the bedrooms. Both were of a good size, and both had double beds, which Enya was particularly happy about after her snug, but tiny, crog loft bedroom at the farm.

"I can ask Sali to come for sleepovers!"

"You can. It's lovely, isn't it?" Seren whispered. "We must say thank you to Jamie again, for organising all this."

But just as she turned to go downstairs again, Seren glimpsed a large box, clumsily wrapped but with a pink bow on top, lying on the floor next to her bed.

"You've got a present!" Enya cried. "Open it, quickly! I bet it's from Jamie, because he bought me a new wetsuit the other day."

"Did he? You hadn't told me that," Seren said, frowning slightly.

Enya squirmed, seeing her mother's expression. "He said it was a secret, and it would help me swim in the winter when it gets colder. Please don't be cross with him."

Sitting on the edge of the bed and feeling herself sink into the comfort of an old-fashioned eiderdown, Seren unwrapped and opened the gift. When she realised what it was, a mix of different emotions whirled through her all at once: happiness, gratitude, fear and anxiety being the strongest. It was a Panasonic Lumex Bridge camera, one recommended by amateur wildlife photographers all over the world, with a zoom and auto-focus that enabled you to take crystal clear pictures of birds and animals without alerting them to your presence. She knew it was expensive, and knew Jamie must have bought it for her, as Lloyd had no money to spare, but what did giving her and Enya such big gifts *mean*? Did it make her and her daughter even more obligated to him, as she could never have afforded such things herself, which he knew full well?

Enya, sitting next to her, was watching her closely. She had become adept at reading adults' feelings from their faces. She was worried.

"Don't you like it, Mum?"

Seren hesitated, and closed her eyes. How could she begin to explain all the things she was feeling without sounding churlish, if not downright rude. Downstairs, the men were also eagerly awaiting her response, but she did not know what to say. When she heard footsteps on the stairs, and Jamie appeared in the doorway, she stared at him for a few seconds, saying nothing.

"Can you go down and see if *Taid*/Grandfather's OK, Enya?" Seren eventually said, to give herself a little time to gather her thoughts. Concerned, Enya left.

"Ah, I see. You think I'm trying to buy your friendship with this small gift, don't you? But that's not how I see it," Jamie said. "We are already friends, good friends, or I hope we are. My aim was solely to give you some hope for the future so that you can take the photographs you have always longed to take. I have money, and I have no future of my own to spend it on, so I..." he stopped, and Seren heard his voice waver. She felt a surge of affection for this man, and longed, once again, to offer him comfort. This was difficult for him, and she was making it even more so. As she now knew what she had to say, she said it:

"Yes, we are good friends, and always will be, I hope. I am very grateful for this – I really am. It's more than I could ever have hoped to buy myself, but I will only accept it on one condition. Are you willing to hear what that is?"

"Er, do I have a choice?" Jamie said. He looked as shy and uncomfortable as he had when she had first seen him, hunkering down on the rocks alone.

"No, you don't. OK, here it is. If you want me to develop *my* talents, you need to use yours too. You told me that you used to have curiosity about the world and want to know things, to find out the truth in your past profession; somehow, I want you to find that again. Do a course, write an article, a story, a novel, anything, but it has to be *you daring to be you* again. I can only accept this camera if you promise me you'll do that."

The only sounds were of Enya exploring downstairs, opening and closing cupboards to see what they contained.

When the silence lasted so long it became almost unbearable, Seren realised she had to be the one to break it.

"It's not easy, I know, but you have to try and dip your toe into life again – we both do. We can't hide away here forever, always looking over our shoulders and shying away from what might go wrong. We have to face life head-on."

Jamie scratched his chin, which was stubbly as he had not shaved again after doing so for their dinner party. "Well, I used to make up stories for Agnes, and write them down. That was one of my dreams once, to write stories," he said, and Seren saw a shadow cross his face. "But I failed at the most important role I had in life, keeping my child safe."

Without them having heard him climb the stairs, Lloyd was in the doorway and had heard these words.

"We all deserve a second chance, Jamie. The past was terrible, but it's gone, that's how I look at it. You need to move forward, into the future. It's been granted you for a reason."

"But my family... I destroyed it," Jamie cried suddenly, burying his head in his hands.

Seren was shocked. What on earth had happened to this man? Part of her longed to know, and to rescue him, even to love him, but part of her wanted to keep her distance and save herself from any more pain. There was danger here.

Lloyd put an arm around his shoulders. "We are your family now. Let that be enough for the time being. It's more than I had for almost thirty years."

"And you *do* have a future, with us," Seren said as warmly as she could.

"Thanks. I don't know what I'd have done without you two, and Enya," he said.

"Survived," Lloyd replied. "It's what we do."

Just then, a seagull thudded onto the cottage chimney, and its raucous, cackling cries dispelled the intensity in the room.

"So, can I keep my camera? Will you agree to my terms? I

have to say it would break my bloody heart to have to give it back," she said, laughing.

"I agree to your terms, but I expect to see your first photographic exhibition with the results of it," Jamie said. "You can do this. I know you can."

"Yes, I think perhaps I can. And so can you."

"Is everyone OK up there?" Enya called from downstairs. They had almost forgotten she was there.

"Sorry, love, we're coming down now," Seren called back.

When they all went downstairs, relief flooded the little girl's face when she saw their expressions, but Seren sensed that something was still not right. As the men unpacked some boxes in the kitchen, she asked her what it was.

"Mum, you left your phone down here, and... it rang. I didn't pick it up at first, but I saw Dad's name on the screen, so I did." she said, her eyes wide. "He said he knows where we are and he wants to come and see us, but he's in trouble and hasn't got any money, so can you send him some? He said he *needs* us."

"Right, OK, let's think about this," Seren said, her heart pounding. She had prayed that Finlay's silence meant he had got the message and was leaving them in peace. He had taken her number against her wishes in Covent Garden, and obviously decided that now was the time to use it. She needed to try and stay calm, however panicked she felt in reality. "We can feel sad that he's in trouble, but, well, how do you feel about Dad visiting?"

A pause, until Enya whispered, "I don't want him to. Please don't give him any money to come."

Seren pulled her close. "I haven't got any to give him, and I wouldn't anyway, so he won't come, love," she said, deleting Finlay's voicemail so that Enya could see it vanish.

"Promise, Mum?"

"Promise."

But when Enya went to find her grandfather, Seren felt all

the joy of the day seeping out of her. Finlay had finally worked out where they were. Could he borrow money from someone else to come? Why did he want to prolong their agony? He was miserable, but he was taunting her. God, how she longed to be free of him forever.

When some of Dylan Thomas' words came into her mind, she said them aloud to the empty air:

"Open a pathway through the slow sad sail,

"Throw wide to the wind the gates of the wandering boat

"For my voyage to begin the end of my wound."

She knew she had, somehow to release them both from this tyranny, but how she could do so, eluded her.

TWENTY-THREE

Luckily, another milestone eclipsed these worries for a while. Enya started primary school in nearby Beaumaris and Seren was busy scurrying around getting everything she needed (and quite a few things she didn't). Seeing her little girl looking so proud in her tiny red sweatshirt and clumpy new black shoes brought tears to her eyes as she held her hand and led her to the school gate on the first day of term. They both greeted Sali and Ruthie happily enough, but it was drizzling, so the gathering of parents was kagoule'd or umbrella'd, which meant nobody could chat easily, or wanted to loiter long.

"*Pob lwc, cariad*/Good luck, love," Ruthie called to Sali, and Seren did a thumbs-up to Enya, but she was painfully aware that her daughter was going into an environment that would be almost totally Welsh. The phrases they had both learnt with Ruthie and Sali were a start, a foothold, but a meagre one.

"I hope they'll look out for each other," she said to Ruthie, who was already heading back to her car. "They look so *small*, all of them."

"They have to find their own way now," Ruthie replied, grimacing at the rain dribbling down inside her collar. "Got to dash, sorry. Busy day ahead," but when she saw Seren's crest-fallen face, she added in a gentler voice, "It's tough, when it's your first, I know. Don't worry, she'll be fine. See you at pick-up time!"

But as Seren walked slowly away, she couldn't suppress feelings both of anti-climax and of disappointment. Ruthie was still the only woman she could call a friend on the island, and she was fond of her, but she had hoped there would be more similarly friendly women at school today for her to get to know. In reality, this was likely to be her only point of contact with other adults. Resigned to a long, lonely day, she saw a woman standing alone by her car, obviously very distressed. Her shoulders were shaking as she sobbed and then wiped her face with the sleeve of the stylishly capacious mac she was wearing. Seren walked towards her.

"Are you OK?" she asked. "I just left mine for the first time too."

The woman looked up, and Seren saw a pretty heart-shaped face framed by damp, auburn curls. Her nose, bridged with freckles, made her look more like a girl than a woman. Her expression was initially one of surprise, followed by one of recognition, which disarmed Seren completely. They had never met before.

"Thanks. It's silly, I know, but it's *forever*, isn't it? Once they start school, they're gone five days a week," the woman said, sniffing and dabbing her bright blue eyes with the tissue Seren had handed her. "Not that I haven't wished for this day a million times, when he's driving me round the bloody bend of course!"

The woman had a soft, North Welsh accent, which gave emphasis to her every consonant and was almost musical to listen to, but there were traces of other places, other lives too.

"I know. It feels too soon, doesn't it, but we'll still have the evenings and holidays to be driven bonkers in," Seren said.

"I know, and they'll survive, like we had to, I'm Del, by the way. So, have you got a boy or a girl starting today? My son's called Macsen, but we call him Max. Don't ask me why."

"My daughter's Enya," Seren replied.

"Another Celtic name – an Irish one in your case," Del said, before blowing her nose loudly and pulling out a huge bunch of keys on a fluffy pink keyring out of her handbag. "Her Dad's Irish, is he?"

Seren hesitated for a second or two. There was no point lying. "Yes, he is, but we're not together." Lowering her head, she noticed that the woman was wearing mismatched wellies, one blue, one pink.

"Ha, you've spotted my deliberate fashion faux-pas! My mother lives with us and we're the same size. She took one of mine this morning, so I had to take one of hers! Pretty chaotic in our house, *dweud y gwir*/to tell the truth."

Seren took a quick breath, and dared to reply in Welsh, "*A fi hefyd*/And me too. *Mae'n chaos yn tŷ ni*/It's chaos at home." She had used an English word and her grammar was probably awful, so she shook her head in embarrassment.

"Hey, don't worry! Good for you, speaking some *Cymraeg*/Welsh! I grew up first language Welsh, but I went away for years to study and forgot the lot, so mine's a bit ropey these days as well. My real name's Delyth, by the way, but it makes me feel like an octogenarian, so please call me Del at all times," she gabbled without pause. Seren began to wonder if she was nervous."

"Hi, Del. And I understand the thing with names completely! I'm Seren, a name which caused me a *lot* of problems in England, to be honest," Seren said with a wry grin.

Del nodded. "I think it's a lovely name. Your mother must have chosen it with care, especially if she was English..." Her piercing eyes were once again scanning Seren's face as if she knew her. "Was she, English I mean, your mum?"

Seren, unnerved, felt a strong need to back away. All this was, well, a bit *strange*. "She was English, but it's complicated, my family history," she said.

"You didn't grow up here, though, or I'd have remembered you," Del added. "Everyone knows everyone up here."

"You're right there. Well, I'd better be off. Great to meet you. See you later, perhaps," Seren replied, now very unsettled indeed. What was going on here?

"Sure. I've got to get to work. See you later, and I promise I won't be weeping next time you see me," Del said.

Watching her drive away, Seren felt a mixture of feelings. This woman seemed kind and incredibly open, but there had been something a bit weird about their encounter. It felt as if Del knew exactly who she was but didn't want her to know that she did. She spent the rest of the day brooding about what this could mean.

When the children bundled out of school at the end of their first day, most of them ran into someone's open arms before heading straight to the playground toys to burn off some energy. Seren scooped Enya up, grateful to feel her small body safely next to hers once more, and to her left, she saw Ruthie and Del doing exactly the same. Luckily, all three children seemed happy and said that school was fun, but Max said that playtime was too short.

"Typical boy," Del muttered. "Already an academic under-achiever."

"Have you met Del and Max?" Ruthie asked Seren. "They live on the farm *yn hollol ganol nunlle*/in the absolute middle of nowhere the other side of Penmon. Our mams grew up together, and were right hippies, the pair of them. Greenham Common, CND demos – they were there. Joined at the hip."

Del rolled her eyes. "They sure were. Had some kind of

'secret women's society', Mam always tells me. Sounds a bit dodgy, I know, but it's stood the test of time. *Chwarae teg*/fair do's, our mams are still close mates."

"They're the two that are left," Ruthie said, casting a quick glance at Seren, who was not sure what to make of this cryptic information.

"So, do you like where you live now, Seren?" Del asked. "Ruthie told me you stayed at their cottage when you first arrived."

Startled, Seren realised that these two women had obviously talked about her. It didn't feel good at all, but politeness overcame her reservations.

"I did, yes, and now we're in one of the row of old cottages above the Point."

"Yes, I know. That Scottish man lives up there, doesn't he?" Del said. "Blew in on the breeze about a year ago, and nobody knows anything about him."

The atmosphere cooled in an instant.

"Well, he's been kind to us, I know that much," Seren said, trying not to sound too irritated. She could not listen to gossip about Jamie. "As to his past, I don't know much about it."

Ruthie said, "I'll bet it's a sad one, poor guy. He's always on his own."

Increasingly uncomfortable, Seren moved the conversation on. "My dad's Lloyd Evans, by the way. He lives right down by the lighthouse, but his place is too small for us to live there," she said.

"Yes, I know," Del said, meeting Seren's gaze for the first time. "My mam Catrin knew yours, back in the day. I think you met her on the beach the other week. Ruthie's mam Enid knew your mother too. Did you know?"

There was a deafening silence in which Seren's mind whirred. A crawling sensation crept across her skin. She stared at Ruthie, who looked sheepish.

"I, er, think I remember you telling me something like that," Seren muttered. Running her hand through her hair nervously, she stepped back. Her growing disquiet was clear to all.

"I should have been upfront this morning, I know," Del said, reaching out for her hand, "but when you didn't say anything when I asked you about your English mum, I didn't like to pry, and Ruthie had told me who you were, and to look out for you at school. In the end, you found *me*, blubbering in a corner, and I'm so grateful that you did."

"And no nasty gossip was involved, honestly," Ruthie said. "We just care about you, as our mothers all cared about each other."

Del went on. "My mam remembers that you went to live with family in London, and how hard it was for Lloyd afterwards."

"But if you knew all this, why did you ask me all those questions?" Seren blurted.

"Look, I was just trying to be a friend, if you needed one. I wanted you to tell *me*, I suppose. It seemed more natural that way," Del said, looking embarrassed.

Seeing the frosty look on Seren's face, Ruthie moved forward to stand almost between the two others. The atmosphere between the women had curdled horribly. "Seren, please don't take offence. Perhaps we do things differently here, with less *pussy-footing around* than down south, but we both just want to welcome you, help you feel at home. Our families have a long and close history, that's a good thing, isn't it?"

"Yes, it is, but I know nothing about that history, and it feels like it's like a prize that's always just out of reach," she murmured. "I don't know why my mother left, and neither does my dad. I don't know why she died in a horrible, brutal way and, well, it's all... too much sometimes, it really is."

As tears began to roll down Seren's cheeks, she felt both

women pull her into a hug and after a stiff second or two, she sank into it.

"It must be really hard for you, *cariad*/love, but wouldn't it be great if we three could be friends, as our mothers were?" Del said softly.

Seren pulled away. "I don't know, I'm not sure," she said. "It's as if everyone that knew Kate has made some kind of weird pact, not to tell anyone that she was planning to leave, or why? Her sister, my Aunt Alice, won't tell me either."

Enya, Sali and Max running happily towards their mothers ended the conversation, and so Del was only able to whisper:

"We genuinely don't know, but I think they all made a promise to keep some secrets, secret. I remember Mam telling me that when I tried to probe," Ruthie said. "She got very shirty with me actually."

"And my mam did the same," Del added, "as she did to you, Seren, on the beach. Couldn't wait to get away, I expect."

"Well, there's clearly some kind of mystery here, but let's try to focus on the here and now. For now, we want you to know how glad we are that you and Enya are back where you belong, *whatever's* happened in the past," Ruthie said.

"Let's face it, we all have things that we'd like to forget. I need to leave those hideous red beaded cowboy boots a *long* way behind me," Del added, winking at Ruthie. "And we really are glad you're home."

And as Seren looked from one kind face to the other, despite her doubts, she felt that this was true.

TWENTY-FOUR

The weeks that followed were amongst the most peaceful Seren could ever remember, and life followed a predictable routine set against a backdrop of spectacular beauty. Their new home was perched so high above the water that she felt as if she was a bird scanning the horizon from its lofty nest. Whereas London could be a little sad in September as the parks' summer displays faded and the trees had yet to blaze in their full autumn glory, Anglesey was still poised between two seasons, summer and autumn, and the weather reflected both in quick succession. As the leaves on the trees began to crisp and brown, the hedgerows glowed with red honeysuckle berries, purple blackberries, scarlet rosehips and the last of the summer's wildflowers. On some mornings, the grass was silvered with a heavy dew, but on others, a vivid blue sky set the colours of summer alight once more and postponed the advent of full-blown autumn, and then winter, just a little longer.

Enya was immediately happy in school, if exhausted with having to try and understand Welsh all day. Luckily, Sali and Max translated what she needed to know, and the language all children share, that of play, ensured that she soon made friends.

Lloyd called into Seren's cottage most days, and Jamie now only occasionally joined them for a *panad*/cuppa and a chat, but he seemed much more quiet and withdrawn of late. If he called at all, he chatted mainly to Enya, asking about her day and what she'd learnt in school. Lloyd rebuffed Seren's concerned enquiries as to why this might be with, "He's fine," "Just leave him be," or "It's a good long while since he came here and left his life behind, so he's probably a bit low, with nothing much to put in its place," but she was not convinced his cooler manner towards them was so easily explained. She wanted to find out what was wrong, and help him as he had helped her at a low ebb. His distancing himself from her had hurt more than she'd expected and made her long for the growing closeness they had begun to share. Had she given him the wrong impression, some- how, or revealed more than she had intended to? She thought she had become skilled at hiding her true feelings, both good and bad; exposing them had got her punished in the past. Like a mouse on a wheel, these thoughts went round and round in her head without progress or solution. It was exhausting.

Ruthie, Del and Seren looked forward to seeing each other at the school gate, but their meetings were always brief as Brownies, netball practice or piano lessons beckoned after school. Whenever Del's mother Catrin, or Ruthie's mother Enid, had to drop off or collect their grandchildren as their daughters were working, Seren did not approach them and they did not greet her, which was disconcerting, but if her asking them questions they had sworn never to answer could upset them, it was not worth the risk. Seren had had enough "upset" to last a lifetime.

As autumn finally began to establish its grip on the island, and wet, windy days outnumbered dry ones, Seren began to feel a dull, leaden gloom which she recognised only too well as the forerunner to depression. Her few shifts at the bistro had dried up as the tourists had gone, Ruthie was busy on the farm and

Del worked part-time as a solicitor in Bangor, so company was sparse. They'd managed one, rather bibulous, night in a wine bar together, but that was not enough to sustain Seren or lighten her mood. She needed to *do* something, rather than wait for something to happen, so she returned to job hunting, but without much Welsh or any useful qualifications, openings were few and none paid well. The only date in her diary was the beginning of the nature photography course in Aberffraw she had signed up for. As it neared, each day began to crawl more and more slowly. There was no more contact from Finlay, but she could not suppress a sense of gnawing dread in the pit of her stomach. This was a far more familiar feeling than the happiness she had first enjoyed on the island. The very possibility that she was doomed to ride this emotional rollercoaster forever horrified her.

Her father, too, seemed to be despondent as the easy days and long evenings of summer faded from memory, so when he told her that they both needed an outing, she leapt at it. He wanted to take her for a ride on the Eye that was set up in Beaumaris every year, and would soon be dismantled for the winter, and then for a slap-up lunch at The Buckley Hotel. Luckily, the day was a glorious one and as she and her father boarded one of the twenty-four romantically named "gondolas" on the huge wheel, Seren felt a buzz of excitement mixed with fear in her belly. The only feeling she could compare it with was the one she had recalled in the dream after her surgery – that of holding her father's hand tightly as they watched massive waves crash against the side of the lighthouse, laughing as their outstretched tongues were coated with cold, salty spray. The fact that she was on the island almost thirty years later, and reaching out for his hand once more as the wheel began to move, seemed almost miraculous. Yes, she had done a good thing, in coming home.

As the wheel slowly turned, and the spectacular landscape on all sides of the glass gondolas was spread out around them, Seren's nerves vanished and she let herself be swept upwards, soaring above this beautiful place. She saw the sea, the mountains, the colourful houses along the main promenade and a few people fishing or crabbing with hooks and lines along the pier. It was all so solid, so grand, that it made her, and her concerns, seem so tiny. What did her moods matter when she looked at the perfection of those heather-coated hills on the other side of the Menai Straits, with the peaks of *Eryri*/Snowdonia beyond them? They would always be there, unchanged and unchanging, as they had always been. As the wheel inched its way up to the top of its journey, she gasped as she saw the black and white lighthouse at Penmon standing proudly just offshore, with Puffin Island beyond and a cloud of white-winged seabirds peppering the sky above it.

"It's so perfect, isn't it, Dad?" she murmured, but when she turned to look at Lloyd's face, he was staring intently at something on the street far below them.

"Isn't that Jamie down there?" he said, squinting to get a clearer view.

Seren looked, and felt a chill pass through her body. It *was* Jamie, and he was walking alongside a young woman whose thick blonde hair was so long it almost reached her waist. She was very pretty, and wearing a vividly coloured coat from a brand she recognised from her city life in London. Seren felt her breath become shallower and her heartbeat quicken.

"I think that's his wife Fiona, you know," Lloyd said, leaning forward, as yet oblivious to his daughter's growing distress. "He showed me a photo of her once. Well I never. I am surprised she's come to see him after all this time."

Desperate for fresh air, Seren slid the window of their capsule open and a chilly breeze rushed in immediately. So did a sudden blast of seagull cries and the low, dull crank of the Eye going around. In an instant, she was part of the real world once more, and not in the dreamy bliss she had been enjoying so much only a few moments earlier. The single word "wife" ricocheted around in her head.

"Are you OK, *cariad*/love?" Lloyd said, once he saw Seren's face, which was now ashen pale. "Feeling a bit queasy up here?"

Seren nodded and attempted a smile. It did not convince anyone.

"*O bechod*/Oh shame, he hadn't told you about her, had he? That they were still married, I mean…?"

Feeling her eyes fill with tears, Seren turned away. "No, he hadn't, but it's fine. I know so little about him – even less than you do, and he has a perfect right not to tell me everything. It's just that, well, he's become such a part of mine and Enya's life, but there are still so many secrets between us. It's not good, Dad."

"There will be a reason why neither of us know all there is to know about Jamie yet," Lloyd said. "All in good time. To tweak some of Dylan's words:

"*This side of the truth,*

"*You may not see, my daughter.*"

"But I need to! So, you knew that they were still married?" Seren said, feeling, for the first time, a flash of irritation with her father's poetry-quoting habit.

"Yes, I did know that, but I have known him for longer than you have… and it didn't matter, as he wasn't in danger of falling in love with me, was he?"

"Or I with him," Seren whispered, feeling her face blaze with embarrassment as she realised what she had just said. "Oh shit. I really don't need this now. What if he's going to get back together with his wife? My life's complicated enough as it is!"

"Life rarely gives us what we need, when we need it, in my experience, and love is particularly prone to shoving a spanner in the works," Lloyd replied. "But believe me when I say that

Jamie is very, very unlikely to be reuniting with Fiona, and he will tell us what we need to know about why she's here in his own time," Lloyd replied.

"I hope so, I really do, because I know I can't ask him. He panics if I try."

"No, you can't, and you mustn't, however hard that is." He paused, before adding softly, "So do you think you could ever love him, Seren?"

She hesitated. "I don't know. I really don't. But we have a... *bond*, I know that."

"That's a good foundation for love, in my experience. I felt just the same about your mother when I pulled her out of the waves. We were joined, destined by fate to travel through life together, however hard that road might prove to be."

"I want to help him, and I know he wants to help me, so perhaps, yes, love might follow for us, too, if the stars align, as Dylan Thomas would no doubt say," Seren said, kissing her father softly on the cheek.

As the Eye completed its slow and graceful circle and brought them back to the ground, father and daughter disembarked feeling that the experience had been more intense than either had expected, but also a sense of relief that they could now speak to each other openly, without the need to edit or pretend. Neither now felt like a big lunch, so they got fish and chips and sat on the bench overlooking the sea instead, taking turns to fend off predatory seagulls.

And as they ate in companionable silence, Seren reminded herself of how lucky she was to have this wise, kind old man as her father. Whatever lay ahead for both of them, she hoped he would always be by her side, and she, by his.

TWENTY-FIVE

The first session of Seren's nature photography course was disappointing. The tutor, Mai, spent the entire session talking about lenses, apertures, zooms and exposures, which left most people both bored and bamboozled. When they were all asked for feedback, an English woman who had introduced herself as Jude spoke for all of them when she told Mai very firmly that she'd hoped they were here "to learn how to take the best photos of some of the beautiful things we see around us and not to do a course in camera tech". Mai, visibly chastened, said she would get to that "in future sessions". Seren made a beeline for Jude in the car park.

"Thanks so much for saying what I was certainly thinking," she said.

"No problem. I work with images all the time in my business, and I'm fine with the bigger, landscape shots, but I wanted to get better at taking crystal clear pictures of the little things, if you know what I mean? I'm rubbish at that."

"I know just what you mean, and I want to do just the same thing. 'Macro photography' it's called – I looked it up. Beth, the woman running the shop over there, said we'd be doing that kind of thing in this course, so let's hope Mai 'takes our feedback on board', as the phrase runs." Seren paused. "Can I ask what your business is called?"

"The Memory Maker, and I'm Jude Parry. Check out my Facebook page, and you'll find me. Sorry, got to dash now and do a shop before school pick-up," the woman said with a broad smile. "You know how it is."

"I do indeed... Jude. I'm Seren Evans, by the way," she blurted, before adding the simple phrase that had now become her story. "I was born here, and have come back."

"Well, it's a bloody good place to come back to. Good to meet you, Seren," Jude said. And with that, she drove away.

When Seren got home, she immediately looked up Jude's website, and was deeply impressed by her ability to blend texture, colours and different media in her work. To commemorate a wedding, for example, she had managed to combine nearly thirty different things, including shards of confetti, pressed flowers from the bride's bouquet, extracts from the hymns and a tiny photograph of the happy couple framed with a coronet of leaves from the old oak tree in the churchyard. It was both beautiful, and deeply evocative of what the day must have been like, but she saw that Jude hadn't included any close-up pictures of single items, or macro photography; that was what she'd hoped to learn about in the course, as she'd told her. Could this woman be a kindred spirit, or even become a friend? She dearly, dearly hoped so.

Seren felt ideas firing off inside her head. Photos of people and places, weddings and celebrations, the traditional fare of photographers, did not appeal to her, but the ability to reveal the minutiae of nature – a cache of pollen on a honeybee's back legs, the sheen on a mallard's head, the veins threading through the petals of a flower were things that had always fascinated her. Kitsch calendars, bland greetings cards and postcard-perfect prints of glorious beaches were everywhere, but the tiny details of life filled her imagination, and she started to spend the first part of each day that week scouring her small world for things to photograph, getting up before Enya to see them before the wind or the tide disturbed them. She was fired with enthusiasm by the time the second class came round, and even brought in some of her best of pictures to show to Jude... but she was not there. Devastated, Seren felt like a child who had come last in the sack race on sport's day.

The class itself was much better, but she felt such acute disappointment that Jude had not turned up that she asked Mai, the tutor, if she knew why.

"She DM'd me saying she's got too much on to commit the time at the moment, what with her business and a new baby," Mai said. "Shame, as we could all have learnt a lot from her – she's a real talent in her field. She said she might come back after Christmas, when her baby's a bit bigger. You can show *me* what you've done off your own bat, though, if you like." There was insecurity in her face and in her tone, as last week's challenge from Jude had clearly hit home. Seren recognised a body blow to self-confidence when she saw one.

And so she showed Mai her pictures, but the tutor's measured phrases, such as "showing great promise", and "a sound foundation" did not fill her heart with joy as she felt Jude's opinion would have done; she would have had much more of an understanding of how much *love* had gone into each and every shot. After Christmas, Seren would have probably started some mundane job, and so would never see Jude again. She decided only chocolate would fend off despair.

Disconsolate, she walked over to the village shop to buy some, secretly hoping to see Beth Williams again, but a rather zanily dressed young man was serving instead. She bought herself some locally made chocolate, *Siocled*, but it was no compensation for not seeing Jude or Beth. How could she ever make friends in this place if she only met possible candidates once before they vanished again into their busy, happy lives? When she got back to her cottage, a wave of sadness washed over her, a thick black tide of gloom that began at her toes and spread throughout her body. She understood the seductive downward pull of depression better than most people, but for Enya's sake, she simply could not succumb to it again. If she could not be friends with Jude or Beth, and Jamie was keeping his distance because Fiona was back in his life for whatever reason, she needed to try harder with Ruthie and Del.

"I need to join them in something they already do," she said to herself. That left only one feasible option: swimming in the sea in all weather, through all seasons, wearing only their swimsuits. They both resolutely refused to call it "wild swimming" and spurned the aptly named local Bluetits group as it cramped their style, but getting into the sea was hugely important to them. Seren understood why to some degree, as she had grown to love it in the summer too. What she was less on board with was going into a very *cold* sea, but she had no choice but to at least attempt to join them, insane as it felt. Her WhatsApp message to both women was suitably light:

> Hi, you two. Fancy a quick dip after school drop-off on one of your mornings off? Really want to join you both in going through the winter. S x

Del replied first:

> Gr8. Welcome aboard! I'll be at Lleiniog Beach at 9.15 a.m. tomorrow. D X

Seren quickly checked the forecast for the following day, 7th October; it did not make hopeful reading and she dearly wished she had seen it before texting the other two.

Scattered showers, some heavy, with a stiff
onshore breeze. Temps low.

When Ruthie's thumbs-up reply pinged on her phone,
Seren knew she simply could not bottle it. Muttering, "If you
can't beat 'em, join 'em," she went to search for Enya's wetsuit
just in case, by some miracle, it was stretchy enough to fit her. It
wasn't. Hard core it would have to be.

The forecast had been spot-on, and it was cold and mizzling
fairly convincingly when the three women arrived at the
beach. Del and Ruthie waved when they saw her, and then
went straight down onto the shingly shore, causing a few
oystercatchers to fly off in a flurry of disgruntled peeping.
Seren joined them, pulling the mac she had again borrowed
from Lloyd tightly around her in the wind. She had come all
ready in her rather frumpy, post-surgery bathing costume
rather than risk changing on the beach, but she was worried in
case her silicone prosthesis slipped out of place. She had yet to
tell them about her mastectomy, and this was the first time
there was any chance of them noticing that her breasts were
not identical. Neither baring her soul nor her body were
things she had ever done in the past, however much she'd
wanted to at times. Enya was the only person she had allowed
to see her flat chest, and what the little girl immediately
dubbed "the chicken breast", her smooth, pink prosthesis
(which did look *very much* like a chicken breast). Paralysed
and shivering, Seren watched as the others peeled off their
clothes gaily as the wind whipped around them. They could
see the hesitation, even fear, in her face, but they did not ask
her any questions, nor urge or tease her. The choice as to
whether to actually join them in the water was hers alone and
she could feel that there would be no shame in their eyes if

she couldn't. They carried on doing what they always did, and let her make up her own mind, in her own time, about what she did or didn't do. It felt like compassion in its truest, purest form.

"So, why did you choose this beach, Del? We don't usually swim here," Ruthie said, tucking her copious curls into a swimming hat. "It's a bit weedy underfoot."

"Yeah, I know, but there's a very good reason. I'll reveal everything once we're out," Del said, unaware of her innuendo.

"We've seen it all before, remember?" Ruthie said, with a huge laugh that echoed off the rocks around the beach.

"Haha. Right, I'm going in. Here goes nothing," Del replied.

Seren watched as Ruthie and Del waded into the water without hesitation, and within a minute, vanished into the froth of an incoming wave. She saw them begin to swim with long, confident strokes, and her doubts as to whether she could actually *do* this multiplied tenfold. The fine rain was easing, but the wind was keen and she was already feeling very cold. Perhaps these two were simply much tougher than her, born and bred on this wild island and almost Amazonian in their endurance and strength? It made sense, and it could let her off the hook...

But as she agonised, other possibilities demanded to be heard too. She thought back over all the times in her life when she had let insecurity overcome her, such as when she had let Uncle Neil persuade her into a degree she had not wanted to do; when Finlay had told her she had no need for friends as he was enough; when she had let him bully her and then hidden, cowering, until her hurt and her bruises had healed rather than tell someone what was going on. Then she remembered how she had faced her cancer diagnosis, her surgery and her treatment head-on, and finally, how she had taken the decision to leave everything she knew behind and bring her little girl here, where she knew nobody, but where she instinctively felt they would both be safe. If she had found the courage to do all that, why was she standing on this beach doubting that she could swim in the sea today?

With a deep breath, she let Lloyd's mac drop to the ground, and then she, too, walked into the water without a backward glance. She waded through the drifts of seaweed without allowing herself to wonder what might be hiding in them. She forgot about her lost breast, her sadness about Jamie's pretty wife, even the years she had wasted being under Finlay's thumb as he wrestled with his own insecurities. With each step, she let the unspoilt beauty of this place fill her body and her mind with strength, hope and pride in who she was, and who she could be. Within a minute, she had joined the others splashing in the cold water, and smiling from ear to ear.

Fifteen minutes later, the three women were dressed and sitting in Del's steamed-up car drinking hot, sugary tea. Seren had never felt so full of life, so sure that she was invincible. Her entire body tingled as if it was on fire.

"I absolutely loved that," she said, "especially now it's over."

The others laughed in unison.

"There's nothing like it, but beware, because it's addictive," Ruthie said. "Right, Del, tell us why we came here today, and not the beach near the Point, as usual? It's time for the big reveal." She held a spoon to her friend's face as if it was a microphone and they all laughed again.

Del pulled a tattered brown envelope out of her bag. When she showed the others the photograph inside it, they all gasped. There were three young women standing on the exact same shoreline that they could see in front of them, all wearing rather saggy swimsuits and waving and smiling at the camera.

"Oh my God! That's my mam, your mam, Del... and, Seren, that woman looks so like you it must be Kate, your mam!" Ruthie cried, moving her finger from one to the other on the photo as she spoke. "And it was taken right here!"

"And look," Seren almost yelled from the back seat.

"There's us three, on a picnic blanket, on the beach behind them. Ruthie's a bit older, and you and I are still pretty small, Del. Don't we look gorgeous in those pink knitted cardis?"

Del nodded. "Yep, there we are in all our glory. You see, I knew you'd understand why we had to come here. I was going through some of my mam's photos when she was out, trying to find some clues for Seren, and I found this, along with quite a lot of other photos of what was obviously a really happy time for them. And look, it says 'The Three Amigos' on the back. Lovely, isn't it, and doesn't it make it even more special that we three are here now, today, doing exactly the same thing?"

"Amazing. *Bendigedig*/Brilliant, in fact," Ruthie said, but when she looked at the back seat, the smile vanished from her face. Seren was sobbing uncontrollably.

"You're right, they *do* all look happy in that photo, but she *left* us not long after that was taken, with no warning, no explanation," she spluttered. "Why would any mother do that? And why won't anyone tell me?"

Ruthie and Del both joined her in the back seat, and wrapped their arms around her until she calmed down a little.

"I don't know why it's all so mysterious, but our mothers *really* don't want to talk about it, in my experience," Del said. "It's like they pull a drawbridge up whenever we dare mention Kate."

"I know. But it's not a choice for me any more. It's imperative. I have to know why she went, why she left us."

Ruthie and Del each took one of Seren's hands and promised that they would try and help her, but she could sense their reservations. Whatever secrets swirled around her mother's departure and death, it seemed to have established some kind of hold over quite a few very strong women. She could see that getting to the truth was going to be far from easy.

TWENTY-SIX

For several weeks after she had seen Jamie with his wife, Seren did her best to avoid him. Now, she understood why he had been giving her a wide berth, replying in kind seemed the best thing to do to retain her dignity. Lloyd's words about Jamie "being in danger of falling in love" with her replayed in her head again and again, and she knew that she had been in a similarly perilous position with her feelings for him, but if asking him questions about his wife, or his past life had been difficult when they were closer, it was impossible now. He needed space, and she had to grant him that. They met only sporadically, and returned to circling each other warily like animals when they did, unsure if the other was friendly. Jamie came with her, Enya and Lloyd to a lacklustre craft fair in Bangor one Saturday afternoon, but the noise and crowds meant they could not talk properly. The weather was too poor to go fishing and nobody offered to organise another dinner. It was a time of stagnation, of frustration, and although Lloyd told Seren again and again that she had to wait, to give Jamie time to sort things out, it was very hard for her to do so.

"Trust has to be earned, remember," was her father's constant refrain. "Be patient. He'll come back to you."

But Seren was not sure she wanted him to. Jamie had never asked her anything more about Finlay, as if knowing that her ex-partner had hurt her and Enya was all he needed or wanted to know. There was no sign of Fiona around his cottage, or in the area, so Seren assumed she had gone back to Scotland, but did he still love her and was that why she had come to see him? This was an especially painful possibility because she had stopped loving Finlay years ago.

Sometimes, when she was alone, she stood in front of a mirror and shouted at herself, "Why do you need another fickle Celtic man to make your life complete? How's that gone for you in the past? You have some friends, a family that loves you, interests and talents and a body that's got you through childbirth and cancer; surely that's more than enough?"

But in her heart of hearts, when tears followed each outburst, she did not believe it, and Jamie's soulful, gentle face still danced across her dreams.

When he knocked on the door of her cottage late one evening, Seren was taken aback when she glimpsed him through the window. Enya was in bed – as Jamie must have known – so he must want to talk to her alone. She pulled her dressing gown around her tightly; it really wasn't visiting hours in her opinion. But when he came in, coy and shy, the wind slammed the door behind him, and they both laughed.

"Oops, sorry about that," Jamie said, blushing.

"No worries. It's pretty wild out there tonight," Seren said. She decided to try as hard as she could to maintain a cool but polite manner. "Long time, no see."

"Yeah, I know. It's been a, well, a tricky time for me. Lots going on."

There was a silence he made no attempt to fill, but Seren waited until she felt prepared with the right words rather than letting her hurt feelings speak for her.

"Can you tell me about any of it, the lots that's been going on I mean?" she asked with more brittleness in her voice than she'd intended. "It's as if you vanished off the planet. Even Enya's been asking why you don't visit us much any more."

"That's one of the reasons I came to see you tonight," Jamie said quietly. "Can I sit down please? I feel like I'm being interrogated at the moment."

"Sorry, of course!" Seren said, flustered. Being even slightly assertive was so unfamiliar a feeling. "Drink? Tea, coffee, or I think I've got some whisky somewhere, as Dad likes a drop 'to warm his bones,' he says. And I didn't mean to be..."

"It's fine. I understand, and no thanks to the drink," Jamie said. "I just need to tell you something and then, if you want me to, I'll go. Please sit down yourself. You'll need to."

The only sound in the room was the crackle and spit of logs on the fire until she heard Jamie take a deep breath, and begin to speak:

"You know that I came here with secrets. Lloyd will have told you that, and he will have warned you off quizzing me about them, because I asked him to. There are still things I can't tell you, for your own safety, but you deserve to know why I haven't been coming round much for a while. It's hard, but..."

He paused and ran his hand through his re-grown beard. He was clearly very nervous, so Seren sat quite still and waited until he was ready to go on.

"When I was working, one of the assignments I was given by the newspaper I worked for was to infiltrate one of the biggest drug gangs in Glasgow. I was tasked with getting them to trust me so that I could expose their operation, because, when I was younger, I'd almost been one of them, and my brother,

Fraser, had been. He never really got his life back on track after that; they wouldn't let him. He's dead now."

Seren felt all the blood drain from her face. "That's awful. A *drug gang*? Oh, Jamie."

"Shocked? I knew you would be, but let me get to the end before you judge me," Jamie said. "So, this assignment was risky ploy, but I was up for it, for the glory, for some kind of *absolution* for Fraser, I suppose. I got very close to them, and even saved one of the main gang members when he'd overdosed, by calling an ambulance, which got me a *lot* of brownie points, I can tell you. I thought I was invincible after that. Very big mistake." He paused again, but Seren said nothing as she had no idea what to say.

"To cut a very long story short, I became obsessed with this job. I was never home, never present for my wife and daughter, because my career, my reputation, meant more to me." He swallowed hard. It was clearly very difficult for him to tell her this. "One day I was taking Agnes swimming, but we were late as I'd been passing on some important info about an operation the gang were planning. We were just about to cross the road where we lived – a nice part of Glasgow, unlike where I'd grown up, when my phone rang again. I let go of Agnes' hand to answer it... but she carried on walking, into the road."

Seren held her breath. She knew what was coming, but knew he needed to tell her himself, to say it out loud.

"She was killed instantly. A joyrider, a young, stupid lad, but when I look back, I think my crime was worse than his, far worse. I was a selfish, neglectful, weak, *useless* father. No jail term can repay my debt, as it's unforgivable. And Lloyd understands that."

A long, long silence followed, in which Jamie's guilt filled the room with a thick, soupy despair and made it almost difficult to breathe. Again, Seren waited.

"My wife, well, as you can understand, Fiona told me to

leave. She couldn't even look at me at Agnes' funeral. I packed in my job, and I came here. I lost everything. My wife, my child and my career, because of my arrogance."

Struggling to speak, Seren said, "That's truly terrible, and I'm, well, grateful that you told me, but before we go any further, I need to be completely honest with you. Can I ask you something a bit... difficult?"

Jamie nodded wordlessly.

"I saw you with your wife a few weeks ago, in Beaumaris, so I wondered, well, what was going on."

Jamie looked at her, his eyes full of sadness. "Yes, Lloyd told me that you'd seen us. I'm sorry if that was a terrible shock for you."

"It was, chiefly because I had no idea you were still married," Seren said, trying hard not to let childish pique colour her words. That was so unimportant compared with Jamie's loss, however powerfully she felt it.

"No, I know, but that's why I've been keeping my distance for a while. Fiona's got a new partner, our divorce has just come through and they're moving abroad, to France. She's pregnant again, as well. She'd told me she wanted to come and say goodbye a few weeks ago, and I didn't want any awkwardness if you two met each other," he said, his expression the quintessence of misery.

"But why do you feel you need to tell me now, when you haven't done so before? Because you'd told Dad?" Seren asked.

"I came to tell you that, even though I am formally divorced, whatever is beginning to happen between us, and I know you feel it too, *can't* happen, or not yet. The work I was doing up there, well, it rattled the cages of some very dangerous people. I refuse to let you and Enya be in any kind of danger, and I will not risk you losing her for my happiness. That comes very low on my list of priorities now."

Seren tried to speak, to ask "what about *my* happiness?" but her voice was a croak. She cleared her throat, and said, "So, what are you saying, Jamie? That we mustn't see each other again?"

Jamie put his head in his hands. "No, that's not it, or rather I hope not, but I am saying that I need to make sure you're safe. This means I need to go back to Glasgow and gauge the lay of the land. If the gang no longer see me as any kind of threat, I'll come back and we can be together, if you want that as much as I do."

"Oh, I do, you know I do, but what about *you*? What might happen if you go back?" Seren cried.

"I know it's risky, but despite their cruelty, their heartless-ness, these people do have a code of honour. I saved one of them, got them to trust me. Ironically, I never used any of the info I'd gathered as I was in pieces over Agnes and my editor pulled the plug on the whole story, so it was all for nothing in the end, but it does mean my cover wasn't blown. I had a massive breakdown and came to Anglesey last year, and I'm quite sure I... wouldn't be here any more if it wasn't first for your father, and then, you and Enya."

Seren nodded sadly. She knew those depths of misery, and she had recognised them in this man when they had first met. They left an imprint on the soul. "I'm still worried that you'll be a target if you go back," Seren said. "Do these people still see you as a rat, even though you didn't use what you'd learnt?"

Jamie took her hand in his. "I have no guarantee of anything. It's a dark, complex world, but it's one I think I under-stand well enough to stay safe. I didn't betray their trust, and I've paid my dues in losing Agnes, and losing everything. I'm hoping they'll think that too."

"Ah, 'honour among thieves', isn't that the cliché?" Seren murmured.

"Let's hope it's true. Can you see that I need to know for certain I can live without fear, not hiding away here avoiding the world when, because of you, I want to be a part of it again?"

Seren nodded. "I understand, yes. But how long do you think you'll be away? I'll miss you, and so will Enya."

"I'm not sure, and I don't know how much I'll be able to keep in touch. Not a second longer than I need to be is all I can say. I haven't forgotten that I promised to protect you both from Finlay either. Lloyd is no match for a thug like him."

"If he comes here, Dad will have a much stronger me by his side," Seren replied. "I'm still hoping he'll remember what I said in London, and leave us alone. He hasn't turned up here yet as he threatened to, so perhaps it was all bluster."

"Here's hoping, my love."

Just as he was about to lean over and kiss her, Enya appeared in the doorway, rubbing her eyes.

"I had a bad dream," she said, flashing a beaming smile at Jamie before she ran and jumped onto his knee. "Will you come up and tell me a story?"

Jamie kissed the top of her head, and looked at Seren. "Can I ask a favour? Please."

She nodded. There was little she would refuse this man now, and she knew her daughter had been right to trust him from their very first meeting.

"Enya, I'm sorry I've not been to see you for a while, but I hope you'll forgive me when I tell you that I've written a bedtime story just for you. Shall I tell it to you now to help you forget your nightmare? I have to go away for a while tomorrow, and I need to know if you think it's any good before I go."

"OK, but I have to be in bed to hear a bedtime story," the little girl said, jumping off his lap, grabbing his hand and leading him upstairs.

For the next twenty minutes, Seren listened to the low burr of Jamie's voice through the floorboards as he told his story.

When he came down, he looked tired, but happy. She stood up to get him a drink, as he clearly needed one.

"So?" she asked, handing him a whisky.

"She said she loved it," he replied. "And she wants me to write more stories for her."

Resisting the urge to ask him what tonight's story had been about, she said, "Then you must. If you send them to her while you're away, I'll read them to her."

Quietly, Jamie put his glass down, walked towards her and took her in his arms. She froze. She had not told him about her mastectomy, but she'd already taken off her bra, as she'd had a bath and been heading for bed before he'd arrived. Panic coursed through her.

"I had breast cancer," she whispered. "I lost one of my..."

But he only drew her closer, pressing her body tightly against his.

"Thank God you're still here at all, every wonderful, perfect inch of you," he said, and kissed her.

When he tiptoed out of her bedroom a couple of hours later, Seren knew without doubt that she would love this man for the rest of her life and that he would love her back. They had not needed to say it to believe it. They had both experienced great sadness, and it was something only each other understood, but it had enriched what they felt for each other rather than detracted from it. She watched him walk down her path towards his cottage, the soft light of the almost-full moon cast a pearly shimmer over the scene. It was magical, as if out of a book of fairy tales and for the first time, she dared to believe in a happy ending. As she snuggled back beneath the bedcovers, some of Dylan Thomas' words that her father had written in his very first letter drifted into her mind:

Light breaks where no sun shines;
Where no sea runs, the waters of the heart
Push in their tides.

TWENTY-SEVEN

Anglesey is a different place once the hordes of summer tourists who block pavements and colonise the beaches with paddle-boards and badly behaved dogs have gone. In October, the season is finally guttering to an end, and the ice-cream kiosks and boat-trip offices close for the winter. Then there is a notable *quietening* everywhere, as if someone has pulled the plug and the bubbling crowds have all vanished down a sink. In many ways, this made life for locals easier, but for Seren, the sense of the island beginning to shut down in preparation for the long cold months ahead, made her uneasy. In London, life never slowed like this, there was always the buzz of rush, of purpose, even if that purpose was a worthless one. Here, days were long after she'd left Enya at school.

Her photography classes were now the highlight of her week, and she took hundreds of photographs as the weather cooled and the colours of the landscape shifted, as if someone had turned a kaleidoscope to reveal a different pattern. This was good, and although Jamie had left, she knew that he wanted their future to be together, but still the waiting seemed endless. Things had changed with Ruthie and Del since their last conversation about Kate. They were still friendly, and they invited her to swim with them, but the water really was too cold for her now. She'd stopped asking them if they had learnt anything new from their mothers about Kate, as they clearly hadn't and trying to prise her mother's erstwhile friends open like reluctant scallops would be foolish. Again, patience was key, but her reserves of that quality were now lower than ever and she had no time for subterfuge or dishonesty.

Thankfully, Lloyd had more free time now the season had ended, and said he didn't feel like farm work at harvest time this year as he was too old for it.

"I'd far rather spend my time with you and Enya than in a draughty tractor cab or smelly cow shed. I'm tired," he told Seren, and she could see that he did look as if he needed a rest. He was often out of breath when they walked along the headland together, which concerned her. She did not see him as an old man, but he felt like one, he said.

"Dad, why don't you book an appointment with the doctor for a 'well man' check-up? It's important, in your sixties, that you begin to slow down and take care of yourself," she said.

"Have you tried getting to see a GP since you arrived here?" he replied. "I'm fine, and don't need any fancy London 'well man' nonsense, thanks very much. I just need to remember I'm not as young as I once was."

Whilst she understood, Seren could not suppress a twinge of disappointment that it did not look likely that he would be able to pick Enya up from school and give her tea sometimes, so that she could find a job. She still scoured local papers and community websites for opportunities, but there was nothing. As a familiar gloom began to settle around her like a cloak of dark despair, she knew it would only lift if she was not alone for hour upon hour, but what could she do here, on this little island in the middle of the sea? In London, marooned in their flat, she had sometimes rung helplines just to hear a human voice. Just as she began to consider doing so again, her rescue came totally unexpectedly, as the best things in life often do.

Seren loitered in Beaumaris, the town where Enya went to school, after she had dropped her off each morning. She usually walked to look with particular longing at the vivid prints and paintings in a gallery in one of the back streets. It was not usually open before 10 a.m., so she stood with her nose pressed to the window, sometimes for up to half an hour, trying to see as much as she could. The gallery specialised in promoting the beauty of the island, and its windows proclaimed that with each picture of a rocky cove, a sweep of sand or a stone cottage surrounded by sand dunes or vivid wildflowers. This solitary morning ritual was not only deeply gratifying for Seren, but it also postponed her return to her silent, empty cottage. One day, she decided to risk having a coffee in a quaint tea shop on the High Street. It felt like an unnecessary luxury, but she needed to hear the babble of other people around her. As friends met, greeted each other and began to chat, she wondered if they, too, had been lonely until they'd arrived at the tea shop, all longing for the comfort of company. How easy it was to be unaware of how other people truly felt.

Within a few days, Seren was recognised as a regular, greeted with warmth and offered a welcome. Within a week, the owner, Ceri (a woman probably in her late fifties who wore enough make-up to cement her features into the same, slightly surprised expression all day) began to talk to her. Or rather, talk *at* her. Seren braced herself for questions she was not terribly happy to answer, but luckily, they did not come, because Ceri was far more interested in talking about herself, which suited Seren perfectly. First of all, it was established that Ceri had come here from South Wales (which she still missed to this day) with her husband, Gwilym, who was from the island (and whom she didn't miss at all as he was a bit of an idiot), who had died of something horrible-sounding ("the docs said it was his heart, but I say it was his liver, the number of pints he drank") over twenty years ago. Thereafter, their everyday conversations usually ran along the lines of:

Ceri: "Hello, love. Ooh, I was up half the night last night with my sciatica, you know. It starts up here, at my hip, and runs down the back of my leg like a bolt of lightning."

Seren: "Poor you. That sounds very painful."

Ceri: "Dreadfully painful. Worst pain ever. A curse, it is – my mother suffered from it too, for years. Like me, she never complained."

Seren: "Sorry to hear that. Does nothing help? Oh, could I possibly have...?"

Ceri: "Nothing relieves it, except my daughter pressing into the back of my leg with her elbow, to release the nerve. She's never keen. Bloody agony it is."

Seren: "I bet. Could I have a flat white, please?"

Ceri: (shuffling off with a sniff and a limp) "Yes, of course, love."

This became the routine most mornings between the two women, though Ceri's ailments could vary, as she also suffered with migraines, IBS, lumbago, eczema, anxiety and trapped wind. Seren, desperate to talk to *someone*, did manage to share she lived in Penmon; had a little daughter at the local school; really needed a job; loved taking photographs and, finally, that her name was Seren, but these revelations were brief, and did not really seem to penetrate far into Ceri's consciousness, as each one was met with either a nod, or "mmm, that's nice". It was almost as if she knew all this information already, and hearing it again bored her. But one, wet, morning in early October, just as Seren was wrestling to accept that the sun might not actually return to the island for a very long time, Ceri was unusually cheery when she came over to serve her. She even brought her coffee without her having to order it.

"Seren, I've got good news for you," Ceri said. As this was the first time she had ever used her name, Seren was shocked that she'd remembered it. There had been such a slew of talk about illness since she'd revealed it to her weeks ago.

"Hi, Ceri. How are you this morning?" she said, trying not to flinch at the grisly symptoms that might now be coming her way.

"Me? I'm fine ta. But guess what? My daughter has just the job for you."

Seren, startled, was lost for words.

"She runs The Seaside Gallery in Ship Street, up behind the main road. Know it?"

Seren could only nod that she did. Her breathing was faster already.

"Well, I told her about you, and she says can you pop up after your coffee as she needs someone to help her in the shop, someone *arty*, like you. The girl she had has gone off to Uni, which was a bit inconsiderate in my view."

Seren couldn't think what to say to this.

"You look as if you've seen a ghost! So are you interested in the job, then?" Ceri asked, her face deviating from the usual surprised expression into one of mild concern.

"Oh yes, I am!" Seren blurted, as if someone had uncorked her. "That would be so, so amazing! I love that gallery," she gabbled, grabbing Ceri's hand.

"OK, OK, calm down, love," Ceri said kindly, but pulling her hand away and rubbing it vigorously. "Arthritis in my hands, see. So, shall I message Angharad and let her know you'll go and see her later?"

"Yes, yes, please. I'll be there in ten minutes."

"Maybe a bit longer than that, or you'll scald your tongue on your flat white," Ceri said, waddling away. Her swollen ankles were clearly playing up today.

TWENTY-EIGHT

It had started to rain by the time Seren left the café to go and meet Angharad. Nerves were bubbling in her belly, but Ceri had told her that her daughter was really looking forward to meeting her, which sounded positive.

"That's because I put in a good word," she said, tapping her nose confidentially.

This was big. Seren knew that if this job actually existed and she could fit it in with Enya, it could be life-changing. When she reached the gallery and the "Closed" sign was in the door, she nearly burst into tears. Turning to go, she glimpsed a young woman inside, waving frantically, her eyes popping as she yelled:

"Wait! I need to turn the alarm off before I open the door! Hang on!"

A few seconds later, the door to the gallery buzzed, and the woman darted forward to open it and flipped the sign to "Open". She looked incredibly familiar, but Seren had no idea where from, as she looked *nothing* like her mother.

Seren, now feeling a bit wrong-footed, was very nervous

indeed. She stuck out a hand and blurted, "Hi. I'm Seren and I'm here about a job."

"Haha, I gathered that, and you come with a glowing recommendation," the woman said. "If my mam recommends something or someone, I have no choice but to believe her or risk disembowelment." A pause. "Mind you, she would probably talk me through disembowelling in long and gruesome detail first."

Seren suppressed a strong urge to laugh. It was probably not a good tactic to laugh at her potential boss's mother.

"I'm Angharad, Ceri's daughter, in case you hadn't guessed. Come on in."

Following Angharad into the gallery, Seren felt as if she was in the slipstream of something truly amazing. This woman exuded an undeniable energy she could not quite pinpoint as she bustled around the large space turning on lamps, an aromatic diffuser and finally, the coffee machine ready for the day.

"I know you're caffeined-up, but I need a coffee immediately," she said, adding, "preferably intravenously. Help yourself to biscuits. They're nothing fancy." Her phone rang, and she mouthed "Sorry" before taking the call.

As the air filled with the mixed deliciousness of coffee and neroli oil, Seren looked around her. She had spent so many surreptitious minutes trying to see every corner of this room through the windows that now she was inside it, she could hardly breathe. Images from around the island leapt from every wall, each one encapsulating a moment in time, or a feeling. There were several delicately coloured landscapes, all within a fairly limited, soothing palette that conveyed peace and tranquillity. Hung in amongst them were brightly hued prints of beaches packed with kite-flying, ball-throwing and sunbathing people, so vivid that Seren could almost hear the cries of joy as the children jumped over the rippling waves in the shallows.

The juxtaposition of all these snapshots of Anglesey life in one room was almost overwhelming in its textural richness; it felt rather like the immersive Van Gogh experience she had once been to in London with her cousin Melissa. Many of them were Angharad's work, and Seren found she liked them most of all. Others were by other island artists, but all were stunning in their own way, and all were true to the spirit of this knub of rock that they all called home – Anglesey. There was also a good selection of more generic paintings, of seascapes, mountains, waterfalls and seaside villages, which added their own charm to the eclectic mix.

The only thing Seren did *not* see on the walls of the gallery were photographs of the wildlife, the trees and flowers or, most surprising of all, the sea, whose fickle moods made the island what it was. She felt a tiny shot of joy at this omission, because if she could put together a portfolio of work that would impress this woman, this could be her chance, her opening into the profession she had always yearned to be a part of. She had always believed, and argued, that beautiful photos had the right to be included in a place that celebrates art, but she reminded herself that today, she had one mission only: to get the job and grab this incredible opportunity with both hands.

"OK, so let's chat about what I need," Angharad said, gulping her coffee greedily the moment she'd finished her call. "Then we'll see if it matches what you can offer. I know you've got a kid in school, like me, so there's that to consider."

Suddenly, a memory clicked. Seren had seen this woman dashing across the playground, her hair flying behind her as she pushed, what was it? a very large buggy towards the school door. In that instant, however, she realised that it was not a buggy at all, but a wheelchair, with a small child hunched low in it.

"Yes, er, I've got Enya in the reception class," she stammered, determined not to let any hint of her realisation show, and risk hurting Angharad's feelings. "I think I've seen you at school. Have you got a kid in reception?"

Angharad's eyes were full of gentle gratitude. "I have, yes. My son's called Gwyn, and he's actually in year 1, though he's so small he looks like he should still be in *cylch meithrin*/play-group, I know. He's got spina bifida, and he's as bright as the proverbial button."

Hearing that "and", Seren wanted to hug this woman for her courage in choosing that word instead of "but". There was a momentary pause, in which there were questions Seren could have asked, and things Angharad could have said, but neither did. Both women sensed that there was plenty of time for them.

"So, Mam tells me you need a job and I'm offering four and a half hours, two days a week, 10 a.m.–2.30 p.m. I'm flexible, but I do need a full day 10 a.m.–5 p.m. on Wednesdays. It's not mega-bucks, but I can't get on with my work if I'm always in the shop, so I need some help. Usual stuff: serving customers, checking stock, keeping the place clean and tidy, making sure records of sales are kept," Angharad went on. "Think it might suit you?"

"I think it could be perfect," Seren mumbled. "I have a photography class on Thursday mornings, but..." her words petered out shyly. Damn. The long day on Wednesday could prove a problem if Lloyd was unable to have Enya.

Angharad looked at her closely. "I think you'd fit in here from what Mam's said, but I do need someone who can talk the talk, you know – chat to the customers, make them feel at home, and happy to part with their cash!"

Seren saw that her hesitation, her reserve was now the main obstacle in her way. She had to blast through it or risk jeopardising this chance. Taking a deep breath, she said:

"Angharad, I'll be completely honest with you. I've had some... problems in the past, with a man in fact, and I came here with Enya for a fresh start. I need to make sure she's sorted after school before I can commit – that's my only reservation. I would *love* to work here."

Angharad looked at her appraisingly. "I get that. I know how hard it is when you want to put your child first, but there are so many other pressures and commitments. But I do need someone I can rely on. Gwyn and I are on our own, so it's all down to me."

"I'm on my own with Enya, too, but you can rely on me. I know I probably come across as a bit, well, *quiet*, but I won't let you down, Angharad. I just need a break."

Angharad put her coffee cup down, and smiled. "Then you're hired for a trial period of a fortnight. I'm all for giving someone a break after man-trouble. Someone gave me one a few years back and helped me set up here, so I'm glad to do the same for you. But if you can sort childcare, when can you start?"

"I have to check that my dad can look after Enya after school on Wednesdays, and let you know asap?" Seren replied.

"Your dad lives locally, does he? What's his name? I might know him – and Mam certainly will. She knows the entire universe within a thirty-mile radius."

Seren thought very fast indeed. If Ceri knew Lloyd, she would also know about his eccentricity, his isolated lifestyle and his daughter having to be brought up by relatives as he'd had mental health problems in the past. That was bad, but even if that was the case, she had *still* recommended her for this job. Seren decided that there was no choice but to be truthful if there was to be any future for her here, or any friendship to be forged with this woman.

"Lloyd Evans, he's called. I hadn't seen him for almost thirty years, because my aunt and uncle brought me up in London. My mother... died, and he couldn't cope, but I came back this spring, because I felt I needed to know him again."

For a few seconds, there was silence, as Angharad's face made it clear that, yes, she *did* now recall having heard Lloyd's story, and thus knew about Seren's. Her expression, when it settled, was one of compassion rather than judgement however, and she did not refer to it.

"Then here's to happy endings," she said. "Welcome to The Seaside Gallery."

When her gaze moved to a customer who had just come in, Seren knew it was her cue to leave.

"I'll be in touch very soon, Angharad, and thank you," she said, opening the door. "I can't tell you how much this means."

"No need to tell me. I can see it. Let me know when you're able to start," Angharad said before focusing her powerful charm on the customer, who was now eyeing up a very expensive painting.

The rain had stopped as Seren made her way back to her car, and the pale blue sky was streaked with milky clouds. She was so happy she almost danced back into the tea shop, where she found Ceri sitting on an old Welsh rocking chair. There were no customers in, so she was having a breather, but there was a real air of doom about her and she was far from her usual bustling, chatty self. When Seren, eyes bright, told her that she had a trial for the job, she looked pleased, but hardly more than that.

"Sorry, *cariad*/love, of course that's great news. I knew you'd smash it. I'm just a bit worn out after a whole summer on my feet, and my bloody bunions are killing me. It's heavy load to bear," she said mournfully. When Seren did not respond, she went on, "But, compared to our Gwyn, what do I have to complain about, poor lad? That's why I never moan, me. Have you seen him, our Gwyn, up at the school, in his wheelchair? You've probably *heard* him at least – never stops talking, that boy."

Unsure, Seren hesitated. Perhaps Ceri's attitude to her

grandson was not as positive as her daughter's, which could prove a minefield if so. "I met him ages ago, actually, at Ruthie Edwards' farm. Angharad just told me how super-bright he is."

Ceri nodded. "Oh yes. Positive little Einstein he is, and he plays the piano beautifully. Wants to be a professional musician, he does. I just, you know, feel for him when he can't play football or run around with the others. Breaks my heart it does sometimes, and it's a lot for Angharad to cope with on her own."

"Seeing your kid missing out is worse than your own pain, isn't it?" she said. "My little girl was so shy and insecure before we came here that she hardly spoke a word to anyone. I was worried sick. I know it's not the same, but..."

"But it is, to you, yes. They're all gifts, these children, in their way. I am thankful he's here... but it's hard sometimes, for both of them – and for me. Don't ever tell Angharad I said that, by the way."

So Seren had been right, Ceri's view of Gwyn's situation was a lot starker than her daughter's. Which one of them was more realistic, she had yet to learn.

"Do you look after him sometimes, when Angharad's working?" Seren asked, wondering how on earth the two women managed, as she assumed the needs of a spina bifida child would require some serious support. It was important to be sensitive, as she knew little about the condition or how it might impact a family, but she could not help but wonder if that contributed to Ceri's slightly martyred air.

"Yes, I do. I close early and pick him up sometimes, if we're not too busy, and I take him to his physiotherapy or his check-ups," Ceri said. "He always comes first, in my book and he knows it, too, little rascal. The old phrase 'Butter wouldn't melt in his mouth' could've been written with that boy in mind."

"I hope my dad feels the same when I ask him to collect Enya on Wednesdays so I can take the job," Seren said. "He says he's feeling tired and old lately."

Ceri met her gaze for the first time. "Well, he probably *is* feeling tired and old. I know I do, but of course he'll help you, because that's what we do. He's been through a lot, your dad. I knew him back in the day, and your mam, bless her. You've probably guessed that."

Seren nodded. "Yes. Everyone knows everything up here, don't they?"

"They do, but it can be a good thing, you know. Lloyd's always been a bit of a delicate flower, but people care about him, and he'll love that little girl of yours all the more because she's brought him something he never thought he'd have again – a family."

Seren suddenly felt very tearful. The people she'd met here were so unafraid to talk about things like sadness, regret, loss and grief; it was an emotional honesty she hoped to learn herself. The fact that Ceri had also known her mother, that she had been an active member of this community, was another piece of the puzzle she hoped to complete one day, but this was not the time to ask questions. She said her goodbyes, more thank-yous, and turned to leave.

"Do you know what the name 'Gwyn' means in Welsh, by the way, and why Angharad chose it when he was born, with his wonky spine and his little legs all twisted up?" Ceri said softly.

"Gwyn? I thought it meant 'white'," Seren said.

"Oh, it can mean that, yes, but up here, the *name* means 'blessed'," Ceri said. "And we are blessed, believe me, having Gwyn in our lives."

TWENTY-NINE

Asking Lloyd if he could fetch Enya from school and give her some tea on Wednesdays proved to be an even bigger deal than Seren could ever have imagined. Her father already spent a lot of time with his granddaughter, more so after Jamie had left for Glasgow, and both were happy in each other's company, but he always knew that either Jamie or Seren was nearby, and available if he needed them. It was clear that the prospect of that *not* being the case seemed to fill him with genuine horror.

"I don't know if I want to be responsible for her on my own," he said, when Seren first asked him. "I'll have to drive her to school, see all the other parents, drive her home, cook for her... it's a lot to ask of me, *cariad*/love, without, you know, having you or Jamie as 'backup'."

Alarmed, Seren resisted the urge just to dismiss his worries and tried more soothing language instead. He would be fine, she was sure, and they had to make this work.

"If you like, you could get the bus to the school, and then take her to the café for her tea that day, and then come to the gallery at 5 p.m. and we'll all drive home together. How about that? Ceri will be around in case you need anything."

Lloyd was visibly shaken by this suggestion too. "But there's only one bus at that time in the afternoons, you know that. What if I miss it, and then *nobody's* there to fetch Enya?"

Seren did *not* say "then you could drive, or ring me and I'll see if Ruthie or Del can take her, or I could even ask Ceri if it's too much bother for you", but she really, really wanted to. This was a side to her father she had not seen since she'd asked him to look after Enya so that she could go to London and see Finlay – an emotional vulnerability, and an insurmountable reluctance to be relied on. But as she walked home and thought a little more about why this might be, a few faint images swirled around in her head before cohering into clear memories. Looking at his scared, anxious face, she was suddenly a little girl again, hiding behind a sofa as things crashed around her and a man made terrible, deep sounds of pain, like a wounded animal. She saw the door open and watched as he staggered out into the rain, howling at the sky. And she began to understand; he had failed once as a parent when he had heard of Kate's death, and he had lost her because of it, and was utterly terrified of doing so again, with Enya. He did not trust himself, and how could she blame him for that? She let the subject drop reluctantly, and watched his anxiety gradually ebb away.

The next morning, the weather was wild, wet and blustery, a typically autumnal mix. Seren went to see her father again as she had to sort childcare for her to be free to accept Angharad's job offer. She found him staring out to sea from his armchair looking like a lost little boy. He sensed why she had come, and what she was going to say. As many people had now reminded her, Lloyd had suffered so much and he was getting old now; she must not forget that. Taking one of his hands in both of hers, she began to speak softly, kindly, about how it would work if he let himself believe he could do this, as she did. So much depended on it, for both of them, but she needed to be gentle with him.

"Dad, I think I understand why you're not sure, but I think it will be OK, I really do. Enya knows you really well now. She loves you, she trusts you, and I love you and trust you too. One hundred per cent."

Lloyd turned to look at her, as if dragging his eyes from the reassuring view of the lighthouse, the steady centre of his world. "*Diolch yn fawr, cariad*/Thank you, darling. But what if...?"

"What if the most awful thing in the world happens again, when she's with you?" Seren said softly. "It can't, Dad, because it's already happened, and you are not the same person as you were then."

"You remember it, do you?" he whispered. "How it was, how I was, that night?"

Seren nodded. "Yes, I do, but only in tiny fragments, like the filaments inside a light bulb. I know that there was nobody for you to ask for help except Aunt Alice, who was hundreds of miles away. That must have been so terrible. I remember us waiting a very long time before she came." She paused, feeling the impact of these recollections hit her full-on for the first time. "But I also remember other people coming to the cottage before she arrived. Yes, and I remember one of them wrapping me up in a blanket, and you, crying in the corner of the room. Who were they, Dad? Did *you* call them?"

Lloyd turned his face away from her, and she felt a shift in the conversation. He shook his head, and when he slowly turned to face her again, there was something in his manner that she had never seen before: fear.

"I don't recall anyone else being here," he said. "I don't remember anything until your aunt and uncle arrived in the middle of the night. It was raining. Pouring, in fact, but I went out in it, I went to the lighthouse. It was calling me, telling me that it would always be there, unchanging, whatever was happening to me, to us. I felt I could somehow reach your mother if I went there, as that was where I had first seen her lovely face. That's all I can tell you."

Seren wanted to ask more, but as she watched him stroke his beard repeatedly, his white hair fizzing wildly around his head as he had not combed it for weeks, she knew she could not. He was as easily broken as a spider's web.

Today, now, her goal had been to get her father to realise that she saw him as fully capable of helping her care for Enya, so that she could take Angharad's job, but now, she was not so sure. It might be the making of him, or, heaven forbid, it might break him. The only way to find out was to risk it as she felt in her bones that she had to do this to move forward. So she did.

"Tell you what, Dad. Let's have a trial run tomorrow, shall we? You fetch Enya, by bus or in your car, your choice, and then you either take her to the café for tea or bring her home, and I'll still be on-hand if you need to call me. Please believe me when I tell you that I trust you, and everything will be OK."

Lloyd picked at the skin around his fingernails, a picture of insecurity. "You might trust me, yes, but I need to trust myself."

"I know that, but you've waited a long, long time to find out if you can," Seren replied. "Take this chance to forgive yourself, however unsure you feel about it, Dad. I need you to at least try, for me. You can do it, Lloyd Evans. You are my rock in the midst of a storm."

"But I let you go. I failed you, my little star."

Taking his hand in hers, she said:

"That was a long time ago, and I don't hold it against you, or judge you, Dad. As Dylan Thomas said:

"*...all your deeds and words,*

"*Each truth, each lie,*

"*Die in unjudging love.*"

Lloyd looked at her and sighed. "Ah, there's so much of your mother in you. I will try, but I am fearful. What about *these* words from old Dylan?:

"Shall the child sleep unharmed or the man be crying?"

"Well, I suppose tomorrow's the day to find out," Seren replied lightly, keeping her slight disquiet at this quotation to herself. "We'll pretend it's the real thing, a working Wednesday for me, and I'll tell Enya what we're doing as if it's a bit of a game. She'll be excited. If it goes well, I can let Angharad know that I accept the job, and if not, well, I'll think again. OK?"

"All right, but you'll be in your cottage tomorrow if I need you?" Lloyd said urgently. "Promise me you will."

"I will, Dad, I promise."

And as they went over the fine details of *exactly* what was to happen again and again, Seren finally understood that what seemed like such a simple thing to her, was a truly momentous one to her father.

At around 6 p.m. on the following day, having followed the plan to the letter, Seren knocked on her father's door, stood back and waited expectantly. There was whispering coming from behind the door, and then some suppressed giggling. She knocked again.

"Hello in there. This is Seren Evans, come to collect Enya Evans after her first session at 'Crigyll Cottage Champion Childcare Services'," she announced.

The giggles now became whoops of laughter, and the door burst open to reveal Enya sitting colouring at the kitchen table, smiling from ear to ear, and Lloyd holding the door for her and almost bursting with pride.

"So, how did things go?" Seren asked. "Did you drive, or take the bus? Did you have tea in the café, or did *Taid*/Grandfather cook for you, Enya?"

"We drove into town in *Taid's*/Grandfather's car that smells of... what's it called? It made me feel a bit sick, whatever it is," Enya said.

"Snuff," Lloyd replied, feigning being hurt. "And a lovely smell it is too."

"Then we had a milkshake in the café and then *Taid*/Grandfather drove us here and he cooked fish fingers and mashed potato and peas," Enya announced, adding in a whisper to her mother, "But I didn't eat the peas because they were hard, like little stones."

Seren looked at Lloyd, whose cheeks were still flushed with the sheer thrill of having overcome his anxieties, and successfully both fetched and fed this beloved child.

"You did it, Dad," Seren said, hugging him. "And it looks as if you enjoyed it too."

Lloyd stepped back, drew himself up as if he was about to make a speech, laying his hand melodramatically over his heart.

"I am a changed man. We have a date, every Wednesday afternoon, *Enya fach*/little Enya. Be there, or be square, as you young folks say!" He sat down, wheezing slightly after his exertions.

Enya laughed and broke into a spontaneous round of applause.

But as they settled down for a *panad*/cuppa together, Seren could see that doing this for her had taken a lot out of her father. This was the first, and therefore the hardest time, but every Wednesday would be a test to some degree, however successful this trail had proved. She had to have faith in him, to give him faith in himself.

"So can I message Angharad, and say 'yes' to the job in the gallery?" she asked both her father and her daughter. "Thumbs up for 'yes', thumbs down for 'no'."

Two vehement thumbs up gave Seren her answer. She could barely find the buttons on her phone to message Angharad, as she was trembling so much. When a reply pinged back almost immediately, she read it out:

Great news. Can't wait to work with you. See you on Monday at 10 a.m. A. X

"I've got the job!" she said and was enveloped in hugs from all sides.

A little later, as Enya was gathering her things before they went back to their cottage, Seren sat next to her father on the sofa, and threaded an arm through his. Having been full of energy earlier, now he looked utterly worn out, and was very breathless indeed.

"I know you won't go to the doctors, but I'm a bit worried about you," she said. "Are you sure you're feeling OK, Dad – in general, I mean?"

Turning to face her, he said, "Never better, *cariad*/love. Never better."

PART 5

LIGHT AND SHADE

THIRTY

Seren found the prospect of a job that could quite literally change her life terrifying. She had never had a job that was important, only ones that paid some bills and kept Finlay in beer and baccy. This one mattered to her very much.

In the days before she started at the gallery, Seren decided to visit some of the beautiful places on the island that Angharad had captured in her paintings. Having not driven regularly for years, the prospect of navigating her way down tiny, high-hedged lanes (many of them with very few passing places if you found yourself behind a herd of cows or a flock of sheep) did not appeal, but she needed to see these places to be able to talk about them to customers interested in buying Angharad's paintings. These few days were her only chance to do so as her time would soon be much more limited.

Dropping Enya off at 8.30 a.m. meant she was out and about early and could visit several destinations before having to be back at the school gate at 3.15 p.m. On her first day of exploration, the weather was kind and the sky dazzled with a blue Seren vaguely remembered from the gorgeousness of summer. The remaining leaves on all the trees were a stunning combination of reds, oranges and glowing yellows, and whiskery strands of Old Man's Beard gave the hedgerows a ghostly cloak. She headed towards a village called Llanddona first, as Angharad had painted a spectacular landscape of the beach from a lay-by on the tiny road leading down to it. Reaching the bottom of the incredibly steep hill was a challenge in itself, but it was worth it as Seren took in the endless expanse of sea and sky. Feeling this limitless *space* around her, she filled her lungs with sea air and threw her arms wide. How small she was, how insignificant, compared to this huge and invincible grandeur! And how lucky, to be even a tiny part of it. Nobody else was on the beach except a very distant dog walker, so she dared herself to do something she had longed to do since the moment she saw the water nibbling at the edge of the beach. She stripped down to her bra and pants and ran into the waves, shrieking both at the cold, and with amazement that she, Seren Evans, the woman who had feared everything and everyone for years, was here, doing this, on her own, and loving it.

For most of the rest of the day, she was underwear-less, as her things slowly crisped on the dashboard of her car in the watery sunshine, but even that felt liberating. As she saw nobody, it did not matter that it was obvious that she only had one breast until she could put her bra and prosthesis back on. This was her, and she was utterly, beautifully whole, just as she was.

Her next stop was Red Wharf Bay, where the outgoing tide had left scores of tiny fishing boats standing proud of the beach on their rudders, waiting to rise up once more when the water returned. The clanking of their halyards – the ropes that ran up the masts – was so evocative, such a uniquely seaside symphony, that Seren knew that, like the mournful lighthouse bell, she had heard it before as a child as she'd drifted off to sleep. She smiled, as another thread took its place in her growing patchwork of memories from those brief years she and her parents had spent together. Drifts of seabirds floated above the estuary that ran down to the sea almost a mile away, and she watched as they seemed to dance in one united movement of companionship and grace, leaving none behind when they silently changed direction or speed. People could learn a lot from birds, she concluded.

Lunch was a delicious prawn sandwich in a pretty café on the seafront in Moelfre, a fishing village that featured in several of Angharad's paintings. Beyond the chocolate-box harbour with its scree of holiday homes all sadly sealed until Christmas, Seren followed the coastal path out past the lifeboat station, and towards a pebbly beach framed by a row of incredibly picturesque old fishermen's cottages. Each one had a brightly painted door and had stood fast against the roaring elements for several centuries and survived intact. The hummock of rock beyond the bay was renowned for its birds and seals, and Seren could see scores of cormorants standing with their drying wings spread wide while loud-screeching gulls wheeled around, as if trying to put them off. The air rang with the raucous sound of hundreds of these seaside scavengers and their cries exuded a frank defiance they would need if they were to survive the bitter winter ahead.

She drove on around the coastline, back towards Penmon, and heard her phone buzz as a message came in when she passed through a rare pocket of good signal. It was only 2.40 p.m., so she wasn't late to pick up Enya, but she could not stop to read it now. Was it a message from Jamie, as she had not heard a word from him since he'd returned to Glasgow? She prayed it would not be from Finlay, who had sent a few texts recently that she had read, and immediately deleted, without replying. The first had been:

> Hi, how's things? Hope you're lovin' life as much as I am.

– at 2.06 a.m., which told her he was drunk. Then came:

> How's school going for Enya? Send me a pic of
> her in her uniform.

– which made her shiver, as if she did, he would then see the *Ysgol Beaumaris*/Beaumaris School logo, and find them. Only a few days ago, and most alarmingly, she'd received:

> Thought I might pay your aunt and uncle
> another visit as you've frozen me out.

Seren's fingers had hovered over the delete key for a few seconds, trying to convince herself that his "thought I might" meant "in fact I won't", but she rang her aunt anyway. When she chatted happily without not mentioning Finlay having been to their house again, Seren relaxed enough to delete the message.

Just as she reached the school ten minutes before the bell rang and the children cannoned into the playground, Seren heard two texts arrive in quick succession. Her heart sank. Finlay always texted in parts, as if he knew that the intrusive, repeated sounds would unnerve her before she even read his words. He was right. When she opened the first message, it dispelled all the carefree pleasures of her day in an instant:

> Still ignoring me? You can't get rid of me that
> easily.

She sat quite still as her thoughts raced. A few seconds later, she opened the second message.

> I know where you are, you selfish cow. You're
> going to pay for abandoning me like this.

She closed her eyes and leant back, sighing. She had to stop this, he had to understand that it was over, and that she would no longer be intimidated. Only one idea came to her, and it seemed so unlike her that she hardly believed her brazenness in acting on it. She texted Jamie, forwarding both Finlay's messages to him.

> Hi. Finlay is threatening us. Here are today's messages. Sorry to ask, but have you got any thoughts about how to make him leave us alone? Miss you. S x

It was a long shot, she knew, but she didn't know who else to turn to. Jamie was a wordsmith, so perhaps he would see a way to get inside Finlay's head and make him realise that she was gone for good and nothing he could say or do would change that. Perhaps, Seren began to wonder, only words as menacing as his own were the only ones he would heed. Jamie could muster those too, she was sure, given his experience with dubious types. Finlay took no notice of anything *she* said, however understanding, patient and/or assertive she tried to sound.

She was shaking when Enya got into the car and leant over for a hug as usual. It was all Seren could do not to just keep driving, to run away again, but they deserved better than that. If Finlay was refusing to listen to her, he needed to listen to someone else and to heed a crystal-clear warning to stay away. Dark times called for drastic tactics.

THIRTY-ONE

Seren slept fitfully that night. She had no enthusiasm for exploring the island any more. It seemed silly and pointless after Finlay's cruel messages. She half expected to see him following her, with his flop of dark hair, his piercing blue eyes fixed on her face, his full mouth sneering at her. How had she ever convinced herself that she loved him, let alone that he had loved her? It had been a battle of *control*, not of love and she had to show him that he had lost his hold over her forever.

The next morning, she sat in the window of her cottage watching the rain dribble down the windowpanes and staring at her phone, willing Jamie to respond. It was one of the longest mornings of her life.

When a call came in just before 1 p.m., she crossed her fingers and picked it up even though the screen read, "Unknown Caller". This could either be Jamie using a different phone to call her for safety's sake, or Finlay, on a borrowed one, hoping to trick her into picking up.

"Jamie?" she said. The sound of harsh, heavy breathing greeted her and she felt skin prickle as if tiny insects were crawling all over her body.

"Sorry, yes, it's me, I've been running, and I needed to find somewhere quiet to speak to you," he said, out of breath but his voice so achingly familiar, his Scottish accent slightly stronger. "Got a new phone, just in case."

"I get that, but are you OK?"

"I'm fine. Something else has come up that I need to tell you about another time, but right now, I'm ringing about your message," Jamie said firmly. "Finlay doesn't sound as if he's mucking about any more. Threats like that need to be taken seriously." This was a different Jamie from the withdrawn lost soul who avoided people and preferred isolation. He sounded in control and she leant into his strength as her own faltered. This was what she'd hoped for from him and she knew he would not let her down.

"Yes, yes, I know," she stammered. "His words were so horrible, so bitter. He said he knows where I am and I'm going to pay. I'm really scared this time, Jamie."

"I know. I can try and get him to leave you in peace, if that's what you want me to do, but I think there's only one way to do that." A pause.

Seren shivered. "Jamie, you can't... *hurt* him?"

"No, not that, for God's sake!" he exclaimed. "Who do you think I am, Al Pacino?"

The relief was immediate, but then came doubt. "So, what's your suggestion?"

"He's always wanted to own you, have you only for himself. I need to tell him that you love someone else now, and that because of that, you will never, ever come back to him," Jamie said. "That's probably the only thing he'll accept as final, the fact that you're no longer his, because you're mine. I reckon he'll deflate like a popped balloon once he sees his threats and bravado mean nothing and I don't think he's got the gumption to follow through."

There was a long silence. Seren pictured a ghastly tableau

of Finlay punching Jamie to the ground, kicking him with a viciousness she had only seen in the horrible games he played. Jamie was right, that wouldn't happen. At heart, Finlay O'Neill was a bully, and "bullies are cowards" as her father had told her. He would probably crumble like the lovelorn boy he was, the child who was never made to feel as if he mattered... but that was *not her fault*.

Jamie spoke first. "I need to know if that's what you want me to do, Seren. You need to be sure. Take a moment to think it through. There's no guarantee how he'll react, but I really think it's our best shot. Call me back. I'll wait." And he hung up.

For a few minutes, she sat quite still, watching a wide "V" of geese cross the sky, their wingbeats synchronised as they began their long journey south. This was a pattern they repeated, every year, without thinking, without doubt. Instinct kicked in and they believed they could do it, so they did it, for their own survival. She had to do the same for her and her daughter's survival. She rang Jamie back.

"Do it. I don't want to hurt him, but he has to understand that we are out of his life for good, that this is what both me and Enya want – and that I am with *you* now... if you still want that as much as I do, that is," she added with a familiar flicker of insecurity. All this, feeling truly loved, was so hard, and so *un*familiar.

"Oh, I do, I really do. I'll do my best and let you know how it goes."

"Thank you," Seren said. "The sad thing is that I don't think he ever really wanted to be with me. He just wanted me to love him because nobody else ever had."

A catch of breath, as she remembered the feeling of being trapped in a hell of her own making in their ghastly flat in London. "But he was so good at obliterating everything that made me, *me*. I didn't know who I was at the end. I was a nobody."

"But now, you do, and you are very far from a nobody, my darling," Jamie said, and she heard the love in his voice. "Sorry to ask this, but are we actually within the law to tell him he can't expect to see his child again?"

"Yes, we are," she replied without hesitation. "He's not on Enya's birth certificate, so he has no paternal rights, I've checked it again and again. She's been scared of him her whole life – she hates him, in fact, and I can't allow myself to feel any loyalty to him any more just because he's her biological father. He loves her in his way, but his way is poisonous. This has to be the end of it."

"I've got his number from the texts you forwarded, so I'll send a message once I've thought through exactly what to say. It may be a few days. I need to be able to contact you, but once I have, get rid of your phone, get a new one and let me know the number."

"Another one?" Seren said. "But they cost so much!"

"Seren, you have no choice. Please get rid of the phone."

"OK, I will," she said, sighing. She hated having to resort to such Bond-like power games. "And thanks, Jamie. I couldn't do this without you."

"You don't have to, but I promise Finlay won't get hurt. It's ironic, given how much he hurt you, but I understand how important that is to you."

"Thanks. I don't want to be cruel to him, as he was to me. What example does that set for Enya? I'll wait to hear from you," Seren said, and hung up.

For the rest of that day, she went through the motions of making a pasta bake for tea, helping her father clear his vegetable patch ready for pre-winter planting and fetching Enya from school, but her thoughts were hundreds of miles away, in their old flat in Kilburn where the windows were painted shut and the drip-

dripdrip of the leaky bath tap nearly drove her insane. Although she would never have believed herself capable of doing what she had done a few hours earlier, there had been no choice. Finlay O'Neill had given her Enya, her precious daughter, but he had taken so much more, and she had let him. Never again. The worm had turned.

The days that followed dragged and she could not focus on anything she tried to do to distract herself. On the Friday afternoon before school broke up for half term, she was so restless that she grabbed her camera and headed out into a bright but chilly day to take some photographs. Any trees that still had leaves were being stripped of them in minutes by the unseen fingers of an increasingly vicious wind, and the air was full of these tiny, lifeless parachutes floating to the ground. Seren walked down towards the beach, and the lighthouse, feeling it draw her towards it in her search for peace of mind as it always had her father. Waiting to hear from Jamie was agonising, but once she had, she prayed it would finally signal her freedom.

As she clambered down the grassy headland to the beach, she could almost picture Jamie the very first time she had seen him, crouched down on the rocks near the water's edge, casting his rod again and again in the hope of a stroke of luck, and a bite. Where was he now, at this precise moment? she wondered. In a pub in Glasgow, catching up with ex-colleagues? Revisiting old haunts? The possibility that he was seeing Fiona one last time before she left the UK popped up in her mind, but she dismissed it immediately. He loved *her*; they loved each other and everything was going to be perfect from now on. If she told herself that often enough, it felt much more likely to be true.

THIRTY-TWO

Every year, on one day in late October, the little town of Menai Bridge is completely subsumed by the *Ffair Borth*/Menai Bridge Fair. It began as mainly a horse and cattle market way back in the 1680s, but over the centuries, it expanded to become a plethora of stalls, hair-raising fairground rides, vans selling dubious burgers and garish candy. It also became, and remains, the event that every single child on Anglesey regarded as one of pure bliss. Most roads in the town are closed to traffic on the day of the fair as the whole town surrenders to the annual event, and many shops close because there is little point in opening. The most magical part of *Ffair Borth* is the fact that, by 6 a.m. the next morning, there is no sign of it at all. The rides are dismantled, the vans gone, the streets cleaned and normality restored. It will have vanished without trace until next year, when it appears once again.

On fair day, the afternoon hours belong to toddlers who circle slowly on the teacups or bounce on the tiny trampolines, but once darkness begins to fall, the schoolchildren arrive, and gradually the streets of the little town are packed with a huge proportion of the island's population, and the air is full of shrieks, the *wheees*, *pops* and *boiinnngs* of the rides, booming music and the smell of candy floss and frying onions. There was talk of little else in all the schools on the island, and every child begged to be allowed to go – including Enya.

Seren had started giving her weekly pocket money, and she had saved some cash to spend, but Enya knew her mother would not be keen, so she enlisted support. Gwyn joined her in a double-pronged attack on Seren and Angharad, but both mothers were reluctant, for different reasons.

"Everyone else is going to the Fair," they wheedled. "We'll use our own money."

Angharad shook her head. "It's so busy, I remember from my own childhood. We may not be able to get your wheelchair up the streets, and I don't know how safe the rides are, Gwyn. That's why I've never taken you before, love."

Seren added, "Enya, you might be scared. I've heard it's really loud and super-crowded. You don't like things like that, do you?"

But the children's faces roundly dismissed these concerns.

"We *have* to go. We want to have fun, like all the other kids," Enya said, and Gwyn added, for extra-special emotional blackmail, "I *deserve* that, don't I, Mam?"

Angharad and Seren did not stand a chance.

Luckily, the day of the fair was a dry one. Everyone told tales of torrential rain being the usual weather, and there were rumours of how unsafe the rides were in the wet, so Seren was very relieved indeed. Angharad offered to drive, as parking in the town would be hellish and she knew some hidden spots where getting Gwyn's wheelchair in and out of the car would be easier. As they drove into Menai Bridge along the winding road from Beaumaris, they glimpsed the flashing arm of a massive ride above the trees, swinging a tiny car with some even tinier feet dangling down from it. Seren shivered. Could they really let their precious kids go on something like *that*? Meanwhile, in the back seat, both of them were almost trembling with excitement, their mouths little "oohs" of anticipation.

Angharad's concerns about Gwyn's wheelchair proved well-founded almost the moment they hit the High Street, now transformed into a deafening, dazzling scrum of rides, jostling people and garish stalls. The crowds were building quickly as everyone finished school and work, and Gwyn was too low for people to see him and his wheelchair coming through.

"Jesus, this is awful," Angharad hissed to Seren. "I'm getting the heebie-jeebies and we haven't even put them on a ride yet!"

They shoved and rammed their way to the ride both children most wanted to go on: a huge, doughnut shaped wheel that spun around, then gradually tilted up on one side until it was almost upright, like a huge wheel, with only centrifugal force and a metal bar holding the riders in place. The queue was long, but when Gwyn saw several classmates near the front, they waved at him to join them, and other people parted to let Angharad push the wheelchair forward. A glance at her son's face showed her how much this simple kindness meant to him. Enya, who was graciously permitted to join her friend, was nibbling her fingernails now, Seren saw, but she was also hopping with excitement. Both children had so much to overcome, so many barriers in their way which others did not have, but if this experience was a positive one, and they had the simple, pure fun they so craved, surely it would be worth it?

When the young lad at the kiosk taking the fares saw Gwyn, his face registered the wheelchair and Angharad had a moment of dread that he was going to refuse to let her son get on the ride. That would be worse than not coming at all.

"Can he go on? Will he be safe?" she said to him, as Gwyn was busy counting out his pocket money, his fingers trembling with anticipation.

"He'll be fine. The bar will keep him in. He's OK with speed, is he? Not going to, you know, freak out or anything?"

"Gwyn's really brave," Cai Owen, a charismatic much older boy from school yelled. "He's had loads of operations and stuff, but he never makes a fuss. We'll all go on either side of him and Enya so they both know it's OK. Come on, *mae'n grât*/it's great!"

Enya beamed up at Cai, as if he was the sun in the sky. She was one of the gang, an accepted member, and he did not judge her for being an incomer, or being so terribly shy when she'd first started school. Everyone would have noticed it, and her. As both mothers watched the lad gently help Gwyn onto the ride and double-check the metal bar he clamped across his body, their hearts were in their throats. Enya, next to Gwyn, was very pale, but her eyes were glistening. They were ready to go.

"Please God, let them enjoy it," Seren said. "I think I'd puke!"

"I know. But I'd never forgive myself for not letting them try," Angharad replied, waving at Enya and Gwyn with a rictus grin on her face.

Then the wheel began to turn, slowly at first, as the riders got used to the flashing lights and feeling of being spun like clothes in a tumble drier. As the speed increased, the two women could no longer see their children's faces clearly as they whizzed around, but both could hear a low buzz of noise rising from everyone as the wheel began to lift up on one side, and the sound from the kiosk screeched a metallic "Up we go!"

And up they went, spinning so fast that all anyone could see was a blur of open mouths and all anyone could hear was a cacophony of yells, screams and whoops. When the wheel was vertical, hanging upside down, held in terrible suspension for at least a minute, many parents covered their faces, but Angharad and Seren looked on in silent astonishment. Gwyn and Enya, right at the very top, were beaming at each other with absolute joy; if they could do this, they could do anything, their faces said, and their mothers believed it.

A few minutes later, with Gwyn back in his wheelchair and Enya, still shaking but still smiling, standing next to him, Cai high-fived them both as he went down the steps and rejoined his mates.

"Same time next year, Gwyn?" he said. "And you, Enya? Enjoy it?"

Enya nodded vigorously and blushed. Cai Owen had just *spoken* to her.

"It's a deal, Cai," Gwyn replied. "Hear that, Mam? No bottling allowed."

Angharad agreed with a slightly wobbly smile. For her son, next year could never be a surety, but she vowed there and then that, if it was humanly possible, she would always bring him to the fair, and let him join all the other children who lived on the island and for whom this day was pure and utter magic.

THIRTY-THREE

Seren did not like to assume that something bad would inevitably follow something good, even though that had usually been her experience. The evening at the fair had filled her with such hope for the future, and such joy at her daughter's incredible transformation, that she decided not to believe anything could ever go wrong again. Still waiting to hear from Jamie, she decided that a positive, can-do attitude was all she needed. Finlay *would* listen to him and all *would* be well, she told herself. Sadly, her optimism was misplaced.

One rainy morning, on her way back from the school run, she decided to call in on her father, but as she pulled up outside his cottage, she was surprised to see his door ajar, banging in the wind as she approached it. It was November, and not a warm day at all, so why was it open? He had been forgetful lately, so she wasn't worried, but as she walked up the path and heard it thudding eerily in the wind, her imagination began to supply terrible possibilities. Praying she was wrong, she knocked, out of courtesy, but did not wait for her father to reply before pushing the door open. When she saw him, she screamed. Lloyd was lying on the kitchen floor, his legs askew, his fingers clutching at the flagstones as he struggled to try and gain enough purchase to get up.

"Dad! Oh my God! Stay right there. Don't move! I'll ring for help," she cried, suddenly incredibly thankful that she still had her phone despite Jamie's instructions. "Are you in pain?"

When her father pointed to his chest, to his heart, Seren felt her own contract.

Kneeling beside him, she rang for an ambulance, but Penmon was a good twenty minutes from Bangor and the nearest hospital; a current of ice-cold dread coursed through her. When Lloyd lifted his face from the floor an inch or two, she was relieved, until she saw him drooling from one corner of his mouth and struggling to speak, his fingers still scrabbling at the floor. It was so terrible to see, and she was fighting an over-whelming need to burst into howling tears; doing that would help nobody.

"Don't try and speak now, Dad, please. The ambulance is on its way. Just stay still, and everything will be fine," she said as calmly as she could. Was he dying? It was a terrifying thing to consider, but if he was, and they only had minutes left together, what would she want to say? Two things came to her, sharp and clear, and without any doubt. She lay down next to him and put her face inches from his. He would want to know that she forgave him, and he would want to know why Kate had left him. She could only answer one of them fully, but that would have to be enough.

"You're the best Dad I could ever have wished for, and I'm beyond glad that I took a risk and came back to find you," she whispered. "I forgive you for what happened when I was a little girl, and I understand why it happened, and I want you to believe that we have so many more happy times ahead of us, Dad."

Lloyd's stricken face relaxed a little, but it was a ghastly grey and his hair was plastered to his head with sweat. As a few minutes passed, and his breathing began to calm, Seren saw a distant look in his eyes that frightened her. His life was ebbing away second by second, as she watched helplessly. She had to say something powerful to make him believe how much she wanted him to stay with her. She had to at least address the second thing he would want to know if not give him the answer he craved.

"And I promise I will try to find out why Mum left," she whispered. "I promise on Enya's life. But I can't do it if you die, Dad. I can't." Then her tears came.

Lloyd wrapped one of his arms around her neck, and kissed her tenderly before slumping back down to the floor. His breathing was shallow, but a little steadier.

When the ambulance arrived, its siren cutting through the wind off the sea and the unending racket of seabirds' cries, Seren only felt any relief when the paramedics assured her that he was stable.

Slowly, gently, as they prepared her father to be taken to hospital, she called Ceri to ask her to fetch and feed Enya, and told her she would pick her up as soon as she could. The old woman agreed without hesitation.

"Just tell her that *Taid*/Grandfather's a bit ill, but he's going to be OK," she said, praying she was right. "I don't want her to be scared."

"She'll be safe with me, so don't you worry about her," Ceri replied.

Just as she was closing up Lloyd's cottage, her phone buzzed – the phone that had just been a blessing and saved her father's life, now cursed her. It was a message from Finlay.

Her heart began to pound, and a hot wave of panic began at her toes and rushed up through her entire body. Did she want to read this now? What might it contain? Had Jamie messaged him, and told him the truth yet? She had assumed she would hear from him first, but, of course, Finlay's response was one *she* was owed, not Jamie. Within a minute, she succumbed. The message read:

> Message received and understood. I've got a new girlfriend anyway. She's still got both her tits. Be happy. F

There was no time to process her feelings or compose any kind of reply. No words were appropriate anyway. As the paramedics lifted Lloyd's stretcher into the ambulance, Seren messaged Jamie instead. She decided not to tell him of her father's situation until it was clear what was wrong. What could he do, but worry?

> Thank you, my dear love. He's let me go. Getting rid of this phone right now!! S XX

With a primeval yelp of fury and determination, she ran the hundred yards down to the sea as the paramedics looked on incredulously, and threw her phone into the churning waves before clambering into the ambulance.

Finally, she was free.

THIRTY-FOUR

In the week that followed, Seren had many reasons to remember the old adage *a friend in need is a friend indeed*. Having never really had friends in the past, she was astounded at how the ones she had made on the island rallied round to help her now. As the possibility of staying on the island permanently became more and more likely, Seren appreciated the support she was offered, rather than wonder about the motives behind it. The only thing that was missing was Jamie, but everything else in her life was shaping up pretty well, she reminded herself when she went to visit a very fragile Lloyd in hospital.

Angharad said she was willing to postpone the start date for the job in the gallery until she was ready, which was incredibly kind. Ruthie and Del took turns to fetch Enya if Seren was with Lloyd in the hospital, and Ceri ensured both Enya and Gwyn were given limitless supplies of food, drink and decidedly unhealthy treats for tea. The two children were now the closest of friends, sharing an intuitive understanding of each other's needs that Seren never dreamt Enya would be able to establish with another child. Now, she believed in herself and she and Gwyn dared each other to test the adults, inventing silly words that nobody else could understand, and playing endless tricks, such as dropping a pea into their coffee, or putting a chip on their chairs. Ceri summed this little miracle up beautifully, saying, "They both have their weaknesses, so they give each other strength." Seren could only marvel at the continuing metamorphosis her daughter was undergoing and resign herself to a lot of mock-shocked exclamations and grease-stains on her clothes.

Lloyd rallied well about a week after what transpired was a mild heart attack, but his recovery was slow. He was so determined to return to his beloved cottage that he paced the corridors of the hospital for hours, his newly acquired walking stick clacking on the hard floor like a heartbeat, tic-tic-tic.

"I need to die near my lighthouse," he insisted whenever the nurses warned him not to overdo things. "I can't stay here much longer. It's calling me, you see."

But Seren knew that her father could not return to his cottage alone. He would need caring for, in case he was taken ill in the night, and she was his only family. She and Enya moved down to *Crigyll Cottage* the day before Lloyd was discharged from hospital. Jamie's continued absence softened the blow of leaving their comfortable cottage to some degree, but they had become used to their isolated home high on the cliffs above the sea, and they had loved it. At Lloyd's house, Enya would sleep in Seren's childhood bed and her mother on an airbed on the floor. It was far from ideal, but until the old man was strong enough to live independently, if ever, this was how it had to be.

Father and daughter soon established a slow, predictable daily routine. Once Enya was in school, they went for a walk, sometimes down the tiny road that led to the lighthouse, but more often along the seafront in Beaumaris as it was flat and made walking easier for Lloyd. Arm in arm, they strolled in companionable ease for at least an hour, every day, whatever the weather. If Seren suggested they didn't venture out because it was windy, or raining, as it very often was at this time of the year on the island, Lloyd's reply was always the same:

"Weather is weather. It's how you deal with it that matters."

She always took her camera with her and learnt so much about the flora and fauna of the island from her father, who pointed out hidden plants, a clump of rare fungi at the root of a tree or a perfectly streamlined seabird just as it speared the water. Seren soon found that she had amassed a substantial portfolio of images – most of them close-up, incredibly detailed and all of them jewel-like snapshots of the natural beauty that surrounded her. She made sure to take a picture of Lloyd too, and always with the lighthouse behind or beside him. They were the two things in her life that were immutable and represented safety; she felt the need to record of them together for when one of them was no longer here.

"It's like you've opened my eyes for the first time, Dad," she told her father one chilly November morning after he'd spotted and pointed out a kingfisher as its blue wings blurred past them in seconds. "I see things your way now, and it's a veritable revelation."

"Glad to hear it. I've found it pays to focus on the small things in life when the bigger ones threaten to overwhelm me," Lloyd said. "Everything you need is here, on this little island of ours. As Dylan Thomas puts it:

"Ears in this island hear
"The wind pass like a fire,
"Eyes in this island see
"Ships anchor off the bay."

And yet still, sometimes, Seren grew deeply restless as she sat watching him dozing for hour after hour, snoring with his mouth open. Everything was still on hold, Jamie was still not back, and had yet to explain what was keeping him in Glasgow:

she missed him keenly. She had accepted that starting her job at the gallery and being out of the cottage for long was not yet possible, but when her father was strong enough for her to leave him for an hour or so, she grabbed the chance. She made him a flask of hot, sweet tea (which he loved) and put a very basic mobile phone in his top pocket with the words "call me if you need me, and press this button if I call you, and we can talk". When she kissed the top of his head before she left, and smelt his unique, snuffy self, a wave of gratitude washed over her at the fact that they had found each other again. He would never work again, his movement was limited and he could be grumpy and frustrated, but this was more love than she had ever expected to be given by another adult, or ever felt for one.

On one of these short hours of respite, Seren walked from the lighthouse towards the old dovecote and priory that lay a mile or so away. She had always found it peaceful, as its ancient stones reminded her of a time before the troubles of modern life, when pilgrims walked for days to reach this holy place. It gave her inspiration for photographs, too, and one clear-skied afternoon, she finally managed to capture the sheer translucence of the water at St Seiriol's Well, an ancient watering hole that had, so legend maintained, mystic healing powers. As she approached the domed stone dovecote with its snug cubbyholes for hundreds of pigeons and doves, she was surprised to see a group of teenagers sketching it. An attractive woman was sitting on a large rock, obviously supervising. Seren watched as the teenagers asked her questions and proudly showed her their work in progress. When the woman noticed that she was being observed, she smiled.

"Hiya. Great-looking camera there. Nice day for photos – it's actually not pouring for once!" the woman said.

"Thank goodness," Seren replied. She reckoned this woman

was perhaps in her late thirties or early forties, but she had an English accent. Her "hiya", and the slight North Welsh twang to her words, implied that she, like her, had come here from England at some point.

"Yes, it's great for taking shots of wildlife, and zooming in. I don't have an iPhone any more, so I got this," Seren replied, aware that the woman was watching her very closely now, which made her slightly nervous. "It's something I've always wanted to do, but until I came here, I couldn't. Too busy achieving nothing very much down south and hating every minute of it."

The woman nodded. "Ah, I get that. I did just the same thing as you about five years ago. Upped sticks with my family and landed here. No regrets, though, despite the fact that I jettisoned one husband and got a better one along the way." She threw her head back and laughed. "I'm Nan, by the way – Nan Parry."

"Seren Evans, and that's so weird, because it seems we *both* got rid of a useless bloke and found a much nicer one!" Seren replied. "Great to meet you."

Nan patted the other half of the stone slab she was sitting on and Seren sat down next to her. This was turning out to be a totally fantastic afternoon.

"No regrets, I hope?"

"None at all. The new man's away at the moment, but he'll come back soon."

"If it's right, they usually do, I find," Nan replied.

"Are you a teacher?" Seren asked. "You seem to be in charge of this lot."

"No, but I bring groups of young people to see the history that's all around them on Anglesey, encourage them to notice it, appreciate it a bit more. Their lives are full of online noise and nonsense, so I think this does them good," Nan said. "Not that they'd admit it, but I think they enjoy it as well."

"There's so much to learn on the island, isn't there? I've only just begun exploring, but my father knows all the old stories and secret places," Seren said. "He's ill at the moment, so I'm pretty tied-up with caring for him."

"I'm sorry to hear that. I lost a dear uncle a few years back, born and bred on Anglesey he was. I loved him dearly, and we lose so much experience and wisdom, when we lose the older generation. I hope your dad will recover."

"Me too. He means the world to me and my daughter."

There was a silence, in which she could almost *feel* waves of sympathy from Nan.

"Will you show me some of your photos? I'm not very artistic, but my husband Harri is. He carved me a seabird out of driftwood once. A gift from his soul to mine, he called it."

Seren looked at Nan's wistful expression, and hoped that one day, Jamie would show her his love so totally and yet so simply. Was he even capable of that, after all that had happened to him in his childhood, adolescence and in adulthood, losing Agnes? She wasn't sure, and each day he stayed away, she became less so.

Flicking through some of Seren's photos, Nan looked particularly impressed with the macro photography she had done, such as the incredibly detailed close-up shots of single whorled shells, dewdrops on a blade of grass and the reflection of the sky in a raindrop.

"These are amazing, Seren," she said. "I think it's important to look closely at things around us, you know. I sometimes do mindfulness with the kids I spend time with, and it really helps them. It stops their brains spinning from one distraction to the next, like an 'anchor' in the here and now."

"Thanks. I do a photography class, but the tutor tends to want us to take scenes, or sunsets. They're great, but what about the smaller things?"

At that moment, two boys bundled out of the dovecote together.

"*Ych a fi*/Yuk! It stinks of bird shit in there," one of them said. "And Gethin's trying to climb up that stone ladder thing in the middle."

Nan got up quickly. "Looks like time to intervene, sorry. Nice to meet you, Seren. Your pictures make people *think* and *look*, and that has to be good. Do something with them. Be brave. Up here you can reinvent yourself, you know. I did."

When Nan went inside the dovecote, Seren heard her tell someone to "get down this minute", and she walked on, smiling, her spirits hugely lifted.

A germ of an idea had begun to form in her head.

THIRTY-FIVE

At Enya's suggestion, when her *Taid*/Grandfather was well enough, they got him a tiny grey kitten from a nearby farm. The plan was that it would keep him company when Seren started work in December, when the gallery would be at its busiest. Dafydd put a cat flap in the back door of the cottage, and the little creature soon settled in, and hassled everyone for attention almost to the point of annoyance. Lloyd called it Cobweb, as it was so light and fragile.

"A puff of wind, and she'd blow away with it," he said, again and again, as his eyes lovingly followed the little creature around the room.

His body was recovering, but it was much weaker than it had been, and the consultants had gravely told Seren that heart disease was usually a progressive illness in someone of her father's age, which did not bode well. He took all his medication and went to all the check-ups, but Lloyd had changed irrevocably. His memory was failing him more and more, as well. Once or twice, he called Enya "Seren", which made them both laugh, but when he called Seren "Kate", neither did. If the genuine anguish in his voice when he realised his mistake was not enough to make Seren keep her promise to try and find out why her mother had left, his whispered words as she tucked him into bed one night certainly were:

"I remember the promise you made, you know, when I thought, when we *both* thought, I was dying. I know it won't be easy – far from it, *dweud y gwir*/to tell you the truth – but I would be so happy if you found a way to keep it."

Ruthie and Del had made no progress at all in getting their mothers to talk about Kate and both women were understandably not keen to risk their relationships by pushing any harder. Reluctantly, Seren concluded that she might have to search for answers elsewhere, but she had absolutely no idea where to start. The one thing she was certain of, however, was that Lloyd needed to know the truth before it was too late for him to hear it.

The weather now heralded the harsh winter months that lay ahead until spring returned to the island. Storms battered the shore, and the lighthouse was sometimes swathed in thick fog until noon, when some slivers of weak wintry sunlight might burn it off. Seren had always hated the long, dark evenings in London, but they had been nothing like the total, blanketing blackness on the island once the sun had set in winter, which was before 4 p.m. on many days. There was no hum of traffic, beeping of horns or clatter of shoes on wet pavements as they headed to the Tube stations at 5 p.m. At *Trwyn Du*/Black Nose, the only sounds were the waves, the wind and the warbling cries of unseen curlews circling the water in the darkness, calling to each other. In some ways, this was peaceful, calming even, but in others, it felt as if there was no life beyond the four walls of the cottage, and it was stifling. Jamie kept in touch pretty regularly, but there was still no talk of his return. He had been offered an amazing opportunity he told Seren, but it was all under wraps for the moment. The excitement in his voice made her feel that he was not missing her as much as she was missing him, and it hurt. Had she been imagining their love for each other? Had it simply evaporated once he'd returned to the real world, beyond the narrow confines of Anglesey?

Her salvation was the day when Lloyd was well enough for her to start work in The Seaside Gallery on 8th December. Miraculously, she felt as if a strong hand was hauling her out of the downward spiral she recognised only too well. She had tiptoed around depression her whole life, sometimes losing herself in it, sometimes managing to skirt around its edges and not fall into the abyss. When she started work at the gallery, however, she felt a rush of confidence, a feeling of independence, of adulthood, that she had never, ever felt before. Her new job marked the beginning of a new *her,* and it was bloody brilliant.

Angharad, already a close friend, was now her brilliant boss. She took time to involve Seren in all the processes of running the gallery and ordering stock, which gave her the chance to look through catalogues of prints, cards and tasteful *objets d'art* that tourists were keen to spend their holiday money on. None of the other paintings had the immediacy of Angharad's own work, but she'd learnt that many people found solace in a fairly bland, unnamed seascape, or a soothing pastel-coloured view, and that was fine with her.

"Never presume that your taste is everyone's taste," Angharad told her, as they both winced at a particularly garish painting of a clifftop near Rhosneigr. "I want there to be something for everyone in here, even if what they like, I don't."

Together, the two women discussed what might sell and what would not, what was a fair price and what was likely to be off-putting. As they spent hours, heads bent over screens and catalogues, they learnt things about each other that neither had told a living soul. They also discovered how similar their respective paths through life had been.

"Gwyn's father reeled me in pretty quickly, I'm embarrassed to confess," Angharad said one morning, totally out of the blue. "He was so *dashing* compared to all the farming lads I'd met, and his cut-glass English accent, well, he had me at 'Hello, my name's Rory'."

"There's something irresistible about accents different to our own, isn't there?" Seren replied. "Finlay was Irish, and when he first spoke to me, I melted and Jamie's 'wee' this and 'wee' that is so endearing. I'm putty in his hands."

"Hmmm, I know, but be careful. I'm not sure that putty is something we should aspire to be," Angharad said. "Accent apart, did you ever actually love Finlay, Enya's dad?"

A pause. "I fell under his spell, for sure, but I knew pretty quickly that it wasn't love. When Enya was born, she cried endlessly. He almost punished me for having her, as if it was none of his doing at all!" Seren said with a bitter laugh.

"Rory was just the same. Horrified, he was, when I told him I was pregnant, and going to keep the baby. He had plans for another 'gap yah' in Indonesia after graduating. He was only twenty-two, you see, and had just finished at Cambridge, so the glittering career in the City he had lined up was on hold while he enjoyed himself for one more carefree year," Angharad said. "Nice for some."

"Did he support you at all?" Seren said. "Finlay tried to, I suppose, but it was always a struggle."

"Rory tried to do the right thing, because his brother had told him to, but once I'd had the twenty-week scan and we knew the baby had spina bifida, he was off." A shadow crossed Angharad's face, fleeting but real. "We were in an on and off relationship for years – the love of my life, I thought he was, from the first time we met. His family had a huge holiday home in Beaumaris, and came every summer – or rather they did, until Gwyn came along. They sold it sharpish then, and I never heard from Rory again. Luckily, his brother Alistair was cut from different cloth."

"How do you mean?"

"Remember I told you that someone had given me a break after I'd had 'trouble with a man', and that's why I gave you one, in giving you this job? Well, it was Alistair that lent me the deposit that meant I could afford to rent this place and start the business. I thought it was a loan, but when I could afford to start repaying it, he told me to keep it, and the money was for Gwyn, and his future."

"So noble souls do still exist," Seren murmured. "They're pretty rare, but I think my dad's one of them as well."

"And your new man – Jamie?"

Hesitating, Seren realised for the first time what an honest answer needed to be. "I thought he was, but now I'm not so sure. I think he might be making a mistake he's made before, putting his career first, and the people who love him second."

"His loss, if so," Angharad said. "You deserve to be put first, every time."

"And so do you," Seren replied, putting an arm around her friend.

Angharad looked at her and said, "But you'll be fine without a man. We both will. You do know that, don't you?"

"Yes, I do, of course. Thank goodness for our kids, though. We're never really alone, as my poor dad was for years, looking out to sea, waiting for me."

"Yes, thank goodness for Gwyn and Enya... the cheeky little gits."

As Christmas neared, all the shops in Beaumaris became busier and busier, days at the gallery passed in the blink of an eye. Seren became adept at guiding customers towards what they didn't even know they wanted, and advising them on gifts for loved ones. Angharad's prints sold well, but the starkness of stormy skies, or a canvas covered only with black, icy waves, were too bleak for many people. Seren knew that they reflected the darker side of her friend, and longed to get close enough to help her see more light in her life, but she was always busy, running to keep up. Caring for Gwyn was exhausting and managing his life and varying needs all-consuming. Ceri helped enormously, but the vast majority of what needed doing was done by Angharad and it took its toll on her.

One Wednesday, Seren's full day at work, Ceri brought Enya to the gallery just before 5 p.m., as she did every week. Sadly, since his heart attack, there was no possibility of Lloyd fetching his granddaughter, despite his protestations that he was more than able. As Enya settled down with her reading book, Ceri sat down behind the till and watched Seren quickly tidy up.

"You even move like your mam, you know," she said suddenly. "She was light on her feet too – she almost danced when she walked."

Seren scented an opportunity. "Did you know her well, Ceri – my mam?"

"Well, I wasn't allowed in their little clique of three, but I always saw her at *cylch meithrin*/playgroup, because I took Angharad and she took you. Nice she was, but a bit like a *tylwyth teg*/fairy, here one minute and flitting off the next."

"My aunt, her sister, would agree with you on that. But why do you think she left so suddenly?" Seren asked as casually as she could. "Nobody will tell me, and my dad, well, I think he needs to know before…"

Ceri shuffled to get more comfortable on the chair and winced. Her sciatica, she didn't need to say. "I agree with you. I have no proof at all, Seren, but I don't think Kate was well. She wasn't herself those last few weeks and she was very *distant*.

She ignored me completely when I asked if she was all right one day, which was very out of character. Kate would talk to a wall."

The only sound in the gallery was the dull buzzing of a fly, lazily circling the main light. Seren could hardly breathe, but knew she needed to keep Ceri talking and try to maintain a calmness she did not feel.

"Did anyone else think she might be ill?" she asked. "I don't think Dad did."

Ceri sighed. "I know what you're trying to do, love, but you need the *truth*, rather than snippets of gossip and guesswork, and I don't know it. All I can tell you is that Kate didn't look like *her* just before she left; she looked like a, well, a *shadow,* if you see what I mean, as if the real Kate had already gone."

"I see. So, you think she might have been ill," Seren said. "Thanks for that."

At last, she had a clue, a trail of breadcrumbs to follow through the forest.

After Ceri had left and she had locked up the gallery, Seren and Enya walked up the High Street and looked in all the shop windows, all of them sparkling with glitter and tinsel and many positively throbbing with fairy lights. It struck her that, by the time she had been Enya's age, her mother had left her, and died a few months later, violently, and totally alone. It was a sobering thought, and she squeezed her little girl's hand.

"Are you OK, Mam?" Enya said, seeing her sadness.

Seren noticed that it was the first time she had called her "Mam" rather than "Mum", but she said nothing. It was a good sign, a sign of belonging.

"I'm fine, just a bit tired," she said, adding, "Who would have imagined this time last year that we would be here, spending Christmas with *Taid*/Grandfather?"

"I don't remember anything about last Christmas except

Dad had that 'axydent' and then his head was bleeding," Enya said.

Seren nodded. She remembered too. Finlay had been very drunk and cut his head on an open cupboard, but luckily Enya had gone to bed before he'd started blaming her for his "accident".

"But you had a new doll, remember? She came here with you," Seren said with urgent positivity. How she hoped that the bad memories would soon fade and the few good ones rose to the surface like oil on water. "Hey, you need to tell me, what would you like *this* Christmas?"

"Jamie to come back," Enya replied without hesitation. "Oh, and Gwyn to be out of his wheelchair, but I know *Siôn Corn*/Santa can't make that happen."

"No, love, he can't, but Gwyn is lucky to have a friend like you, who wishes that it could," Seren replied deeply moved.

As to Enya's main wish, there was nothing she could do to make that one come true either. It appeared they were not seen as a part of Jamie's life at present. He professed his love, how much he missed them, missed the island and how upset he was to hear of Lloyd's illness, but he did not mention when he would return. The situation saddened Seren deeply, but she tried to remember Angharad's words:

"You'll be fine without a man."

Try as she did to believe this, Seren's heart told her that to have a man like Jamie by her side, who understood and accepted her so completely, would be even finer.

THIRTY-SIX

As Christmas neared, life was busier than ever for Seren. In between running the household, looking after Lloyd, going to the carol service and the *Sioe Nadolig*/Christmas Show at Enya's school, she was working in the gallery as many hours as she could. She was increasingly exhausted, and sleeping on the airbed was uncomfortable and chilly, but there was no choice. Lloyd seemed stronger, but he was far from content, and leaving him was starting to become difficult as he didn't want to be alone left any more, he told her plaintively. He often asked about Jamie, but she had no answers for him. When, one day, she heard him murmuring to Cobweb, his kitten, and calling her "my only friend on earth", she realised that he felt his erstwhile friend, whom he had welcomed into his life and his family, had abandoned him. Seren decided to call Jamie and get some answers to the questions that ricocheted around her head in the small hours for weeks. Her first attempt went to voicemail, which flustered her, as she wanted to sound *un*flustered, but couldn't pull it off. When she tried again, she left a message she hoped was suitably non-committal:

> Hi there. Wondering how you are, as we haven't been in touch for a few days. Busy here, but we miss you. S x

When a day passed without a response, she tried once more, deciding that this would be the last time. If she heard nothing, that was it, it was over... but the very thought of that possibility sent shivers right through her. When Jamie picked up, it was impossible to hear him as the roar of traffic was so loud wherever he was, and they were forced to hang up. Upset, Seren reminded herself again that the world he was in was so very different to this one, on this tiny island. She had been happy to say farewell to city life, to the bustle and rush, but perhaps he wasn't, and wanted it when given the choice to have it again. His career had always been so important to him, and it was obviously on the up once more. When a text pinged into her phone, her heart leapt and she read it eagerly.

> SO sorry we couldn't talk. I'll ring this evening. On a big job. Love you. X

That evening, she waited until 11 p.m. for him to call, but he did not. After an agonising hour or so, she decided it was best for her, and for her father and daughter, that they tried to get on with their daily lives without expecting, or hoping, that Jamie would be a part of it. Unless he explained, she felt she had no choice but to conclude that, for now, he had chosen a different path. Nevertheless, she cried herself to sleep.

About a week before Christmas, a huge snowstorm hit Anglesey, with needle-sharp winds that whipped snowflakes into thick, whirling flurries that buried everything in whiteness. The land down to *Crigyll Cottage* was impassable, so Seren could not get to work and Enya's school was closed. Even with the heating on and the fire blazing, cold permeated the old stone walls and ill-fitting wooden windows, and Lloyd sat, wrapped in blankets, with his knees almost touching the fireguard in his efforts to get warm.

"Dad, perhaps move back a little," Seren said gently. He was cold, and miserable, but the possibility of an accident was very real as he was so wobbly these days. For the first time ever, her father snapped at her.

"Stop telling me what to do, girl! I'll sit where I want to in my own house, thank you very much."

Enya looked up from her colouring, alarmed. She recognised a flare of real anger when she saw it.

"Shall we go outside, Mam, and make a snowman for *Taid*/Grandfather to look at?" she suggested.

"And why would I want to do that?" came the bitter response from Lloyd.

But when Enya got up and went to her mother for a hug, his face fell.

"I'm sorry, *cariad*/love. I just feel so helpless, sitting here all day. I've looked forward to a Christmas with my family for so long. I've had years of lonely ones, and sometimes I pretended it wasn't Christmas at all, and now I'm useless to one and all and so I can't even enjoy it. It's not *fair*."

Enya nodded understandingly. Then she unfolded herself from Seren's arms, went over to Lloyd, taking one of his wrinkled hands in her, small, soft one.

"I'm looking forward to this Christmas too, *Taid*/Grandfather. It's going to be the best one ever," she said. "It might even be white!"

Lloyd ruffled her hair fondly. "*Dos allan i chwarae, Enya fach*/Go outside and play, little Enya. Make a big snowman and give him a sprinkling of snuff from me!" He handed her the dented and battered tin of his favourite snuff.

After half an hour outside piling snow into something

vaguely resembling a human, Enya and Seren were clapping their frozen gloves together and their noses and cheeks were scarlet. Lloyd stood at the window as they started throwing snowballs at each other to warm up and Seren could see him laughing when she skidded and landed on her bum with a softened thud.

"Right, I'm frozen through, so let's go inside for a hot drink," she said, dodging a final snowball from Enya.

"Wait, the snuff!" she cried, sliding over to their snowman and sprinkling a pinch of brown powder on what might be called an arm, as he had no hands. "Right, all done. Look, *Taid*/Grandfather!"

But when they both looked at the window, Lloyd had vanished. Seren knew in an instant that he had not stopped watching out of boredom. Something had happened. She raced towards the house, her boots slithering on the ice-crisped snow. Enya followed behind her, eyes wide in fright.

"Dad! Dad!" she shouted, until she pushed open the door and saw him once again sprawled on the floor, gasping, his lips blue and his eyes wide with fright.

"Enya, *Taid*'s/Grandfather's not well. Dial 999 and ask for an ambulance," she shouted, getting down to roll her father into the recovery position.

This time, the ambulance came faster, but the wait still felt like an eternity. Enya, pale and trembling, sat silently in Lloyd's chair stroking Cobweb while Seren cradled Lloyd's head and tried to keep him warm with blankets. He was breathing, but struggling to do so. This was much worse than last time, as he was already weakened. She had to keep him conscious, and hopeful.

"Stay with me, Dad. I'll keep my promise, I'll find out why Mum left, but please give me a little more time and stay with me," she whispered, as tears rolled down her cheeks.

When the paramedics arrived, one of them remembered

both Lloyd and even his father, Aled, before him. They all greeted him warmly and respectfully, which brought a broad smile to his lips and gave Seren a glimmer of hope that he would recover again. Wheeling him towards the ambulance, one of them turned to Seren and Enya.

"You'd better follow on this time, as the little one can't come with us. Anyone you can leave her with for a while?"

Seren did not hesitate. "Yes, yes, a friend will look after her, but please tell Dad I'll be there with him as soon as I can."

"Plucky little thing, to make the emergency call and ask for the ambulance," the paramedic said, smiling at Enya. "Well done, young lady."

Enya smiled back, and said, "I've done it before, when Dad hit Mam."

Seren wished she had not seen the horrified expression on the man's face as he joined Lloyd in the back of the ambulance and closed the door.

Several, very long, hours later, Lloyd was stable on the men's ward in *Ysbyty Gwynedd*/Gwynedd Hospital, looped with wires and tubes, and the nurses said he was responding well to treatment. The fact that he felt well enough to be perusing the supper menu with remarkable engagement reassured Seren that they were probably right.

"The toad in the hole sounds good," he said.

Seren could only laugh, and suggest the jam roly-poly and custard for pudding.

When she finally stood outside the main entrance with the usual gaggle of surreptitious smokers, it was dark, and she was exhausted. There was no more time for doubt or hesitation. She drove to a nearby phone retailer, bought yet another phone and called Aunt Alice from the car park. The familiar theme tune of her favourite soap opera was blaring in the background.

"Hi there. Sorry to spring this on you, Aunt, but Dad's really ill, and he's in hospital with heart disease. He's being treated, and he's doing well at the moment, but the doctors say it's not good at all – in the long term, if you see what I mean."

A sympathetic sigh. "Oh, I'm really sorry to hear that, love. He was a kind man."

"What? He's not dead yet, and he's *still* a kind man!" Seren said, shocked.

"Oh, I'm so sorry, I misunderstood, I didn't hear correctly," Alice stuttered, wrong-footed. The television was suddenly turned off.

"What I meant is that his time might be... short, and he needs to know why Mum left before, well... Look, you're the only person who can tell him." Seren paused, before adding, in a low voice, "Oh, Aunt... Alice, I'm begging you, please help me now."

As she waited for a reply, Seren could hear the familiar sounds of London – a screaming police siren, a pelican crossing beeping and the incessant hum of traffic. How glad she was to be no longer living her life to that soundtrack. When Alice replied, a whole endless-seeming minute later, her words were unexpected.

"I have been thinking about this a lot since you left, and I think you're right. He does need to know, and so do you. There are some... things I need to do, and Christmas is almost upon us, but after that, I'd like to come and visit, and we'll talk about Kate, about everything I haven't been able to tell you all these years. It's time."

Seren was almost lost for words. All she could muster in reply was, "Thank you, from the bottom of my heart. And Happy Christmas to all of you."

THIRTY-SEVEN

Seren thought about her conversation with her aunt long after it had ended. As a child, she had always been conscious of the fact that she was a guest in her relatives' house in Wimbledon, and not a true family member, however much her cousins tried to persuade her otherwise. She had never looked forward to Christmas and having to be grateful for gifts, food and attention she told herself she neither wanted nor needed. Now, she looked back at her lack of grace with shame; they had tried so hard to include her, but she had petulantly turned her back on their kindness for years. She would put that right, in the future.

As for Enya, her feelings about Christmas had always been directly linked to how much her father had drunk, and how angry and disappointed he would be by the end of the day. This year, both mother and daughter were one hundred per cent determined that, despite Lloyd's illness and Jamie's absence, they were going to have FUN.

Lloyd was discharged from hospital on 22nd December and seemed in better spirits than he had been before his second heart attack. He could not travel anywhere, so Seren did something she had never done in her life before – she invited all their closest family friends over for a meal on Christmas Eve. She could not invite everyone they knew, but Angharad, Gwyn and Ceri had been so kind to Enya, and so flexible in the gallery, that she wanted to show them her appreciation. She hoped that Lloyd would enjoy their company too, and was sure he would like Angharad and her ever-chatty mother. Yes, she would surround him with companionship for what might well be his last Christmas, making it one he would never forget.

Shopping for her first ever dinner party was a stressful experience, but with Enya's help in pre-planning the menu and writing the shopping list, the tiny kitchen in *Crigyll Cottage* was filled with delicious smells that afternoon, and both Lloyd and Cobweb sniffed appreciatively whenever a lid came off a pan or an oven door was opened. The snow had melted, but it was a cold night, and a harsh frost was already crisping the grass when the guests arrived, but the warmth of the welcome they received was matched only by the one they gave.

Seren had put all the small tables in the house together to form one long one, of varying heights and widths, with a special place laid for Gwyn where it would be easiest to park his wheelchair. Candles flickered in jam-jars all the way down the middle of the white lacy table runner she'd found in a drawer. Lloyd told her Kate had brought it from her childhood home and warned her:

"It was her grandmother's, so don't get wax on it."

Gifts were exchanged and when everyone was finally sitting down, the beef was carved and plates piled high with crisp roast potatoes, perfectly cooked vegetables and gallons of gravy (made, at her insistence, by Ceri, who wanted "the proper South Welsh stuff, not brown water"). Seren proposed a toast and everyone raised their glasses to friends and family. It was the happiest she had been for a long while, and all the bad, sad things in the past faded into the companionable joy that was the present. For a good five minutes, the only sounds were the clattering of cutlery and groans of pleasure at the deliciousness of the food. Lloyd fed Cobweb tiny pieces of meat from his plate, and everybody pretended not to notice, and Gwyn ate a remarkable eight roast potatoes, which Angharad said was just the warm-up. Almost every morsel was eaten, even the sprouts, which Enya consented to try and pronounced "a bit metally but OK".

There was a piano in one corner of the room, which Seren knew her father had never once played, so her mother must have done. When Gwyn wheeled over to it, blew the dust off the keys and began to play Christmas carols they all knew and loved, and they sang them, all together, the evening was complete.

"I told you he's brilliant," Ceri said, blinking. She'd had more than a couple of sherries. "Doesn't even need the music – he just *plays!*"

Just as they were pulling crackers and trying not to think about the crumble and custard that was coming for pudding, Seren saw car headlights outside.

"Who on earth can this be?" she muttered. "There's no food left for them, whoever they are."

A loud knock at the door silenced everyone, and all eyes turned to see it open to reveal a very tired, but very happy-looking Jamie.

"I hope I'm not intruding, but I..." he managed to say before he was winded by Enya's rugby tackle of a hug. As she danced around him happily, he greeted each of the guests, none of whom he had met before, with remarkable ease, before kneeling beside Lloyd's chair. The old man's face was wreathed in smiles, and his eyes glittered with tears.

"You came back, Jamie," he said, clapping him on the back

with surprising force. "I knew you would. Well, I hoped you would. *Croeso 'nôl*/Welcome back. I've missed you."

"Thank you, old friend. I've missed you too. We need to get out fishing again, show those bass who's boss."

But when Jamie turned to Seren, neither could find the right words to say. She did not feel like jumping up and hugging him, or shouting her relief at his return, and he knew better than to take her in his arms unbidden as he had some explaining to do. Instead, they exchanged a smile, which said, without words, that they would talk later.

The rest of that evening was one of more singing, more laughter and a great deal of pudding. At just after 9 p.m., Angharad wheeled a reluctant Gwyn towards the door with Ceri tottering behind her. She turned to Seren before opening it to admit the waiting chill of winter. Jamie immediately stood up ready to help her get Gwyn into the car.

"This has been the most amazing evening, Seren. Thank you, from the bottom of my heart, from the bottom of *all* our hearts. Your coming here has made my life so much better, in every single way."

"Ditto, my friend," Seren said softly.

"Hear, hear," everyone in the room chorused.

"Right, *Nadolig Llawen pawb*/Happy Christmas, everyone," Ceri cried, as she fumbled in her bag and then popped an indigestion tablet.

"Hope *Siôn Corn*/Santa Claus comes, Enya," Gwyn called over his shoulder.

"Ditto, my friend," she replied with a *very* cheesy grin at her mother.

Jamie left soon afterwards, to return to his lonely cottage which they all knew would be very cold and damp after such a long time lying empty. There was no room for him at *Crigyll Cottage* even if Seren had wanted him to stay, which she did not. She invited him for lunch tomorrow, on Christmas Day, but more than that, she was not sure about yet.

Yes, she was glad to see him, very glad, but there were things she needed to know before she could fully trust him with her heart. As Angharad had said, she deserved to come first, every time, and she intended to make sure she did.

THIRTY-EIGHT

Christmas Day was bitterly cold, but dry, and the sky was a vivid azure that seemed unfeasible in the middle of winter. Seren had put the turkey in the bottom of the range to cook slowly overnight, so they all awoke to the smell of it, sniffing like cartoon characters at a passing pizza or enormous steak. Enya was delighted with her modest gifts from Santa, and even more delighted with the refurbished bike her mother and grandfather had bought for her, complete with a front basket with plastic flowers tied to it and a very loud bell. Before noon, the stabilisers were off and she was riding, rather wobblily, up and down the lane outside the cottage, an excited Cobweb scampering behind her.

Jamie arrived for lunch at 1p.m., as instructed, and Seren smiled when she saw how handsome he looked in his smart blue lambswool sweater and corduroy trousers. He had clearly been shopping in Glasgow, as they were a huge improvement on the tatty clothes he had always worn on the island. When he finally removed his woolly hat, she saw that his hair, newly washed and combed for the occasion, was well-cut, and it suited him. Lloyd and Enya greeted him warmly, and she gave him a peck on the cheek, but a part of her was still guarded. Watching him laughing with her father and tickling her daughter, she felt once again that she could love this man forever, but did he feel the same? She had been asking herself that question on repeat for so long. Today might reveal the answer, as she was determined to confront him about his lengthy absence.

Lunch was a great success, much to Seren's delight. This was only the second large meal she had ever cooked, the first being the previous night's gathering, and she was very proud of herself when all went well. Contentedly full, both Lloyd and Enya fell asleep in front of *It's a Beautiful Life*, a film made in 1946 that Seren had been forced to watch every Christmas Day in Wimbledon as it was a much-loved tradition in Aunt Alice's family. She had always thought she despised what she saw as mawkishness, but today, she relished every second of its celebration of what really mattered in life and what made a good person, good.

"I have to pop back to my cottage to get my gifts before it gets dark," Jamie whispered to her. "I was so nervous earlier, about coming today, I forgot to bring them."

Seren knew that she had made him nervous by her less than enthusiastic welcome last night, but she was secretly pleased to hear him acknowledge he had noticed it. What she felt, mattered.

"Shall I come with you? These two are out for the count. I'll leave them a note, and I'll have my phone if they need me," she said.

"That would be great. We need to talk, don't we?"

Her expression as she pulled on her boots, coat and hat confirmed that they did. She hung her camera around her neck. The sky was streaked with pinks and oranges as the winter sun slowly set and she wanted to capture the end of this, very special, Christmas Day if she could.

. . .

A breeze had sprung up, sending flurried ripples across the surface of the sea as they walked along the beach and up onto the headland, towards Jamie's cottage. A few crows picked at the banks of seaweed washed up by the last high tide, but there were so few signs of life that it seemed that even the natural world had paused the daily grind for today. Out on the horizon, two huge tankers were moored, their voyage to and from wherever they were going suspended for at least a day. Taking a photo of them silhouetted against the blazing sky, Seren hoped the crews were celebrating their strange cut-off Christmas and not missing home too much, wherever home was.

The path to Jamie's cottage door was overgrown with weeds, ragwort, bindweed and Herb Robert being the main culprits. It looked uncared for even before he had opened the door, but when he did, a rush of cold air came out, laden with the thick smell of damp. This had never the best-kept cottage in the row, but now it looked as if all hope had abandoned it. The cottage Seren and Enya had borrowed was faring better, but even that needed warmth and maintenance in the long, Welsh winter. She hoped the couple who owned it would make sure that happened, as too many second homes fell into disrepair when the island was cold and rainy, and a coastal mini-break did not appeal.

When Seren followed Jamie inside, she could tell immediately that it was no longer a home, but a place he was "camping" in temporarily. His open suitcase was on the kitchen table and a box of breakfast cereal, pint of milk and a loaf of bread seemed to be his only provisions. She deduced that he had no intention of staying for very long, which was worrying. Their upcoming conversation would therefore be a brief one. She would need to stick to her pre-prepared script.

"Sit down, I'll make us a cup of tea," he said, but as he moved around the room, there was a wariness to him that Seren had not seen since the first time she had seen him fishing out on the rocks. He skirted around her, as if scared to touch her in case it made her angry. It was time to ask the questions she needed to and, if necessary, say goodbye to what could have been between them.

"Jamie, I need to ask you..." she began, but when his beloved face turned towards her, the measured words she had rehearsed in the darkness of her bedroom slipped away. "God, I don't know *what* I need to ask you, apart from everything."

"Let me talk first, perhaps, and then you'll feel able to," Jamie said, putting a mug of tea in front of her and sitting down. "It's not as bad as you think. In fact, it's really good – for me, and for us. Honestly."

Seren shivered, grabbed her mug and wrapped her hands around it for comfort and for warmth. The next few minutes could decide the course of the rest of her life. No pressure, she thought to herself, putting her camera carefully on the table before bracing herself to listen.

"OK, I'll begin at the beginning," Jamie said. "As you know, I went back to Glasgow to sort out my life and see if there were likely to be any repercussions from the gang I'd infiltrated. As the material was never used, and I'd done a good deed in saving one lad's life, I discovered my cover was still intact, as I'd hoped. That was a relief, but also a massive anti-climax if that makes any sense. I was safe, it was behind me, but for Fraser, nothing had changed – no good had come out of it all."

Seren, who had no siblings, could only imagine how it would feel to lose one. "Anyway, for about a week, I festered in the house, drinking beer and eating crap, while everything sort of recalibrated itself in my mind. The old me was gone for good, but who the hell was the new one?" He paused to sip his tea, and Seren resisted the urge to say "the one who told me he loves me?" "It sounds pretty feeble now, I know, but I needed to feel sure of who I was, before I came back and committed to being the partner you deserve and Enya's co-parent. It took time for me to get there, more time than I'd expected, but I did."

"Glad to hear that," Seren said, rising anger beneath her words. What typical self-indulgence from a man! She, thinking he had broken her heart, had carried on working, caring, managing, of course whilst he had wallowed in self-pity. "Not sure if you've convinced me that you deserve *me* yet, to be perfectly honest, but do go on."

Jamie's face blanched, but he went on. "OK. When I had a plan, I went in to talk to Fergus, the editor of the paper I worked on. We talked for about two hours, and he was genuinely pleased that I'd come such a long way since the state I was in after losing Agnes, and all the stuff with Fiona afterwards. I won't use that stupid phrase 'I'd moved on' because how can anyone really leave something like that behind them completely, but you know what I mean?"

Seren said nothing, as she wasn't sure that she did. The jury was still out as far as her feelings were concerned.

"I told him about you, too, and he said you must be an amazing woman to have wrought such a positive change in me."

"I hope you told him he was right," Seren said, feeling a tantalising sliver of hope flood her body like a sip of good whisky. Could he have chosen her, after all? Listening to this man's musical voice, and irresistible accent, always made her feel better than she had ever felt, with anyone else. Being with him was like being wrapped in the warmest, softest of blankets, he was her place of safety, of comfort, but she knew there was much he still hadn't told her, and waited for him to do so before allowing herself to be happy.

"I told him about Anglesey as best I could, how wild it is, and yet how nurturing I'd found it, how it sort of scoured away the blackness I felt inside. I told him about Lloyd, and night-fishing, and the lighthouse which became a beacon of hope for me in the darkest of times chiefly because *it was always there*, whatever the weather, however I felt. Does that make sense?"

Finally, something he said chimed with Seren. "Absolutely. I dreamt about it for years before I came back here, and felt it was pulling me towards it, as if calling a ship beset with storms to safe harbour. It's a constant, when so little in life is."

"That's just it!" Jamie exclaimed. "But now I'm getting to the best bit of all. I finally came up with an idea for how to take my career forward that did not involve putting anyone, including myself, in danger, but still used my observational skills and my 'writing panache'. I'm quoting Fergus, there, by the way, and he knows his stuff journalistically."

"Remind me to bow down before you in future," Seren said, laughing.

"Haha, very droll. To cut a long story short, I asked Fergus if I could spend a few weeks travelling the Highlands and Islands in the North of Scotland, and submit articles on what I saw, the people I met, the history of each place and how being out in the wild affected my mood, how I felt in myself. He wasn't convinced by the idea at first, but I guess he was taking a big risk both with me, Mr Liability, and the paper's budget. I told him that there's a big push for getting back to basics, to uncluttered simplicity, at the moment and that it could really go down well and be *worthwhile,* which matters to me, especially after Fraser's pointless death. Finally, he agreed to let me travel for a few weeks and submit some copy, and he gave me enough to cover my expenses."

Seren sipped her tea thoughtfully. "But why didn't you tell *me*, Jamie? I just thought you'd abandoned us, and... fallen out of love with me."

Jamie leant over and took her hand in his. "I think I needed to believe it myself, first, after all the things I've done wrong. I couldn't face failing you as well as Agnes. Every time you and I spoke, I tried to find the right words, but they never came, so I had to wait until now, until I could come back and tell you face to face."

"So, Fergus has approved it, has he?" Seren asked warily.

"Not yet, but he liked what I've done so far, so I'm hopeful that he will. I'll be writing under another name, of course. Mine is still associated with, well, less than wholesome assignments I've always been given because of my past contacts. Now, it's time to shed that reputation, but I can live with that. New name, new profession, new attitude to life, if it all works out."

"You're going to change your *name*? Bloody hell, Jamie."

"No, but I'll write under a different name, like a pen name. I fancy Ewan Nairn. It's a sound Scottish name, at least. What do you think?"

He looked at her, his eyes almost pleading. This was all rather weird to Seren. She took her time to think, before replying.

"As long as you stay 'Jamie' for us, I guess we'll cope," she said.

"Thank God for that! Once I've got the final green light from Fergus, I hope I'll have a regular, weekly column focusing on something that strikes me about the way we live, and makes me think about the wider context and how vital being in nature, as it's called, is for everyone, wherever they live."

He paused as Seren slowly took in what kind of life he was outlining to her. Her first thought was, does that mean you won't be here, but travelling all the time? He answered her question without her having to ask it.

"I want to get Fergus to agree, for an initial trial period of three months, to letting me come back to Anglesey and start by writing a series of articles about the island, as it's so rich in well-being source material."

Seren frowned. "Rich in *what*?"

"Sorry, silly jargon. I mean natural beauty, stunning wildlife, history, community, language and age-old traditions and stories. It's like a microcosm of lots of very good things, this little island. I feel so lucky that, purely by chance, I came here at my lowest ebb, and found it."

"Sounds amazing, because small really is beautiful," Seren said, her mind whirring. If he agreed, this opportunity could be good for *both* of them. "I need to show you something." She quickly passed her camera over the table to him. Studying his face as he scrolled through her pictures, she could see he was deeply impressed. "This sort of stuff is called macro photography, apparently – homing in on the detail, the astonishing perfection of one, often small, thing. I think you can capture the distilled *essence* of natural beauty with photos like these," she said, proud of her knowledge. "I did a photography course in Aberffraw before Christmas."

He looked up at her, his expression undeniably proud. "They're bloody brilliant, and I reckon I can use some of these in my articles, if Fergus agrees. But you knew I'd say that, didn't you?"

She nodded. "Yup. And I know someone else who can help us. She's called Nan Parry, and she knows everything there is to know about the history of the island."

"Fantastic. We'll need detail, locals' knowledge and experience for this to be authentic, and I will probably need to venture further afield further down the line if this all works out, perhaps over to Ireland, or the Channel Islands, but I'll make sure none of the trips are long, or that you and Enya can come with me," he said, his face glowing with excitement. "You see, I want to use some of the money from the sale of the house in Glasgow to buy us a camper van, so that we can travel independently, up into *Eryri*/Snowdonia, or down the *Pen Llŷn*/Lleyn Peninsula, for instance."

Seren's face registered surprise. "You speak Welsh now?"

"I've started learning, and yes, I know their Welsh names," Jamie replied. "I believe that every corner of this amazing part of the world has its own story, its own history and we need to convey that to other people."

Seren smiled. This was amazing stuff. "Helping others see what joy can be had from seeing your environment as a living, breathing thing. Sounds great."

"Yes, and one that can heal even the deepest of wounds," Jamie said, adding in a sadder voice, "One of the many regrets I have about Agnes is that we spent so much time apart. She was always in crèches, childminders' houses, nurseries and, in the end, school, rather than with Fiona and I, which makes me sad when I think back. So much lost time." He paused, as his voice was breaking. "And I hope you agree that Enya could miss a few days of school from time to time to come with us, and experience somewhere completely different? That was an integral part of my plan for the future. I don't want us to be apart for long ever again."

Seren had a big lump in her throat. "I think that would be wonderful," she croaked.

"So, we can live together, and work together, as a family! I want you to fulfil all those dreams you've held on to for so long. They can come true, my love, but before that, I need to go back to Scotland for a few more weeks, to get things sorted, get the house on the market and shut down my former life. I'll never be going back, I know that now. Fiona's living in a farmhouse in France and wants her share for renovations. I promise I'll keep you in the loop from now on too. Just believe that I love you, and I want to be with you, always."

Without saying a word, they stood up as one and moved towards each other with a purpose neither doubted. Both had learnt through bitter experience that life was short, and happiness rare. Yes, their future would always be together.

An hour or so later, when they set off back to *Crigyll*

Cottage in the velvet black darkness of the night, they felt as if they were taking the first steps into that future, and that it would be better than either of them could ever have dreamt.

PART 6

BEGINNINGS AND ENDINGS

THIRTY-NINE

Jamie left for Glasgow on 5th January, to persuade Fergus, his editor, to fully commit to his proposal and allow him to begin writing on Anglesey. He took some of Seren's photos with him, as he was sure they would enhance his articles. Explaining to Lloyd that he would be writing under a different name was surprisingly simple, but Enya was unsure, and upset. She had grown to love and trust a man called Jamie, and it had not been easy for her to do so, but now he was inventing a different persona for himself. It reminded her of Finlay's fickle moods, and that she had never known how he was going to be, from one day to the next. She thawed only when her grandfather reminded her that her favourite actor in a *Star Wars* film they'd watched together was called *Ewan* McGregor.

Before he left, Jamie had distributed his Christmas gifts, and his thoughtfulness was not lost on anyone. He had been away from them, but he had not forgotten them. He gave Lloyd a beautiful silver snuff box, engraved with the words *Lloyd Evans: A friend, when I needed one*. He presented Enya with a leather-bound book of stories he had written for Seren to read to her, all based on places and things she would recognise on the island and would add to their meaning. He'd woven a story around children's wishes being granted if they tossed a pebble into St. Seiriol's Well near the priory, another about a dove that was excluded from the dovecote until it revealed its beautiful singing voice, and one about the light-house, whose surrounding waters became a refuge for a family of whales that had lost their way crossing the ocean. Enya was entranced.

Seren had had advance warning of his gift to her. After they had made love on Christmas Day, he'd shown her the diamond ring he'd bought in Glasgow, hoping against hope that, if he proposed, she would accept him, but fully aware of how he had made her doubt him over the time he'd been away.

"As I tried to explain, I had to be sure myself before I asked you if *you* were," he'd told her. "And I am sure. But am I right for *you*, Seren?"

"You are perfect for me," she murmured, but she insisted that he asked for her hand formally in front of her father and daughter, as they had to approve too.

When he went down on one knee, and Lloyd and Enya looked on, their cheers left nobody in any doubt of their feelings.

There was no time for moping when Jamie left, because Aunt Alice arrived, by train, First Class, at 1.25 p.m. on the following day. Seren was looking forward to seeing her, and showing her how happy she and Enya were, but when she met her at Bangor station (after a fifty-minute delay due to rolling stock issues) Alice's first words were not promising.

"Goodness, this place feels as godforsaken as it always did."

On the drive over to Penmon, Seren was able to fill her aunt in on Lloyd's illness, her job at the gallery, Enya's incredible mastery of Welsh and, finally, her recent engagement to Jamie.

All were greeted with real warmth, and Seren even spotted a few, modest, tears in the corners of her aunt's eyes.

"I'm delighted for you, dear, I really am. Whatever you may think of me, I have always wanted and tried to do what's best for you over the years," Alice said.

"I know you have," Seren replied with equal warmth. Finally, she understood that, yes, she had never felt a full member of their family because her true, real, *blood* family was here, and had been all the time. The Montagues had done their best, which, as Lloyd was very fond of saying, was all anyone could do. But to Seren, what they had offered her had never come close to what she felt now.

Aunt Alice was staying in the Bulkeley Hotel in Beaumaris and had booked a suite overlooking the sea and the mountains beyond them, but she insisted on going to see Lloyd and Enya before even checking in.

"I want to see them first and then I have some other things to do. After that, we can talk," she said, folding her hands over her handbag in a way that precluded any protests or questions.

Lloyd had not been looking forward to seeing Aunt Alice again. It was almost thirty years since the night she came to take Seren away, the very lowest point of his life and a night that had marked the beginning of decades of loneliness and despair for him. He did not blame her for the huge loss he had suffered – none of it was her fault, he knew – but he had no wish to revisit it with her either. It had been the best decision for Seren, and that was that. The fact that Alice was adamant that she wanted to talk to him filled him with absolute horror.

"Tell her that I'm too ill to see her," he told his daughter plaintively. "She'll upset me, bring up an old trauma and make me *stressed*." The word "stressed" sounded particularly alien in the old man's vocabulary. Seren could not help but wonder if he'd done some research about mental health or even ventured into the current populist strands of self-care and personal well-being. If he had, well, perhaps that could be a good thing overall.

"I'll be around except when I have to fetch Enya from school, so if you want me to politely usher her out, I will, or you might just have to do a bit of acting, and say you're not feeling good."

"I won't need to bloody well act! I'm *not* feeling good," he replied bitterly. "But I'll try, for you, if not for her."

And yet, in the end, nothing was anything like he'd feared it would be. Aunt Alice came through the door, dropped her suitcase and rushed over to him with a gasp of fondness, and wrapped her arms around his neck. Lloyd found himself instinctively hugging her back, and within minutes both of them were looking at each other, laughing, and taking in how time had changed them, and how it had not. Seren made a pot of tea, occasionally glancing at them in astonishment.

"You look just the same, Alice," Lloyd said. "Except, perhaps, your hair is a slightly different colour now."

"I think you need stronger glasses, Lloyd, but thank you," she replied, blushing.

"And you look so like... *her*," he added. "Oh, it's like having Kate back with me, in this very room. And now I can see that Seren looks like both of you, doesn't she? *Anhygoel*/Incredible." He shook his head at this veritable wonder.

At this, Aunt Alice sat down and dabbed her eyes with the perfectly ironed cotton handkerchief she always, always had up her sleeve.

"I miss her still, you know. And think about her, every day," she said softly.

"Do you?" Seren spluttered. "You only ever told me about how selfish she was, how she only ever did what felt right for her and how she hurt you."

When Aunt Alice looked at her, her face was riven with sorrow. "Oh, Seren. I know that's true, but I had my reasons. It was something we felt I had to do, to make you forget your mother, not pine for her. It was terribly hard, and I hated myself for having to do it."

"We?" Seren said. "Who the hell's 'we', as it certainly wasn't Dad?"

Alice hesitated, and looked at her watch. "Almost three o'clock – time to go and fetch Enya from school, I think. If you don't mind, Seren, I need to be alone with your father now for a little while. Or rather, we need to be alone with him for a little while."

Seren turned around slowly to see two women standing in the doorway: Del's mother Catrin, whom she'd met on the beach before Christmas and at the school gate, and Ruthie's mother Enid, who sometimes collected Sali. They smiled at her, but their gaze was drawn to Lloyd, who was almost overcome, his hands trembling in his lap and his lip quivering with emotion.

"Dad, are you OK?" Seren said, feeling panic lap at her heels. "He's had two heart attacks, you know. He mustn't get agitated." Yes, she did need to fetch Enya, but she was really worried. Alice had promised she would talk to Lloyd, tell him some truths he needed to know, but perhaps this was all too much for him.

"Don't you worry, cariad/love," Catrin cut in, her voice low and gentle. "We know he's ill, and we won't upset him, but there's something Alice said you feel he ought to know. We've come to tell him, nothing more."

When her father said, with a solemn but calm face, "I need closure, you see," she knew that he had prepared himself for this day as best he could.

"O, da iawn di weld di eto, Lloyd/It's very good to see you again, Lloyd," Catrin said, sitting down next to him and stroking his arm tenderly, as if he were a child.

"If you're all sure this will not overtax Dad, I'll go and be back in a bit. Call me if you need me, or for anything at all," Seren said, but her father wasn't listening. Instead, he was patting Catrin's stroking hand as Enid poured them all a cup of tea and opened the packet of chocolate biscuits she'd brought with her.

Seren and Enya returned just over an hour later. They'd lingered in Ceri's café for a while to give everyone some time at home (and done some tidying as Ceri's lumbago was playing up). Enya gave Aunt Alice a rather wary hug, but she brightened up when she was handed a smart green plastic box and read out the label saying it was a bait and tackle box.

"Your mother told me you're a keen fisherman," Aunt Alice said.

"Fisher*girl*," Enya replied immediately.

Seren glared at her with her best "be polite or you're in big, big trouble" look.

"Thank you. I really love it! I'm going to go outside and find some worms to put in it right now for next time Jamie takes me fishing. The fish don't mind if the worms are dead, you know," she trilled, oblivious to the paling of Alice's face.

"Well, she's certainly gained a huge amount of self-confidence, as you told me, dear," she said. The slight crispness of her words was softened by her smile, however, which Seren decided summed up Aunt Alice to a tee. "Come and sit down. We need to talk to you."

As Seren sat at the only empty chair around the table, she looked over at her father. He looked very tired, drained even, but he looked calm. Whatever the revelation had been, it had been a good one, at first glance.

"We're going to be as brief as possible, as this is not the time for waffle. I get far too much of that from your Uncle Neil," Aunt Alice said. "Shall I begin, ladies?"

The ladies nodded.

Alice took a deep breath and sat up very straight. "Right, 'here goes nothing', as my children will insist on saying all the time. Seren my dear, your mother, Kate, loved you and Lloyd more than anyone or anything else on earth. More than her parents, more than me, more than herself. I want you to know and believe that before we begin. But I know you've heard that before, haven't you?"

This time, Seren nodded. Yes, Aunt Alice and Catrin had both assured her that her mother had loved her deeply in the past, but only now, did it feel real.

"Kate was a free spirit, a wanderer in life, and when she found a lump in her breast, she ignored our mother's pleas to go to the doctor. Mummy had had breast cancer in her thirties too, but it was found early enough thankfully. A miracle in those days. Kate carried on doing what Kate always did, gambolling through life like some woodland fawn, until it was too late, and the cancer was very advanced."

Aunt Alice paused; four people breathing was the only sound in the room.

"Enid and Catrin were her dearest friends. They were 'The Three Amigos', as I know Ruthie and Del have told you. Well, they rang me and told me about Kate's diagnosis, and said that she'd begged them not to tell Lloyd the truth as she knew it would break his heart to know that he was going to lose her. Instead, she'd told them that she wanted to leave without saying a word to spare him the pain of watching her suffer and not being able to help, or stop her dying. None of us were at all sure about it, but we agreed not to tell him why she'd left, and that one of them would watch over you both and tell me if I needed to come and get you if Lloyd was, well, not coping."

Sitting absolutely still, Seren felt the kaleidoscope of her scattered memories slowly begin to shift, and form a new pattern. "And so when he *wasn't*, they called you and you came and took me away," she said, her voice almost a whisper. "But why did she... kill herself *like that*, so horribly?"

Across the room, Lloyd cleared his throat to mask his distress.

"I can't tell you that, and believe me when I say none of us had any idea that was her intention. She spent a few months investigating alternative treatments, all kinds of nonsense in my view, but that was her choice, her decision. All I know is that when nothing helped, and her pain increased, she probably decided that she had to do something. Kate would have wanted things to end quickly, involve nobody else and not provoke too many questions. Apparently, she was drinking at a bar and bought the motorbike on a whim from a man in a pub and drove it away, without a licence or any experience, straight onto a motorway in the middle of the night. You know what happened next." The older woman paused, before continuing, "It was easy to dismiss what she did as nothing but drunken stupidity. Her dread was that the police might investigate which would risk Lloyd finding out the truth – that she'd done... what she did... deliberately." Her voice began to waver. "To be honest, we were convinced too. The very thought of her on a motorbike was so terrifying that none of us expressed surprise that she'd crashed it. The inquest verdict was straightforward: accidental death."

Seren felt her heart pounding in her chest as she tried to take in what she had heard. It made sense, and yet it seemed so outlandish. Would a handful of pills not have been easier, for her mother and for everyone who loved her, but when she pieced together all she now knew about Kate, a defiant gesture like the one she chose seemed far more like the warrior-woman she had been. Going out in a blaze of glory was the only option her brave mother would have chosen.

"I still don't understand. Why couldn't she just tell Dad that she was ill, and say goodbye to us properly? It would have been terrible, but what she did made us feel she didn't love us, and made me feel it was something bad I'd done and had to be punished for," Seren said. Across the room, Lloyd tutted sadly and shook his head.

"That wasn't her intention, but I told her that's how you would feel if she did something rash, the last time we spoke," Alice said. "She wouldn't listen. She would *never* listen. She was so distraught, she was beyond reason, saying she had to go without saying a word to you or to Lloyd."

But Seren was distraught. "And anyway, cancer doesn't have to be a death sentence. I'm still here, aren't I – I survived it? I'm sure they could have treated her somehow."

"Perhaps, but back then, things were different," Catrin said gently. "Thank goodness treatment has progressed from the early days, but for Kate, there was no hope, and she knew it. She hadn't gone to a doctor in time, and it was a very aggressive cancer, you see. When she asked us to keep her secret from you and your dad, we had to respect that."

"She prayed that Lloyd would get over her, find someone else, and be happy, but you loved her too much, didn't you, you daft old man?" Enid said.

"Nobody could compare to Kate," Lloyd said. "But I do wish she'd told me the truth, so that I could have nursed her. I could have borne it. It might have been easier than thinking she'd never loved me for over thirty years." Tears rolled slowly down his cheeks and were lost in his beard.

"But now you know she did, Lloyd. She loved you to the very end, but it felt like breaking the most solemn promise 'The Three Amigos' had ever made to tell you why she did what she did. It was her secret, that she'd asked us, as her friends, to keep. So, we did."

A silence, punctuated by a few sniffs and some long, slow breaths.

"Seren, we know you asked Ruthie and Del to ask us questions about Kate, but we just couldn't break our word, even now, all these years later," Catrin said.

"She begged us not to if we loved her, and we did, we really, truly did," Enid added. "We all miss her, Seren – every single day, but we see her in you."

"Yes. You are so very like her – courageous, daring. But it was so hard. She was my little sister, and she wouldn't let me help her, and she wouldn't go to a doctor either," Alice sobbed, a sight so very out of character that Seren instinctively reached for her hand. Now, she understood why her aunt had insisted she was checked within days of finding her own lump.

When, a few moments later, Seren looked at the four care-worn women in the room, she knew without doubt that they were only breaking their solemn promise now because she had begged them to. Like her, they could not bear this faithful man to go to his grave without knowing why Kate had left him, and understanding, finally, that none of it was his fault.

This revelation, so long in coming, was tragic, terribly tragic, but it was also cathartic – she could see that on her father's face. A huge weight had been lifted and his relief was palpable, but she sensed an emptiness too, as if the heart of him had been hollowed out and only the shell remained. Peace came at a price.

"How do you feel, Dad, now you know the truth?" she asked him.

He sighed, smiled at her weakly and murmured, "Never better, *cariad*/darling. Never better."

FORTY

January is the bleakest of months on Anglesey, as it is in many places. Days are short, nights are endless and there is little to celebrate. It is a time of waiting, of hoping, until the first brave snowdrops peep through the leaf litter and promise better times to come. In Penmon, there was precious little optimism even when they did that year.

Lloyd's state of mind was calmer, but his mood was darkening and his confusion growing a little more each day. He missed his working life, be it the myriad essential seasonal jobs on farms with old friends or being out on the boat showing visitors why he loved his island home, and the sea that surrounded it. On one day, Seren found him trying to turn the TV on with his mobile phone and on another, feeding Cobweb squares of chocolate instead of pellets of cat food. He was safe, for now, but she knew that something in him had changed fundamentally. Learning the truth about Kate seemed to have lessened a tension that had hummed inside him for so long, but he seemed unable to gather his depleted strength to carry on with life. He often refused to eat, and spent hours staring out at the horizon, his face blank and expressionless. Now that he knew he had always been loved, he told Seren, "My rage has gone, but my soul has gone with it." This made her deeply anxious every time she left him to go to work. If that powerful emotion had left him, what had replaced it and who could live long without their *soul*? Not this intense, loving old man, she was sure.

Other things were faltering too, and she began to feel as if the fragile new life she had built was made of matchsticks and could be felled by the push of a finger. By the middle of January, Angharad had no choice but to consider reducing Seren's hours in the gallery as there were so few customers. She had done well over Christmas, but margins were always tight, and paying an extra wage was impossible if she and Gwyn were to survive financially, she told her.

And Angharad was deeply worried about her son. He had developed a racking cough at New Year which had lasted for weeks, keeping both him and his mother awake as he struggled to breathe and to sleep. For most children, such common winter ailments were to be expected, and they recovered quickly, but Gwyn's every cough and wheezing splutter sent slivers of ice into Angharad's heart. He needed to stay strong and healthy to cope with the other things his condition made him susceptible to, and he was eating very little, which weakened him further. Every winter was a white-knuckle ride until warmth and sunshine returned, and the main risks of illness abated, but this winter was a bad one and she was scared.

"I cannot lose him," she told Seren one day. "If he stops fighting, I know I'll stop too."

When Angharad had to break the bad news about her shifts to Seren, both were a little tearful. Seren had watched Angharad struggle since the New Year, and Enya had visited Gwyn most days and seen just how poorly he had been. Once she had sympathised and dismissed any guilt her friend might feel about cutting her hours, however, she decided to raise a subject that had been on her mind for a while, but it had never seemed the right time to air. The gallery's profitability was fragile, as paintings and original prints were pricey. This meant that locals were unlikely to afford them except on special occasions and therefore, when wealthier tourists vanished, so did their money and the gallery's profits plummeted. Photographs were cheaper to produce and could be used in a variety of ways, so rather than give in to despair, Seren decided to risk sharing her idea with her friend. Given Angharad's mood, it could go very wrong indeed.

"Can I run something past you?" she began, once she had made a clearly exhausted Angharad sit down, drink a cup of coffee and devour the *pain au chocolat* she'd picked up in the Co-op on the way to work. She knew her friend would not have had breakfast herself, as her efforts would have gone into ensuring Gwyn had eaten and Ceri was briefed on looking after him for the day. "It's a business idea, actually," Seren went on, "but if you don't like it, just forget it. It's probably crap." Her old habit of self-denigration clearly died very hard.

"Great. Spill the beans," Angharad said, munching contentedly. "I'm open to any idea right now that doesn't involve my doing anything much at *all*."

"It doesn't, because I'll do it," Seren replied, feeling her courage rise.

She refilled Angharad's coffee cup and began to show her photos of small things she had seen on the island that captured a moment, a mood or a feeling. Each image represented a different aspect of island life, be it a weed-stranded lobster pot, a silvery mackerel, a drift of razor shells on a beach or a cluster of sea pinks on a cliff edge, but each one was a crystallisation of beauty. She told her about the photography course she had done, about Nan Parry, the woman she had met who believed, as Jamie now did, that focusing on small but perfect things in life encouraged mindfulness, and was a good way to live (and very on trend at the moment).

Angharad was speechless when Seren had finished... for all of thirty seconds.

"Bloody hell, they are amazing, girl," she said, beaming. "But I'm not sure how this macro photography is going to help us in an art gallery, or tackle the fact that I can hardly make ends meet out of season."

Seren laughed. "I was getting to that bit! Don't you think that photographs can be art too? I do, I really do, and we could reproduce and sell prints of some of my photos alongside the prints or paintings, as print technology is so good these days. We could generate island-based calendars with an appropriate seasonal image for each month; we could do greetings cards, coasters and placemats, posters and large, framed prints for those with bigger budgets. I was wondering about putting together a book encouraging mindfulness in nature, and perhaps working with Nan Parry who has links to the university and people who run relevant courses. I'm sure I can track down her number easily enough. Jamie has some contacts in publishing, too, and I know he'd be more than happy to help us. We could set up a website, too, and sell some prints online if we can cover costs or even put together some courses, with a holistic approach to art, nature and well-being." She paused, breathless, to gauge Angharad's reaction. She was smiling but looked rather shell-shocked too, so Seren carried on. "And finally, before you think I've completely lost the plot, I want you to know that one of the things that really helped me heal when I came here was the sheer natural beauty we're all surrounded by here, the tiny gems of perfection that fill this glorious landscape and so often go unnoticed. They fed my soul, and I want to see if I can help them do the same for others."

"Bravo! I'm convinced," Angharad said, clapping. "But I have to say, who would have thought that shy woman who hid from everyone and who beamed in here a few months ago would become the truly fabulous *you* I see before me today?"

"Not me, that's for sure," Seren replied, laughing. "But hear me out, or I'll never say everything I need to say! Look, I know I can do all these things and more in the time I'm *not* working here all day. I know what we sell, what we don't sell and perhaps what we should sell, so if I can get some money together to get my pictures ready to be printed, I can be beavering away until trade picks up at Easter and we're ready to launch our new stock."

"Ah, and there's the rub. Money. I haven't got enough to pay you, let alone help you form a start-up," Angharad said glumly. "*Does 'na ddim pres yma*/There's no money here. Sorry."

"I've thought about that too. Dad's state pension is pretty generous, and he's already told me he's got savings as he's never spent much at all, and he wants Enya and I to use them if we need them. I'll ask him if I can invest some of his capital in some basic materials to get us started – it won't be much, but it'll be enough. I've got a great camera, courtesy of Jamie. Oh, and he hopes to make good money with his articles too, in time." Seren paused, as excitement at her words, at these incredible possibilities, surged through her. "Who knows, I could even be able to persuade Dad to come on a cruise, and see a bit of the world as a treat, and as a big thank-you for his investment. He needs to have something to look forward to and get his *joie de vivre* back, so it could tick two boxes at once. Can I stop now?" Seren said, almost out of breath.

Angharad nodded, beamed, and the two women shook hands.

"It's a deal, and fingers crossed it works," she said.

"You rescued me, so I'm going to do my level best to save you and Gwyn," Seren said. "Oh, and Ceri, of course, as I know she's worried about you both."

"Yes, she is, though she hides it well. For all her self-obsession and endless ailments, she'd cut off her right arm for me and Gwyn, I know."

Seren grinned. "You know what I'm going to say, don't you?"

"Yup. She'd talk me through the amputation, step by grisly step!"

FORTY-ONE

Jamie kept his word and kept in regular touch whilst he was away this time. He told Seren that Fergus was keen, but had to run things past the newspaper board and see samples before he could commit some serious money to this project. This was very frustrating, but there were some green shoots of hope, he assured her. The house that he, Fiona and Agnes had lived in as a family was on the market for less than a week before it sold, so that was good. He was buzzing with ideas and plans, which was also encouraging. He also told her that he hoped to be back permanently by the end of March, and was missing her desperately, which cheered her up, but he kept repeating that he couldn't leave yet.

"I want no loose ends, no splinters left under the skin to sabotage us," he said. "I've been having some grief counselling, and it's helping me with losing Agnes. It was an accident, and a terrible one, but it didn't happen to punish me for being *me*, if you get me."

Seren said she did. She had no choice but to do so as she loved this man. She was missing him, but was also pretty busy herself, putting her plans into action. Lloyd had given a very enthusiastic go-ahead, and he was very keen for her to use as much of his savings as she needed. In return, she was trying to encourage him to engage with life a little more by walking to the lighthouse with her each day after lunch. They celebrated his birthday in February with his favourite cake, chocolate, and he seemed content enough, even happy, but Seren found her fragile optimism about the future beginning to dwindle as the weeks passed, even though there were tantalising signs of another spring. She loved the island, and felt the shift of its seasons keenly, but she began to worry that the task she had set herself, plus the relentless greyness of January and February, were sapping all her energy and diluting her enthusiasm for life. She longed for sunshine, and for warmth.

Soon, Seren started to join Lloyd in having an afternoon nap between lunch and fetching Enya from school. Sometimes, she had to cover Angharad in the gallery so that her friend could spend some time with Gwyn, who was slowly regaining his strength, but even these occasional shifts left her as exhausted, as unutterably drained as she had felt... *since the first trimester of her pregnancy with Enya*, she realised suddenly one afternoon at the beginning of March when her limbs felt like lead as she walked up the stairs to the bathroom for the fifth time that hour.

"Oh my God! I think I'm bloody well pregnant!" she cried, half expecting a "No you're bloody well not," from her body in response. But that rebuttal did not come: instead, absolute surety settled around her like a soft, familiar mantle.

And then, a maelstrom of contradictory reactions began to whizz around her brain so furiously that she felt like it was *fizzing* in there. It was wonderful, and yet it was stupid and they should have been more careful. Enya might be happy to have a sibling after all this time, but she might also be jealous. Would Lloyd be disapproving and insist on a shotgun wedding? By the time she'd been to the pharmacy and weed on the stick of one of the four-pack of pregnancy tests she'd bought, she was numb, and felt almost resigned to whatever the plastic strip told her; she just needed to *know*.

It was positive. Curling over the sink, her head in her hands, she rang Jamie from the bathroom.

"Hi there. Sorry to disturb you, but I've got some news," she said in as wobble-free a voice as she could manage. "'Are you sitting down', as the phrase goes?"

"You're pregnant, aren't you?" Jamie exclaimed. "I knew it! Oh my goodness, that's brilliant, Seren, and just in time. I think I'll be back by the end of March."

"How did you guess so easily, may I ask?" Seren said.

A pause. "Sorry, but, well, Fiona and I only, er, had unprotected sex once, and Agnes was the result. Super sperm, see?" he said with a chuckle.

Seren could almost see the cheery look on his face as he waited for her reply. She made him wait, and wait, and wait, before she said, very quietly, "I think you mean super *egg*."

"Hahaha, sorry, of course I meant to say of course it's the winning *combo* of our wondrous reproductive powers, but I'm so happy, darlin'! It's going to be ace, and Enya and Lloyd will love it. A new baby in the house, oh, I can't wait to come home! Are you feeling all right, any sickness, tender boobs, all that stuff as you must be about two months along by now? I remember Fiona was..."

But Seren had stopped listening. She didn't want to hear about Fiona, or the downsides of pregnancy right now. Her thoughts were suddenly with her father, who must have had this exact same joyful news from Kate once, and probably been just as excited about what lay ahead for his little family as Jamie was about theirs. Life had been unbearably cruel to her parents, and she prayed with all her heart for more luck than they had been given.

"I'll tell Dad later, once I've done all the tests in this packet, and then Enya at bedtime, after I've read one of your stories to her *again*. I have to read them on a bloody loop, you know. I think I know them off by heart!"

"Sorry not sorry. Glad she likes them. And let me know how the news goes down."

"Oh, I do hope they'll both be happy for us. It will be a huge change for everyone. I mean, where will we live? I'm knackered sleeping on an airbed as it is."

"Let me worry about that. Irons in the fire, and all that," Jamie replied. "I have a cunning plan, but this might mean I have to fast forward a bit. Lloyd put the original idea in my head, actually. He got really excited about it, said it was the hand of fate. Maybe he's a psychic and he knew this baby was coming! Is there no end to that man's talents?"

Seren laughed. "Please, calm down a bit! I can only take so many bombshells in one day. Let me get over this one before you tell me about the wacky scheme you and Dad have cooked up."

"You'll love it, I promise. It's our destiny, written in the stars, the path we're meant to follow, the fate your father and I have planned for us..." Jamie babbled.

Hearing the almost hysterical boyish excitement in his voice, Seren was not so sure that he and her romantic poetry-quoting father should be fully trusted with anyone's fate, let alone hers.

But Jamie was right on one count. Lloyd and Enya were as happy about the baby news as he had been, and Seren saw more animation in her father's face than she had seen for many weeks. It was all going to be all right. In fact, it was all going to be *great*.

Later that week, as she felt her baby wriggle inside her for the first time, she knew that, whatever lay ahead, her beloved dad would never be alone again.

FORTY-TWO

Easter was early that year, and it was a rush to get the first of the new photographs, greetings cards and placemats ready to sell in the gallery in time for the arrival of the first of the tourists. Jamie was still not back on the island, but he would be very soon he assured Seren, because a) he didn't want to miss another minute of her pregnancy and b) he needed to tell her about his and Lloyd's Great Plan, as he now called it. His house sale had gone smoothly, and the money was already in both his and Fiona's bank accounts. Having seen some drafts, Fergus had finally agreed on a budget and a schedule for Jamie's planned articles about the island, and all looked set for a fantastic summer... until, cruelly, life delivered a blow that crushed them all.

Early one Saturday morning, just as the trees around his cottage were exploding in the fresh green of new, spring leaves, Lloyd had another heart attack. This time, it was Enya, reading in her bed, who reached him first, running, screaming from the top of the stairs to call her mother. Seren, who had already heard the thud as his body hit the floor above her, raced upstairs to find her little girl clinging to Lloyd's limp body and sobbing uncontrollably while trying to lift his head from the floor as she had seen her mother do the last time this had happened.

"I wanted to ring the ambulance again, but *Taid*/Grandfather told me not to leave him and your phone was downstairs and so were you," she wailed.

Seren, shocked at her father's stricken face, pointed downstairs and said, "I'm sorry I wasn't here. Go and ring for the ambulance now. My phone's on the kitchen table. Everything will be fine, Enya."

But her brittle composure evaporated when she knelt down next to Lloyd, she knew it was different this time. His breaths were short and rasping, and his face drained of all colour. When she asked if he was in pain, he mouthed, "Not any more." When she rubbed his hands, as they were almost blue with cold, he smiled at her, but it was terrible to be quite so certain she was witnessing life slipping away from him, second by second. When Enya ran back into the room, shouting "the ambulance is coming!" Seren sent her downstairs again, ostensibly to get her *Taid*/Grandfather a glass of water but in reality, to ensure she was not in the room when he died.

After a minute or two, his breathing changed again to slower, longer breaths. Wrapping her arms around him, she laid her head on his chest. He seemed calm and she closed her eyes to *feel* his deep, resonant voice flooding through her body, as she had felt it as a little girl when he spoke:

"Don't worry, *cariad*/darling. Unlike Dylan's father, I am going '*gentle into that good night*', and I know I will see my Kate when I get there."

He did not speak again.

Jamie came back to the island immediately, arriving at the cottage in the early evening, just as the undertakers were taking

Lloyd's body away. He ran towards Seren, who burst into tears as soon as she sank into his arms. Enya then ran out to join them, wrapping her arms around their legs to unite them all in a tight huddle of grief. They watched the undertaker's black van drive off into the darkness until there was no more of it to see.

After a simple meal of baked potato and beans, eaten only because they had not had lunch and knew they should be hungry, Seren took Enya upstairs to bath her, and get her ready for bed. Routine, and the safety it offered, was important for her daughter now, as this loss could jeopardise all the emotional confidence she had gained since coming to live here; Lloyd had left her, and she had loved him beyond words. Jamie read her one of his stories, but neither he nor Seren left her until they saw her eyes close, and sleep arrive. Cobweb was asleep at the bottom of the bed, and would stay there throughout the night, they knew.

Downstairs, they sat next to each other on Lloyd's battered old sofa, holding hands, but saying nothing for a while. When Seren moved Jamie's hand over onto her belly and he felt their baby kick, he began to cry, soundless tears, for the friend who had saved him, and who would now not give his daughter away when they got married later that year, or meet his new grandchild.

The following morning, after a largely sleepless night, Seren decided not to send Enya to school, as she was red-eyed and very tired. Instead, once they had spoken to the undertaker and the vicar had made an appointment to visit them the next day to discuss the funeral plans, they all headed out into the spring sunshine together.

"Dad wouldn't want us to waste a day like this. Let's go to some of the most wonderful places on the island," Seren said, moving her car seat back to accommodate her belly. She had not driven for several weeks, but doing so showed her how rapidly her baby was growing.

First, they visited Aberffraw, which had become Seren's second favourite beach, after the pebbly one at Penmon. They walked along the estuary and turned the corner to be blasted by the wind off the sea, filling their lungs with its icy purity. Afterwards, Seren popped into the village shop, where Beth Williams was working that day, and remembered her.

"Congratulations are in order, I see," she said, beaming at Seren's belly. "*Bendigedig*/Brilliant!"

Seren blushed like a schoolgirl.

"Oh, and to embarrass you even more, my husband told me that Mai, the photography tutor on the course you did, said you were really gifted. I hope you use that gift."

Seren blushed even more. "That's kind of him to say. Actually, I've just started producing cards, prints and calendars, and The Seaside Gallery, in Beaumaris, where I work, is stocking them. We've got a website, too, if you want to check us out." She handed Beth one of the crisp new business cards that had arrived last week and glowed with pride.

"Ooh, very impressive. Ioan and I will have to come over and have a look. I'm thinking of stocking some cards here too, as people always want them, and it would be great to support another local business."

"Fantastic," Seren said, before adding, slightly self-consciously, "I wanted to tell you, Beth, how much I loved the mural your husband painted for your wedding day. Our class was in that room, of course, and I couldn't take my eyes off it."

"I'll tell Ioan. He's painting all the time now, so he's as happy as Larry. Let me give you my number, and perhaps we could all meet for coffee sometime and share ideas. Ioan loves Angharad's work, I know."

And at that moment Seren knew that this woman and her husband would become her friends, another thread in the tapestry of her new life.

Their next stop was Porth Nobla, a stunningly wild rock-framed little cove on the west of the island. They ate the fish and chips they had bought in Rhosneigr hunkered down in front of the dunes, letting the weak spring sunshine warm their faces. As they were eating, a woman passed whom Seren recognised – Jude Parry, who had been to her first photography class and ran an amazing business called The Memory Maker.

"Hiya, Jude," she said. "How's life? I really missed you at class after you left."

"Busy, as yours is going to be, by the looks of it," Jude replied, smiling, "but more under control now. Well, a *bit* under control."

She pointed out her home, a gorgeous cottage just above the beach, and was filled with enthusiasm for what Seren was trying to do with macro photography.

"Perhaps we could work on something together, as I need photos in the collages I put together, and it's hard to get really good, detailed ones," she said. "I'm more of a landscape girl myself these days."

"Great idea, but it may have to be a long-term project, for obvious reasons," which made Jude laugh.

"No rush. That's how life is up here, as I hope you're learning," she said, before walking off along the beach with her dogs, a perky Jack Russell and a beautiful Welsh collie, running alongside her.

"That's yet another connection in the Anglesey art world in the bag, my love," Jamie said. "It's all about contacts, you know."

"And talent, my love," she replied, digging him in the ribs.

Their final stop was much nearer home. It had started to cloud over, threatening a shower, perhaps a storm, but Seren still drove her little car right down to the edge of *Trwyn Du*/Black Nose, as she had never done before. Today was a day to feel life in all its wildness and unpredictability. As Enya got out and began seeing what the tide had washed up, her mother and Jamie sat in the car and watched the breakers crash against the lighthouse, filling the sky with arcs of sea spray that, when the sun shone through them, created tiny rainbows in the air. Neither of them needed to say that they were thinking of Lloyd, and imagining him there, in the place he loved most, the place that had anchored him through all his years of loneliness; they both knew.

"He's out there now, free and happy, I really believe that," Jamie murmured.

"And she's with him, flitting over the waves like a *tylwyth teg*/fairy," Seren said.

"That's a wonderful phrase. Welsh is the language of poets, as Lloyd never stopped telling me!"

"He was right, and I do remember my aunt, who was the least poetic person I've ever known, describing my mother as a sort of otherworldly being, a creature who danced through life, and never, ever stopped dreaming," she said, pausing. "And I think she loved her all the more for it too."

"I think we all need dreams and love and hope and kindness," Jamie said, kissing her lightly.

"We do indeed," Seren replied, waving at her daughter down on the beach.

FORTY-THREE

There were few people at Lloyd's funeral, as he had known few people, but there were enough to make it clear that he was respected in the community, and would be missed. Aunt Alice and Uncle Neil came up from Wimbledon; Ceri, Angharad and Gwyn were there, as were Dafydd, Ruthie, Sali and their sons Harri and Jac. Del and her mother Catrin sat near the front, with Ruthie's mum Enid, all belting out the rousing hymns Seren had chosen. Everyone gave generously to a charity researching heart disease, before coming for a modest gathering back at the cottage. Luckily, the day was dry, so people spilled out into the small garden and admired a view like no other, one they knew that Lloyd Evans, and his father and grandfather before him, had always loved.

"I will always think of him standing here, looking out over the sea, waiting for me to come back to him," Seren said to Jamie once everyone had left, and they were watching the sun set over the water. "He was sad, and I was, too, but I *did* come back to him in the end. I'm glad I got to spend time with him, get to know him. We were so happy to be together again."

"I know. It wasn't a long time, but it was a miraculous time. He was one of a kind. There aren't many Lloyd Evans' in this world." He paused. "Darlin', I think today might be a good time to tell you about our Great Plan, if that's OK with you?"

"Why not. Nothing could surprise me any more," Seren replied, before adding, with a wince, "Or perhaps it can..."

Jamie led her to the bench in front of the cottage, and they sat down, wrapping their coats around each other as the air chilled. It was April, and there was a hint of warmer weather, but it was only that – a faint hint, a promise.

"Did you know that your grandfather, Lloyd's father, used to live in one of the big old coastguard's houses right down there, overlooking the lighthouse?" Jamie began, his voice low and gentle, as if telling a story. "He was forced to move to *Crigyll Cottage* when the upkeep became too much, and it was sold first as a private home, and then as the Airbnb it's been for the past ten years or so... but guess what?"

"What?" Seren said, feeling her heart begin to pound. She, like Enya, had rarely found surprises to be good things.

"I've bought it," Jamie replied, clapping his hands. "It's what Lloyd had always wanted, he told me very soon after we met, to have it back in the family, and it's going to be our family home, as it was once his. Isn't that the most amazing thing?"

"Oh, I see. And I know," Seren replied in a monotone. Her response was clearly not what Jamie had hoped for, as his face fell, but she was tired, getting cold, and simply could not muster much enthusiasm. She went on, "I know, because Dad told me that was his dream too, but it's *huge*, Jamie, with at least six bedrooms, and it's right on the edge of the land. Think of the draughts, the bills, rising sea levels and all the bloody housework!"

Jamie's face fell even further.

"But, Seren, it's *stunning* inside, and I had to act fast as a property developer was circling like a shark. We'll have enough money to do it up, and we'll just have to have lots of kids, to fill it." He kissed her cheek, which forced a smile from her. "I did it for you, my love. For us."

Out over the sea, herring gulls were cruising on the last of the day's warmth, hoping for a final stroke of luck, and some more food. When Jamie spotted a seal, its whiskery nose poking just above the water as it looked around, he showed Seren. "Look, he thinks it's a great idea, don't you, mate?"

She let herself smile. "OK, if the seal says so, we'll go and have a look around tomorrow, but right now, this body needs to sleep," she replied, getting up to go into the cottage. Her movements were slow, and her fatigue, almost overwhelming. It had been a very long day. "And right now, the thought of six kids is *not* one I want to entertain."

"I get it. Perhaps I chose the wrong moment, but let me know when you change your mind on the six kids, though. Remember, we're the 'hole in one' parents," Jamie said, grinning as she stuck out her tongue at him.

The baby was due in mid-September, and the coastguard's house was vacant, ready for them to move in when they wanted to, but there was one more thing both Seren and Jamie wanted to happen before those huge life events took place; they wanted to get married.

The day they chose was a Saturday in mid-May, and they thanked the weather gods for making it the only dry day in an entire week of rain. The sky was clear and the air and sea sparkled.

Finding a dress for her pretty heavily pregnant body was not a task she relished, but, once more, fate intervened. Clearing her father's cottage after his death was sad, but she wanted to at least start the task before the baby came. In a trunk up in the crog loft of Lloyd's cottage, she had found some of her mother's clothes, all neatly folded and wrapped in age-softened tissue paper. Amongst them was the voluminous white cheesecloth dress that she had seen her mother wearing in the old photograph of their little family. In that dress, she had wafted through life, adrift on her hopes and dreams and deeply in love with her handsome Welsh husband. Seren knew instantly she had to wear it on her wedding day, and when she did, it made her feel as if her parents were with her on the happiest day of her life, and wished her well. Jamie wore a kilt, a crisp white shirt, a sporran, a waistcoat, and traditional socks called kilt hose. He refused the garters his Scottish relations suggested, in case he looked daft.

"I did that last time, with Fiona, and I'm not doing it again. They made me feel like Malvolio in Shakespeare's *Twelfth Night*, where he dresses up like a twerp in yellow stockings thinking his mistress wants him to. She doesn't. Bad news."

Seren thought very hard about who to ask to give her away, as Lloyd was no longer here to do so. For a long while, she considered walking up the aisle alone, as some women had done recently in high profile weddings, but in her heart, she knew what the *right* thing to do was. Uncle Neil was deeply touched to be asked, and when he squeezed her hand when they arrived at the church door, Seren felt, for the first time, that this man loved her. Aunt Alice was clearly moved when she saw them progressing together up the aisle in the tiny church. The previous evening, she'd burst into tears when Seren presented her aunt with a book filled with photos of her as a shy child on Christmas Days in Wimbledon, scowling on holidays to Majorca and a few of Enya during the many times they had sought sanctuary from Finlay. On those occasions, Seren realised only now, she had felt both safe, and loved. There were some later, happy photos too, of Lloyd, Enya and Seren after they had returned to Anglesey, so that Alice could see that their family line still flourished and that she had always been a part of that. She had been a strong and loyal sister to Kate, however hard it had been to be one.

Gwyn carried the rings on his lap and as his flower-bedecked wheelchair came towards Jamie and Seren, he handed it over with a broad smile, and a wink at Enya, who was the only bridesmaid. "Smashed it," he mouthed, before wheeling over to the electric piano Angharad had brought from their home. He was playing all the hymns as well and had not yet mastered the organ. Everyone knew it was only a question of time...

For years, Seren looked back on her wedding day as the one that finally bade farewell to the sadness, the loss, she had always carried within her, buried deep within. She was loved, and had always been loved, even if she had been grafted onto another family until she found her own, and that was enough.

As fiddle music floated above the marquee that was set up right next to the beach, her heart was full as she went outside to breathe in the chill freshness of the salty air. She looked up, and saw the palest flickers of pink, of green, dancing across the sky in fluid movements, free and joyous, unfettered and unique: the Northern Lights. For a few, perfect minutes, she watched them and felt that her mother was dancing amongst them, colourful and free.

"What a gift," she murmured, as the lights faded and then vanished. "I don't need a photo of them, because I *saw* them."

Down on the shore, a heron was fishing in the dark halo around the lighthouse, statue-still, poised, and as she watched him, some of Dylan Thomas' words came into her head, and she could hear her father saying them:

The heron, ankling the scaly

Lowlands of the waves,
Makes all the music.

"Rest in peace together, Mum and Dad," she murmured, as the beam from the lighthouse cast a band of light over the water, making all things safe around it.

EPILOGUE

Seren's baby was born in a rush, before the midwife could arrive to help. Only Enya and Jamie watched her slip into the world, and take her first breath. They called her "Kate Alice", and she was a redhead, and "a true Scot", her father said.

In the year that followed, Jamie's articles about the importance of nature, and its powerful effect on mental as well as physical health, became a very successful feature and Jude's knowledge of local history and Seren's stunning photographs were integral to that. There were plans for him to travel further afield to experience how life was in other places and convey their particular beauty to others, but he had one proviso: wherever possible, he wanted to take his little family with him. This would not always work, because Seren had two children and a thriving business to run, as she told him on a *very* regular basis, but it was the foundation of his immutable new work-life balance.

And things continued to change, as life rarely stands still for long. Seren was now at the very centre of the island's thriving art community, and had taken over The Seaside Gallery in Beaumaris and stocked some of Nan's memory-inspired collages as well as Ioan Williams' stunning paintings. Angharad had stepped back from running the business when Ceri was, genuinely, too unwell to care for Gwyn very often, so now she painted at home and could always be nearby if he needed any help (which he always insisted he didn't). Alistair still refused to accept any repayment of the loan that had set her up in business. He insisted it was to be used to fund Gwyn through music college when the time came. Del, Ruthie and Seren now called themselves "The Three Amigos, Mark 2". Enya was still a keen fishergirl, and won a fly-fishing competition at the age of seven. Jamie assured her that Agnes, the daughter he lost, would have been full of admiration for her elegant casting technique which made her doubly proud.

Often, at night, when the children were asleep, Seren stood outside her new home and surveyed the sea and the sky, her precious new world. The house was now refurbished and looking as solid and dignified as it had been when the role of the coastguard was a prestigious one, respected and admired in the community. Yes, the sea lay all around the Point, as it always had, and the susurrations of the waves lulled her and her children to sleep at night, as they always would.

Sometimes, as she looked up at the stars that threaded like the finest lace above the island, Seren thanked them for all that she had, and for all the people she loved, and who loved and had loved her. And as the world around her settled for the night ahead, she knew, without a shadow of a doubt, that there was nowhere else on this earth that she would rather be.

A LETTER FROM THE AUTHOR

Thank you for reading *The Lighthouse Keeper of Anglesey*. I really hope you enjoyed getting to know my characters and finding out about Penmon and the lighthouse at *Trwyn Du*/Black Nose, as the locals call it. It is a very special place on Anglesey and one which I have always loved. I went there the day my own mum Ruth died, and felt, as Seren feels, that she was with me in spirit still.

If you'd like to join readers in hearing all about my new releases and some bonus content too, you can sign up for my newsletter.

www.stormpublishing.co/caroline-young

If you enjoyed this book enough to take the time to leave a review, that would be very helpful to other readers, and much appreciated by me. Even a short review can make all the difference in encouraging a reader to discover my stories for the first time.

Thank you for coming on this journey with me, and do stay in touch. I look forward to sharing more stories with you, as I have lots more of them to tell.

Caroline

 facebook.com/caroline.young.9250

ACKNOWLEDGEMENTS

This book is a celebration of the things that bind people together, and the enduring power of love, in all its many manifestations. Life is often far from easy, but we need to remember what we all share rather than focusing on our differences. I hope that this story celebrates the fact that we all need the same, very basic, things to thrive – to feel safe, to love and be loved.

Luckily, I have many people around me who offer support when I doubt myself and encourage me to say what I *want* to say in my stories rather than what I feel I *ought* to say. As ever, my husband Geoff has diffused many a crisis of confidence and been a calm voice throughout the, often arduous, process of writing and editing a novel. I must once more thank Idris Jones for checking my Welsh and always seeming surprised when I give him a bottle of wine for his troubles. As well as friends further afield who seem to enjoy my books, I am lucky enough to have a wonderful gang of local "fans", who love reading about our part of Wales. Thanks for all your support, Sara, Rosie, Ann, Annabel, Jane, Carol, Julie, Jo, Liz, Una, Julia and Rachel. It means a great deal to me. I would like to thank Anne Gardner for showing me her stunning photographs of some of nature's smallest gems, and introducing me to the world of macro photography. Finally, another big round of applause for Kate, my editor at Storm, who understands what I am trying to say even if I'm not sure of it myself. Thanks for keeping the faith, Kate.

When I started writing, I think I was hoping to write a prize winner, a work of fiction that would stun the critics and emulate the literati I had studied at Cambridge. Instead, I found myself writing about ordinary people and how they live their lives on a little island off the top of North Wales. There is much to be learnt from such things, I believe.

Printed in Great Britain
by Amazon